# His breath caught in his throat...

as he watched her in the mirror, the satin gown hugging her curves. A wave of intense longing washed over him, threatening to drown him. He wanted her, yet he was afraid of what he'd learn about himself in her arms. Without even knowing he was crossing the tile floor, he came forward and put his hands on her shoulders. In the mirror he saw her lips part, as though to ask a question, but the words were never spoken.

Their lips met in a searing kiss that spoke of need and longing, and they were both breathless when they finally drew apart.

Eden searched his eyes, as a smile formed on her lips. "It really is you, isn't it, Mark?"

The tenderness went out of his face, replaced by pain and a cold expression that gave her a sudden chill. "You're wrong, Eden." He glared at her. "You're dead wrong."

Dear Reader,

Our "Decade of Danger & Desire" continues! To help celebrate and to thank you for your readership these past ten years, we've brought you a very special gift—Rebecca York's PEREGRINE CONNECTION.

Since its original publication in 1986, the PEREGRINE CONNECTION trilogy has been a favorite of romantic-suspense readers—some of the most sought-after books, according to booksellers.

It's our pleasure to make them available to you once again. Whether you'll be reliving the danger and desire, or discovering it for the first time, enjoy!

Debra Matteucci
Senior Editor & Editorial Coordinator
Harlequin Books
300 East 42nd St.
New York, NY 10017

# Rebecca York
## Talons of the Falcon

## *Harlequin Books*

TORONTO • NEW YORK • LONDON
AMSTERDAM • PARIS • SYDNEY • HAMBURG
STOCKHOLM • ATHENS • TOKYO • MILAN
MADRID • WARSAW • BUDAPEST • AUCKLAND

To Lydia, who shares our love of adventure,
and dares to take a risk

First published by Dell Publishing Co., Inc.

ISBN 0-373-22298-X

TALONS OF THE FALCON

Copyright © 1986 by Ruth Glick and Eileen Buckholtz

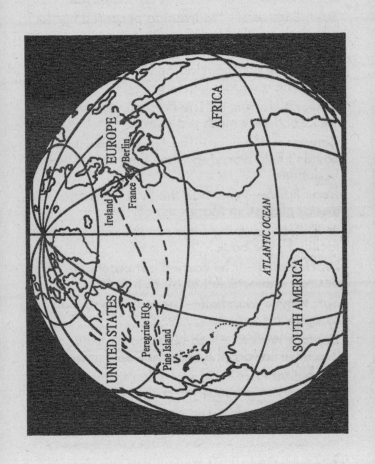

# CAST OF CHARACTERS

*Eden Sommers*—No training prepared her for what she saw in Mark Bradley's eyes.

*Lt. Col. Mark Bradley*—His face was changed, his records missing. Had he been brainwashed, or was he a deadly imposter?

*Amherst Gordon*—"The Falcon" was alive and well...and very much a player.

*Constance McGuire*—The Falcon's assistant couldn't help worrying when their agents were in danger.

*Hans Erlich*—What had the East German doctor planted in Mark's mind?

*Maj. Ross Downing*—He ran the Pine Island facility by the book.

*Dr. Hubbard*—If he carried out orders, he'd destroy what was left of Mark Bradley.

*Sgt. Wayne Marshall*—The male nurse took his assignments very seriously.

*Captain Walker*—Had his minority status made him bitter toward the Defense Department?

*Lieutenant Price*—He saw Eden's presence on the island as grounds for a turf battle.

*Captain Yolanski*—Did his smart-aleck character hide ulterior motives?

## Author's Note

We were delighted when Harlequin Intrigue told us they would be republishing our Peregrine Connection trilogy. They are some of our favorite stories, and we had a wonderful time creating daring women and dangerous heroes and catapulting them into plots swirling with high-stakes intrigue and jeopardy.

With the fall of the Berlin Wall, the collapse of the Soviet Union and the restructuring of Eastern Europe, the world has changed at warp speed over the past eight years since the Peregrine novels were written. Yet with spy scandals at the upper echelons of the CIA and even a terrorist attack at the World Trade Center, themes of preserving peace and the balance of world power are just as relevant today as they were in the eighties, when the Peregrine Connection was written.

In 1985, when we wrote *Talons of the Falcon*, we wanted to create a different kind of thriller—a romantic adventure featuring heroines just as strong as the heroes. We also reached into our own backgrounds and drew on travel experiences. For example, since Eileen grew up near Robins Air Force Base and could vouch for the strength and courage of the men and women in blue, we gave psychologist Eden Sommers and Lt. Col. Mark Bradley air force careers. Eileen also used her memories of family vacations at Jekyll and St. Simon's islands off the Georgia coast to create the feel of the fictional Pine Island facility where Eden is sent to assess Mark's condition.

On a research trip to Europe, Ruth discovered a wealth of details that added to the richness of the story—such as finding the right rocky secluded spot on the coast of Ireland for Mark and Eden to hide before escaping to France. The IRA is also featured in the story. Ruth got the idea for using the organization one evening in an Irish pub when the guy at the next table asked her and her husband if they'd like to make a donation to buy guns for terrorists.

Ruth's familiarity with the Washington, D.C., milieu, and Eileen's career with the Defense Department also helped bring an authenticity to the novel's compelling portrayal of politics and power.

After rereading *Talons of the Falcon*—and all the upcoming books in the Peregrine Connection— we were pleased with how well the books stood the test of time. We hope you think so, too.

Rebecca York (Ruth Glick and Eileen Buckholtz)

# *Prologue*

"What if Eden Sommers gets herself killed on this little assignment of yours?"

"Now, really. You're acting as though the Pine Island business were some personal whim of mine and not a matter of national security," Amherst Gordon grumbled.

The thin, aristocratic-looking woman pursed her lips but said nothing. She knew from long experience that Amherst wasn't finished, and there was no sense trying to interrupt the man once he got started.

"Besides," he continued, "you should think more positively about Ms. Sommers. The woman's not only got spunk, she's got exactly the background we need. Isn't that so?" As he spoke, he reached up to rub the curved beak of the red and green parrot that perched on the shoulder of his tweed jacket. The bird regarded him with one shiny black eye, but it didn't answer.

Constance McGuire looked down through her half glasses at the computer printouts spread among the teacups and jam pots on the wrought-iron table, and she sighed. A query of their extensive data base had produced only four candidates for this very dangerous assignment— each with a Ph.D. in clinical psychology and a unique set of strengths and weaknesses. But in the end there had been one overriding consideration, one factor that set Eden Sommers apart. "You're right," she conceded. "This woman has never worked undercover before, but everything else is damn near perfect—including that fortunate stint at Griffiss Air Force Base four years ago.''

Gordon kept his lined features impassive. His assistant never swore—unless she was worried about the safety of one of their people. And although he would never admit it to her, this time her worries were justified. To the outside world Pine Island was nothing more than an oceanographic monitoring station. But he and Connie knew that the supersecret installation was really an isolated, well-fortified interrogation facility. Its handpicked staff had a single mission—to squeeze the information they needed out of one Colonel Mark Bradley. And damn the cost to the U.S. government—or Bradley himself.

Gordon was more of a pragmatist than Constance. He knew there was simply no alternative to the course of action they were setting into motion. Eden Sommers had to come through on this one for them. If she didn't, Bradley could kiss his twenty-year military career—and maybe even his life—goodbye. But there was a great deal more at stake here than one man's life—or one woman's, for that matter. Otherwise he and Connie wouldn't be contemplating this admittedly risky plan.

''What's Sommers's ETA?'' Gordon asked, pushing himself stiffly out of the chair and reaching for the silver-headed cane he'd picked up on one of his tours of duty in Britain. The parrot fluttered its wings momentarily as he rose, but remained on his shoulder.

His administrative assistant was all business now. ''She should be arriving at 1300 hours. She left Vermont just before breakfast.'' Constance glanced at the gold watch on her narrow wrist. ''Jim's probably pulling up at National Airport in the Aviary courtesy van just about now—unless the traffic on Route 50 was unusually heavy this morning.''

''Good. Very good,'' Gordon murmured. He could always count on Connie to take care of the details. Whether she approved of an operation or not, she did what needed to be done.

For the first time that morning, he permitted himself a slight smile as he slowly crossed the flagstone floor of the solarium and paused to look out one of the French doors that gave access to the well-manicured lawn. The irony of running a top-secret operation called the Peregrine Connection from an elegant Virginia country inn never failed to amuse him. But then, hadn't he picked the Berryville location—and supervised the restoration of this perfect cover site—himself?

Long ago he'd developed the philosophy that anything worth doing was worth doing right, and so any stinginess in government funding for this site had invariably been rectified with his own resources.

Unconsciously he flexed the rebuilt kneecap that had made it possible for him to walk again. A lot of people in the Intelligence community would be surprised to know that the Falcon was still alive. That was the way he and the Secretary of Defense wanted it. If he didn't exist anymore, he couldn't be doing anything illegal. And if he did happen to get caught at it, the secretary would deny the association.

There was the troubling issue of morality, of course. Like Saint Jerome, he had thought long and hard about ends justifying means. But Gordon, in his role as the Falcon, had come to terms with all that long ago. There were some operations that the attorney general could never approve. Yet that didn't mean they weren't vitally necessary.

"Don't you think it's unfair to send Dr. Sommers in there with only part of the picture?" Constance questioned from behind him, unconsciously echoing his own momentary twinge of conscience. Apparently she felt compelled to point out the doubtful ethics of this situation one more time.

Despite his resolve, Gordon's brow wrinkled. Connie was right. What they were about to do to Eden Sommers was a little like dropping an angelfish into a tank of piranhas. But if they told her the whole story, they would prejudice her judgment. What they needed from Dr. Sommers was not only her expertise but also her unbiased opinion.

"The other side doesn't play fair, Connie," he reminded her. "And that means sometimes we can't afford to play fair either."

# Chapter One

Nothing Amherst Gordon could do or say would make her take this job, Eden Sommers told herself as she settled more comfortably into the courtesy van's padded seats and tried to relax.

"We'll be there in a few minutes," remarked the wiry young man who'd picked her up an hour and a half ago at National Airport. These were the first words he'd spoken in almost an hour. He had been chatty enough as he'd swung her overnight case into the custom vehicle and headed out of the airport parking lot, but when she'd tried to pump him about his employer, he'd suddenly developed an absorbing interest in a rock station.

Eden had been left alone with her uncertainties. In the atmosphere of secrecy that surrounded the whole affair, those uncertainties had only multiplied. This was the oddest private-duty assignment she'd ever been summoned to. Only the knowledge that the request for her specialized services came from the highest echelon of the government had made her agree to hear out this man called Amherst Gordon. But she had no doubt that as soon as he'd spoken his piece she was going to head back to the safety of the private clinic in Burlington, Vermont, where she'd been working ever since she'd left the air force.

The van pulled off a secondary road and turned into a narrow drive flanked by redbrick columns and a wrought-iron fence. A beveled white sign announced:

## THE AVIARY
### NO VACANCY

Eden craned her neck for a better view as they made their
way up the long, curving driveway. Despite her apprehension, she couldn't help being impressed by the understated
elegance of the setting. The winding lane led up through a
stand of red oaks and Southern magnolias toward a wide
and well-manicured greensward. At the top of the hill,
commanding a view of the surrounding countryside, was a
stately red brick manor house that looked as though it had
been there since plantation days. But if the facade had ever
been scarred by age, it was now meticulously restored. The
triangular pediment at the roofline gleamed with a new coat
of white paint, as did the carving around its bull's-eye window, and the antique brick had been repainted.

The surrounding topiary contributed to the well-tended
effect with hundred-year-old boxwoods that had been
sculptured into the shapes of large birds that now proudly
guarded the building.

Eden had barely stepped out of the van when a tall, dis-
tinguished-looking woman emerged from the house. She
walked quickly down the steps, projecting a sense of energy and purpose.

"Dr. Sommers," she said, offering her hand. "So good
of you to come. I'm Constance McGuire, Mr. Gordon's
assistant. Would you like to freshen up before your interview?"

"Thank you," Eden murmured. She wasn't going to
mouth the usual platitudes about being glad to be here
when she certainly wasn't.

As Eden stood in the bright sunlight giving the Aviary the
once-over, Amherst Gordon noted the strong set of her jaw.
Even with the slight distortion of the closed-circuit moni-
tor, he could tell that she resented being here. Good for her,
he thought. At first glance, those wide-set blue eyes and
that shoulder-length light brown hair might give an impression of innocence. But there was more to this woman

than met the eye. He had expected that from reading her service record.

Gordon continued to study Eden as his assistant led her down the hall toward the powder room. She was slender and of medium height. Even under what must be very trying circumstances, she carried herself with a sense of confidence. His gaze flicked back to her almost classic profile as she closed the door. Her air force picture hadn't done Eden justice. She was a damned attractive woman. And that wasn't going to make things any easier for her down on Pine Island.

Behind the closed door, his visitor was making her own last-minute observations. "Remember," she told her reflection sternly as she compensated for what she saw as her lack of color with a bit of lipstick and rouge, "you've got control of your own life. Nobody can make you do something you don't want to do." She'd used the line often enough with her patients. She only hoped she believed it herself now.

The pep talk had a salutary effect. When she emerged a few moments later, she had convinced herself she could deal with whatever persuasive techniques Amherst Gordon was going to try.

He was waiting for her in the solarium. The huge sunny room was splendid with potted ficus and schefflera trees and alive with the sounds of tropical birds. A flutter of red and green caught Eden's eye. As she watched, a parrot winged its way from one of the trees to the slightly stooped shoulder of a man standing near an ornate bird cage apparently feeding a pair of cockatoos.

Gordon turned and smiled in her direction. His left hand gripped the head of a cane. There were deep lines etched between his mouth and his nose—and at the corners of his eyes. His thick hair was almost entirely silver. But it was the eyes that really drew her attention. They were an unusual shade of green, with a keen intelligence that seemed to see right through the mask of composure she had affected.

His first words, however, were not for her but for the bird on his shoulder. "Thank you for announcing Dr.

Sommers's arrival, Cicero.'' The parrot squawked and flapped its acknowledgment.

"Settle down so you don't scare her," he warned.

Obediently the bird nestled against the gray tweed of his jacket.

"Won't you have a chair?" he asked Eden, gesturing toward a cushioned seat beside a wrought-iron table. As he moved forward, he leaned heavily on the cane. So that, at least, was no affectation, she thought, smoothing out the skirt of her blue suit as she sat down.

She was sure the rest of the scene had been carefully calculated to create a certain mood for Mr. Gordon's purposes. However, Eden wasn't going to allow him to slowly feed her bits and pieces of information the way he had been feeding the cockatoos.

"Exactly what is all this about?" she challenged.

He smiled. "Anxious to get started?"

"Anxious to hear what you have to say so I can go back to Vermont."

"Second thoughts already? And you haven't even heard my proposition."

"I'm waiting."

Gordon cleared his throat. "The bottom line is that I need the services of a psychologist who's rehabilitated victims of, shall we say, stressful enemy captivity."

"I've already guessed that much. But if you've looked at my records, which you obviously have, you know I haven't accepted a case like that in two and a half years."

Gordon nodded, reaching up to stroke the parrot's beak. "I'm hoping I can persuade you to make an exception. Let me tell you a little bit about the individual involved." He paused. "By the way, I've had your Alpha clearance reactivated, otherwise I wouldn't be able to disclose this information."

Eden's eyes widened. She'd have thought reinstating her clearance would have taken months, not less than twenty-four hours. Before she could comment, Constance McGuire appeared with a tray of small sandwiches, an ornate silver teapot and cups and saucers.

"I thought you might like some refreshment after your trip," the woman volunteered.

Eden thanked her and took a chicken salad sandwich quarter. She'd been too nervous to stomach the congealed eggs and greasy sausage on the plane that morning. She watched as Constance poured three steaming cups of tea and then took a seat at the table.

Gordon waited while the food was served, and Eden found herself wondering if he were trying to heighten the anticipation. "The story really starts eleven months ago, with a highly classified air force weapons project," he finally began, as though he were an old-time radio announcer embarking on a tale of suspense.

Despite herself, Eden leaned forward slightly. "And?" she prompted.

"There was evidence that some of the details of the project were showing up in unfriendly hands, so I was asked to put a man on the team who could double as an engineer while he discreetly investigated the security leak."

Why had Gordon—and not air force security—taken on that duty, she wondered, but suppressed the urge to ask. If she wasn't going to work with this man—and she probably wasn't—she was better off knowing as little as possible about him and his high-placed connections.

"I had the perfect agent for the assignment," Gordon went on. "He was a brilliant air force engineer who had been integral to a number of high-tech projects. He had also worked for me on several occasions, although his official orders always covered any suspicious absences from regular duty. He was everything I needed—loyal, dedicated and smart. More than once I'd put him in the uncomfortable position of having to choose between his personal life and service to his country. And he never failed me when I needed him."

Eden bit her lip. She thought she knew what kind of sacrifice he was describing. It took an emotional toll—in fact, one that had been too high for her to pay over the long term.

Gordon noted the young woman's reaction and pressed on. "I think he came through for me this time, too. He had sent a coded message that he had identified the leak and was on his way back from Berlin with the evidence." He paused for dramatic effect. "But his plane crashed in East Germany."

Even without knowing this engineer, Eden felt herself shudder at the price he'd apparently paid for his patriotism. When she thought back over the past year, however, she couldn't remember an incident like that coming out in the press.

Gordon answered her unspoken question. "It didn't make the papers," he said. "He was necessarily a loner with no family. And we didn't want any publicity."

"But, if he died . . ."

"That's just it. Six months later, the other side notified our Secretary of State that he was safe in one of their medical facilities. It seems they'd pulled him from the wreckage of his plane and managed to save his life. He'd been pretty badly burned and had a dozen broken bones. But they'd patched him up, and as a 'gesture of goodwill' they were returning him to us."

The tea in front of Eden was growing cold, but she'd forgotten all about it. "If they had him for six months, God knows what they did to him," she whispered.

"Exactly."

Despite her professed lack of interest, Eden found herself asking, "Where is he now?"

"For two months a special air force security unit has had him down at a facility called Pine Island off the Georgia coast. They're trying to debrief him, but he's not saying anything at all. I think he's afraid the information he learned before the accident is going to get him into more trouble. But that's not how air force security sees it. They're convinced the other side has brainwashed him—and gotten the specs on the weapons project he was working on. So they've decided he's expendable, and they're going to extract what they can out of him, no matter what the cost."

"They don't know he was actually working for us,"
Constance interjected. "We can't tell them without tip-
ping our hand to whoever it was that sabotaged that plane
in the first place."

Eden drew in a ragged breath. Sabotage. She had been
thinking the East Germans had taken advantage of an unfortunate accident. Now the drama had become even more
complex. But she still thought she understood why Gordon had sent for her. "You want me to go down to Pine Island and referee," she stated.

"Not exactly. There's an opening on the staff for a psychologist. Evidently they've decided strong-arm tactics
aren't working, so they're going to give the persuasive arts
a try."

Gordon had effectively drawn her into his story, but
Eden wasn't going to let herself become personally involved. Pushing back her chair, she stood up. "I'm sorry.
But you can count me out of the party." Working with
torture victims in the past had all but burned her out.
Turning to a less demanding job had been a matter of preserving her own sanity.

Connie looked from the agitated young woman to Amherst Gordon. At times like this she almost hated him. His
face didn't show it, but he was holding the ace of hearts and
had no qualms about using it.

"Would it make a difference," he asked Eden slowly, "if
I told you that the man in question is Lt. Col. Mark Bradley?"

A sharp pain seemed to knife through Eden's heart, and
she sank back into the chair. The horrible things this man
had described couldn't have happened to Mark, not the
Mark Bradley she remembered. But Amherst Gordon's
green eyes told her that it was all true.

"Dear God, no!"

Constance reached over and put an arm around her
shoulder. "I'm sorry," she murmured.

"I'm not going to ask you to make a decision without
more information," Gordon was saying as he got up and
walked stiffly across the room to transfer the parrot to a

T-shaped perch. "Maybe I've made a mistake, and you really aren't the right one for the case."

From a shelf near the window he picked up a manila folder. "Why don't you look over Colonel Bradley's file and then take some time to think the assignment over?"

Constance stood up also. Without further comment, they left Eden alone in the sunlit room that now unaccountably seemed a bit chilly.

Eden looked down at the cream-colored folder in the center of the table. Finally, with fingers that were far from steady, she flipped it open. The first thing she encountered was a large glossy photo of the man in question. In the picture he was smiling at her with that very masculine, slightly rakish grin that had captured her attention when they first met. Her gaze swept over the raven hair slanted across his forehead, the aquiline nose, the jaw that would have dominated his face had the other features not been so strong. The lines at the corners of his dark eyes had deepened slightly, but they only added a touch of maturity that hadn't been so apparent five years ago. Mark's dashing good looks had attracted her first. But she'd learned there was a toughness hidden by that devil-may-care exterior.

She could see his broad shoulders below the twill fabric of his uniform, but the photo had been cropped so that only the first two buttons of his shirt were visible. Against her will, her imagination began to fill in the rest of the picture—the brawny strength of his arms, the crisp dark hair that spread across his chest and arrowed down his long torso to his trim abdomen, the narrow hips, the well-muscled thighs. The way his naked body had felt pressed to hers. The rough texture of his chest against her breasts. That last incredible night he had made love to her, she had been sure he was going to ask her to marry him. The morning after, he had walked out of her life.

They'd been good friends for almost a year and lovers for nine months. But it wasn't just the physical relationship. They'd both seemed to find something vital they needed in each other. Mark had taught her how to capture the unique joy of each moment together—like fine champagne bursting from an uncorked bottle. At the same time, he seemed to be reaching out to her in a deeper way, as if he were finding roots he'd never had time to put down before. She'd thought the two of them had had something very special together. Apparently she'd been wrong.

She resented the way Amherst Gordon had carelessly ripped apart the scar tissue that had formed over her old wounds. Yet now, with Mark's folder in front of her, Eden couldn't help twisting the knife. As though under some sort of compulsion, she began to read on.

The file was a summary of Mark's service record, plus the special assignments he'd undertaken for Amherst Gordon. The language was bland, but the words gave her a sense of how much danger this man had lived with during the ten years he'd been an agent for the Peregrine Connection.

It was hard to take in. But the part that really wrenched her heart was the medical report from the air force facility where Mark was being detained. Eden felt a wave of nausea sweep over her as she began to read the dispassionate accounts of the subject's present mental and physical condition. He'd suffered everything from multiple fractures and internal injuries to major skin grafts. Only a man with an iron constitution could have survived.

Apparently he was on his way to physical recovery. But his mental state was another matter. Withdrawn, depressed, uncooperative and quite possibly psychotic—the terms leapt out at her. And from the prescribed course of treatment so far, it looked as though he was going to stay that way. Gordon must be right. Someone down there was desperate to break Mark Bradley—at any cost.

When Eden looked up from the folder, she knew that she had been manipulated by Amherst Gordon. But after what she'd learned, she really didn't have a choice about her decision.

She was staring off into space when the feeling of being watched made Eden look up toward the doorway, where her gaze collided with Gordon's.

"You bastard," she whispered. The accusation was as much a release of her own tension as an epithet directed at the man in the doorway.

"I take it that means you've decided to accept the assignment," Gordon observed dryly.

"You knew I would."

The silver-haired man acknowledged her capitulation with a slight nod. "You're right. I don't play by the rules. But I didn't have time for two weeks of gentle persuasion. You'll be leaving for Pine Island tomorrow morning, and we have a lot to do between now and then."

## Chapter Two

As the motor launch picked up speed, the salty wind blowing off the bow whipped Eden's shoulder-length hair back from her wide forehead. The spray felt good after the stifling humidity of the Savannah airport. The young woman sighed. In the space of thirty-six hours she'd gone from cool Vermont to muggy Virginia to the even muggier Deep South. But her final destination—Pine Island—was just ahead.

Shading her eyes against the slight glare from the choppy water, she peered into the distance, trying to make out the distinguishing characteristics of the island. All she could see was a white sandy beach and beyond it occasional stands of trees and some low buildings. Amherst Gordon had told her the holdings had originally belonged to a millionaire industrialist who'd lost his fortune in the recessions of the early seventies. The heirs had deeded his white elephant to the government in exchange for settlement on the back taxes.

The man behind her controlling the tiller coughed and she turned. "Best sit down," he advised above the steady hum of the motor. "Bound to be a bit rough out here."

For emphasis the boat gave a little lurch, making the lone passenger almost tumble onto one of the padded bench seats. There was no more conversation. Instead, Eden pulled her navy cotton skirt around her knees and kept her blue eyes fixed on her destination. It wasn't really a long ride, but too far for her to swim back to the Georgia mainland through the choppy water.

She knew why that particular thought had crossed her mind. During his exhausting briefing at the Aviary, Gordon had warned her that once she arrived at this well-guarded outpost, she probably wouldn't be allowed to leave until her job was finished. But what if she needed to get away quickly? What then? She simply didn't have the answer.

And there were other questions troubling her. Even though she'd held an Alpha clearance, she'd never been involved in undercover work. Was she going to be able to help Mark without letting his jailers know what she was doing? She felt like an actress thrown into an important role without time to study the script.

Eden scanned the shoreline, trying to pierce the facade of rich-man's playground that the island presented. Gordon had told her as much as he could about the frightening drama being enacted there. In order to play her part, she'd have to keep a lid on her own doubts and emotions.

The launch was close enough now that she could make out more details—gnarled oaks heavy with Spanish moss and a rambling stucco house reminiscent of a squared-off sand castle, only it was pink. But the charm of the picture was marred by a number of large signs posted around the shoreline:

Private Property
Trespassers Will Be Prosecuted To The
Full Extent Of The Law

A young man with blond, close-clipped hair waited on the narrow private dock. Dressed in blue jeans and a white T-shirt, he was obviously meant to be mistaken for a handyman. However, Eden noted that he walked with a definite military bearing. From reading Gordon's briefing sheets, she knew he was Sergeant Blackwell.

Even his weaponry was not standard military issue. She drew in her breath when she noticed the double-barreled shotgun leaning casually against a bench.

As he saw her eyes flick to it and then quickly away, he grinned. It wasn't a friendly gesture. Instead it was calculated to establish immediately who had the upper hand at this supersecret installation.

"Come into the guard station," he said as soon as she disembarked and her suitcases were deposited on the pier. The words were an order, not a request.

Silently Eden followed him along the rough gray boards to what looked like a shed meant to hold fishing tackle and other paraphernalia. Inside, however, it was equipped with a computer terminal and a telephone. There was no attempt to hide the closed-circuit TV camera mounted in one corner. The red light under the lens was on.

Without offering his visitor a seat, the guard picked up the receiver and dialed. "Sir, Dr. Sommers has arrived," he announced.

Eden couldn't hear the other side of the conversation, but it was punctuated on her end by frequent *Yes, sirs*. When the guard finally hung up, his face was impassive.

"I'll have to get your fingerprints and search your luggage," Blackwell relayed. "But Major Downing is busy now, anyway, so the delay won't make much difference."

Eden had been warned about security precautions, but not something like this. "My luggage . . ." she began.

"Could inadvertently contain materials that are off-limits here. I'm sorry, Doctor." The clipped cadence of his words told Eden that he wasn't.

Trying to appear unconcerned, she watched as he opened a suitcase and began to feel through the contents, unfolding blouses and skirts at random. He even sifted through the contents of the small jewelry bag tucked in the corner. One piece seemed to be of particular interest: an antique pin Connie had said would look nice with Eden's good dress. Blackwell held up the ornate piece, inspecting the amethyst and gold design curiously.

"Not much chance to wear something like this down here," he muttered.

Eden remained impassive. But when he pulled out a lacy bra and held it up for special scrutiny, she had to bite back a protest. There was no use calling attention to her clothing. Although supplied by the Peregrine Connection, the wardrobe fit her slender, five-foot-seven frame as though she had bought it herself. Constance McGuire had assured her that everything had been washed so that it would look broken in. Would the ploy work? Eden's reception committee of one made no comment.

Mindful of the camera and trying to appear serene, she gazed out the window. It was already well past dinner, and the setting sun had painted the western sky a rich shade of pink tinged with orange.

Finished with Eden's luggage, Blackwell brought out an old-fashioned fingerprint record card and opened a black stamp pad. Taking her right hand, he rolled each finger in turn across the spongy surface and then pressed it to the form. He didn't comment on the coldness of her skin. The procedure made her feel like a criminal being booked, not a well-trained professional on a sensitive assignment. She suspected it was supposed to have that effect. Major Downing obviously wanted to create a certain impression at her reception. She wasn't going to give him the satisfaction of knowing how much he had unnerved her.

Just as she was wiping her hand on a paper towel, another blue-jeaned young man arrived with a luggage cart. Small and compact with an olive complexion and coarse dark hair and brown eyes, he fit the description of Airman, Third Class Ramirez. But, as with Blackwell, she'd better not use his name until she'd been officially introduced.

"I'm to take you to your quarters," Ramirez announced laconically, as he began to load her belongings. No one here was making an effort to be friendly.

"If Major Downing is going to be tied up for a while, perhaps I could speak to Dr. Hubbard," she ventured.

"That won't be possible until after you've talked to our chief of station."

The cart's wheels crunched against the gravel path as she and Ramirez made their way between moss-hung live oaks toward the main compound. Besides the pink stucco house there were tennis courts, a pool that might have been designed for a Hollywood celebrity, and lush gardens in obvious need of attention. In fact, as she drew closer, Eden could see that the whole estate was somewhat neglected. The net on the tennis court was little more than a few sagging strings, and several of the statues around the pool were crumbling.

They were almost at the main house. Glancing up toward the red-tiled roof, she noted that the upper windows were covered completely by black, intricate grillwork that looked as effective as prison bars. Further to the right and left were several other buildings that might have been enlisted-men's quarters or offices. Heavy curtains blocked any view of the interiors.

As her guide opened the wide front door, Eden was hit by an inviting gust of air-conditioning, but it was one of the house's few modern improvements. The furniture had obviously come with the total package. While it must have been luxurious in its time, it was now showing the ravages of the wet climate. A faint mustiness tinged the air. Eden could imagine there was an enlisted man assigned to scraping the mildew off the overstuffed chintz-covered furniture and carefully oiling the old oak tables and chairs so they wouldn't crack.

Her room was upstairs on the front. Once Ramirez had left, Eden quietly closed the door. Now that she no longer had to maintain a controlled demeanor, her hands trembled slightly as she looked around at the sparse surroundings. Upstairs, the fading antiques had been replaced by standard government issue. The only furnishings besides the narrow bunk were a tall chest of drawers, a night table and a desk—all of olive drab metal. Not very cheery—and a far cry from the colonial elegance of the Aviary, where she had spent the night before.

Reaching up with long fingers, she massaged her temples and forehead. She hadn't realized what a strain it would be trying to act as though this were just another job. After the brusque reception her insides were churning like a rotary mixer.

Her first inclination was to pace back and forth until she was summoned, but by allowing her tension to build like that, she'd be playing right into Downing's hands. From his file, she knew that he was good at his job. And that included finding any weakness in an opponent and exploiting it. Apparently he wanted her off-balance during their first interview.

Her suspicions were confirmed when Ramirez knocked on the door again about twenty minutes later. He was holding a covered tray.

"I'm sorry, the chief of station sends his apologies. He's too busy to see you tonight. But he has asked me to bring you up dinner, since you missed the officers' mess this evening."

Eden silently took the tray. She was smart enough to recognize she'd just been very effectively snubbed by Maj. Ross Downing.

"Thank the major for his consideration," she told Ramirez.

He remained in the doorway.

"Yes?"

"I'm directed to tell you that breakfast is between 0700 and 0800 hours. It's an informal buffet."

Eden acknowledged the information and closed the door. Crossing to the desk, she set the tray down and lifted the white cloth napkin. The plate contained a slice of baked ham, speckled butter bean, and corn bread. Very Southern, she thought, taking a bite of the warm bread. Everything was good. But with her stomach still tied in knots, she could barely force down a few mouthfuls.

Why couldn't Downing have spared a few minutes to see her tonight? She had been primed for the confrontation. But he must have known that.

She wished he'd sent up Mark's classified case history along with dinner. Deception had never been her strong suit. Sooner or later she was going to slip up and mention something that she wasn't supposed to know.

Sighing, she pushed back her chair and looked over at the pile of luggage Ramirez had stacked in the corner. Somehow she just didn't have the energy to cope with unpacking now. Probably her best strategy was to go to bed early. That way she'd be rested and ready for whatever Downing decided to hit her with in the morning.

Rummaging in her overnight case, she found her toiletries and carried them into the private bathroom—the one luxury her room afforded. Though the plumbing was antiquated, she'd never appreciated a shower more, she mused, as she shampooed her hair and then let the lukewarm water wash away some of her mental and physical fatigue. But running water couldn't completely ease her tension.

After she dried her hair she slipped into one of the sleeveless satin nightgowns from Constance's instant wardrobe. Her own tastes ran to more practical cotton, and the new acquisition felt sensuous against her skin.

Reaching out, she turned off the lamp on the bedside table. Dim light filtered through the translucent shade, casting lacy patterns from the grillwork over the window. The darkness didn't help to soothe her inner restlessness. In the space of a day and a half, her entire universe had been turned upside down. But her training had taught her that the human mind needed time to adjust to a massive shock. It was only now that she was beginning to realize the full implications of what Amherst Gordon's revelations meant to her personally.

Her thoughts spun back to the personnel folder he'd shown her in the comfortable solarium at the Aviary. It had contained more than a simple account of Mark's double career. When she'd come across her own name in the log from five years ago, she'd blanched. She hadn't realized that outside observers were taking notes on her personal relationship with Mark. But as she read further, she drew an even sharper breath.

The note Mark had left her after their last incredible night of lovemaking hadn't explained where he was going, nor had it held out any hope that she'd ever see him again. At first she'd been hurt, then angry.

Now she knew that he had left her bed to be smuggled into a turbulent Middle Eastern country where he'd spent months negotiating the return of three American military officers being held by an antigovernment terrorist group. At the time, she'd assumed that her lover had simply walked out on their personal relationship because he hadn't wanted to make a commitment. After reading his dossier she had a completely different perspective. Mark Bradley had chosen duty over personal happiness.

But why hadn't he come back to her when it was all over? What had she really meant to him? There was no way of knowing without asking. And he might not be in any kind of shape—might never be in any kind of shape—to tell her.

Long ago she thought she'd come to terms with the knowledge that he didn't care. Now she couldn't help torturing herself with what must have been in his mind that last night they'd been together.

The aching loneliness that pierced through her was suddenly more than she could bear. There hadn't been many men in her life since Mark, because there'd simply been no substitute for that particular man.

It had been a long time since she'd permitted herself to consciously think about Mark Bradley—or to hunger for his caress. Instead she'd put her emotional energy into her work. But now that she was so close to him, she was helpless to hold back the flood of memories that seemed to overwhelm her. Closing her eyes, she remembered their last night together. It was all there, every endearment, every touch, every kiss.

"I need you so badly, Eden," he had whispered, his breath warm on her lips just before his mouth had captured hers in a kiss of fiery intensity. He had pulled her tightly against his lean, muscular body before his strong hands had begun a journey of exploration across her passion-roused flesh. It was as though he was trying to memorize her body's every nuance. Perhaps that had really been in his mind. She murmured his name in the darkness, conscious of how close he was. And it was a long time before she finally fell asleep.

EDEN WOKE TO THE SOUND of heavy feet on the stairs. For a moment she was disoriented. Then she remembered that this was Pine Island. With the realization came the knowledge that she was anxious to get on with her assignment.

The clock on the bedside table told her it was well before seven. Apparently the enlisted men ate before the officers. Perhaps while they were occupied she could do a bit of exploring—and maybe even find Major Downing.

After dressing in one of the A-line skirts and cotton sweaters from her new wardrobe, she opened the door and stepped out into the empty hall. Her low-heeled sandals made very little noise on the worn carpet of the stairs. There was no one in the foyer when she gained the first floor, although she could hear the sound of clattering silverware and masculine voices drifting from the end of the hall.

She paused before one of the wide front windows and looked out at the overgrown gardens and the beach beyond, where sea green breakers curled against the white sand. This place could have been a resort gone to seed—except that it wasn't.

Turning away, Eden looked down the hall in both directions. One of the wings of the house must contain the office complex. She decided to try the one to the right. But the only evidence of the area's use was a slight smell of antiseptic in the dim hallway. Perhaps this was the medical facility.

Eden was about to retrace her steps when a door several yards in front of her swung open.

She could hear a slightly mocking voice saying, "Time for your yummy oatmeal."

At that moment a large man swung into her line of vision. His back was to her and she had time for only a fast impression of sandy brown hair and massive shoulders. Eden straightened her posture as he turned. She could see now that he had been maneuvering a wheelchair out the doorway.

Her heart skipped a beat, and her breath caught in her throat as her attention focused on the occupant of the chair. He was wearing loose-fitting gray sweatpants and a matching short-sleeved top. A wide canvas shoulder strap bound him firmly to the chair. Nevertheless, he was sagging forward and looking down so that his face was hidden. Only the top of his dark hair was visible. It had a dull, lifeless quality.

The bulky attendant was the one who spoke. "Dr. Sommers?"

Eden couldn't have responded at that moment, even when she heard her name repeated.

"This area is off-limits until after 0900 hours."

She was busy fighting to keep from gasping, not at the words but at the visage of the man who had finally raised his head to stare up at her from his mobile prison. Neither Gordon's report nor her own imagination could have really prepared her for this moment. Would she have recognized him as Mark Bradley if she'd encountered him in a private psychiatric hospital? She couldn't honestly say.

Her mind struggled to cope with the details of his ravaged appearance. Underneath the loose clothing he had lost considerable weight—as well as muscle tone. The dark hair was now a vivid contrast to the whiteness of his skin.

It struck her suddenly that he looked like someone who had spent long months shut away in a dungeon. The lines at the corners of his eyes no longer suggested laughter but an experience so devastating that laughter might never be possible again.

Apart from the effects of the injuries, this was not quite the face she remembered. But then the plastic surgeons might not have had a good photograph to work from.

Anxiously, Eden sought some sign of recognition in his eyes. For a second she thought she saw a flash of pain in their obsidian depths. Then the eyes seemed to go flat. She had the feeling she was looking into an empty, pitch-dark room. And the knowledge that Mark Bradley lived in there was chilling.

The male nurse studied her speculatively. "Colonel Bradley looks a lot better than he did a month ago. But that isn't saying much. I was hoping to fix him up a bit before you met him this afternoon." The whole speech completely ignored the presence of the patient himself, who in turn seemed oblivious to the exchange.

Eden struggled to get a grip on her composure. "Thank you, Sergeant Marshall," she said. As soon as the name was out of her mouth, she realized she'd made her first slip. She shot Marshall a glance, but the fact that she knew his name before he'd introduced himself didn't seem to have registered.

Her next words were for the man in the chair. Since they were also supposed to be strangers, she'd have to be more careful in carrying out the charade. "Colonel Bradley, I'm Dr. Sommers. I'll be working with you from now on."

The patient didn't acknowledge her words.

"Well, I'll be looking forward to seeing you later," she added warmly.

With that, she turned back to Marshall. "I was trying to find Major Downing."

"His office is at the other end of the hall. He's usually down there at the crack of dawn."

"Thank you."

Before moving away, she risked one more look at the man in the wheelchair. The Mark Bradley she had known had been in superb mental and physical condition. *Oh, God, what have they done to him?*

# Chapter Three

Eden was suddenly aware that she was standing on the front porch of the main house staring blindly out at the breakers washing against the deserted beach. Her mind kept replaying that brief encounter with Mark. The emotional impact was as strong as the relentless force of the surf pounding the shore.

Finally the rhythm of the waves helped calm her. As her pulse steadied she found herself watching a piece of driftwood tumbling up the sandy slope, only to be pulled back into the green water by the force of the undertow.

In a way she was like that piece of flotsam. She'd been tossed into a troubled sea by Amherst Gordon—and he'd left her to sink or swim by herself.

But she wasn't going to be swept under, and she wasn't going to let Mark down, either. Turning, she pulled open the heavy wooden doors and strode briskly through the foyer and down the hall in the direction that Marshall had indicated.

When she reached a door with a polished brass nameplate that said "Major Ross Downing," she hesitated. Inside, a chair squeaked. Before she had a chance to reconsider her course of action, the door was flung open and she was standing face-to-face with the island's security chief.

He looked momentarily surprised. "Dr. Sommers. I didn't expect to see you quite this early."

"Well, I'd like to get started with Colonel Bradley as soon as possible. But of course I felt I should check in with you first." The last was a pointed reference to her reception—or lack of it—last night.

He took a step back. "Then come in."

She followed him inside. The office was the first room in the old house that showed any extensive redecorating. Apparently the major had fixed his private domain to suit himself. The floor was carpeted in a muted tweed. One wall boasted a display of Civil War swords and pistols. On the other was a framed poster featuring a white chess piece against a black background. "Make security your first and last move," it advised judiciously. It was a far cry from what she would have chosen.

The wide oak desk looked as though it had been salvaged from the estate's library. It was clean except for one crisp manila folder, a mug with the air force security service crest and an old-fashioned manual typewriter of the kind she hadn't seen in years.

But the man himself dominated the surroundings. Like his staff, he was in mufti, although instead of jeans he wore light gray slacks and a blue knit shirt. Even in the casual attire, he exuded an aura of command, as though he expected his orders to be executed without question. From where he stood now behind the desk, he seemed to tower over Eden, and his frankly male assessment was an instant reminder that she was the only woman on this isolated, high-security base.

Eden met his confident gaze as they exchanged the stiff greetings of wary strangers. She suspected that Maj. Ross Downing's blond Viking appearance would appeal to a certain kind of woman—although he wasn't her type. From Gordon she knew that this man had been a security officer for the last fifteen years and had an unmatched reputation for toughness. Yet he also had a record of being fair. So why was he coming down so hard on Mark Bradley?

"I'm sorry I wasn't able to see you when you arrived," he began, settling into a comfortable chair behind the oak desk. Somehow the apology lacked sincerity.

Without being invited, Eden took a seat across from him.

"Perhaps you won't be as anxious to get to work when you see what you're up against."

"Oh?"

"Dr. Sommers, the guy we have down here has been so badly messed up that all you've got to work with is a human shell, as empty as a coconut that's been sucked dry."

Aware that he was watching her reaction, Eden struggled to maintain her facade of professional composure. A few minutes ago, when she'd seen Mark, she'd been shaken by very similar thoughts. Now the chief of station's confirmation of her feelings was like a hot knife slicing through her flesh. Downing was simply describing a man who had been brought to him for interrogation. Her fears were for someone she'd cared very deeply about.

"Dr. Hubbard agrees with your diagnosis?" she asked quietly.

"Hubbard's just an M.D.," Downing said, with a gesture of dismissal. "His comments on the patient's mental state aren't worth beans. But just for the record," he added, "bringing a clinical psychologist in on this case wasn't my idea, either."

Eden took in the set line of his jaw. Apparently he couldn't tolerate losing control of the situation. Hubbard's weak questioning of his decisions was simply an annoyance. She, a psychologist, had the potential to challenge his authority. Last night he must have been trying to deny her presence at Pine Island while asserting his domination over the base.

"I have very little faith that your fancy methods are going to work with Colonel Bradley," he continued.

*Apparently* your *methods haven't worked either. Or I wouldn't have been called in,* she thought.

"However, I always follow correct procedures," he added. "That means I want a report from you on the patient's present mental state as soon as possible."

"You'll get my written psychiatric evaluation within the next ten days," Eden returned.

"I don't have ten days. I need results now."

"Major, I'll do the best I can." She paused and then continued. "You must know if you've studied my past cases—or those of anyone else in the field—that no one can guarantee success overnight. I've got to gain Bradley's confidence before I can get anywhere with a therapy program. That means I need a free hand, without your team's interference."

Downing's eyes seemed to bore into her head. When he finally began to speak, his words were clipped and precise. "The last thing I'm interested in is a therapy program. Our mission is to find out what Bradley told the East Germans. If you don't start getting something out of him pretty fast, I have other options."

Gordon had told her about those other options. They had made her blood turn to ice. Was Downing frustrated because his own tried-and-true methods hadn't worked? Or was the major trying to protect himself by making sure that Mark never recovered? Finding out would have to be part of her hidden agenda.

The chief of station glanced at his watch. "Since you're so anxious to get started, I'll call Dr. Hubbard. He can fill you in on the medical details."

Downing phoned the doctor and then looked back up at Eden. "He'll be here in a few minutes. Apparently, Bradley got too much of his sleep medication last night and he's a little dopey this morning."

"What? I assumed the colonel would be drug free while I was working with him," Eden shot back. Downing's casual mention of a drug overdose had hit a nerve. But she instantly regretted having lost her composure.

"I just want Bradley alert when I'm working with him," she stated with less vehemence.

The man on the other side of the desk pursed his lips thoughtfully. "That's your choice—for the time being. But Colonel Bradley suffers from nightmares, I'm afraid. If you take him off his knockout drops, you'll also have to keep him quiet so the rest of us can get some sleep. I assume you won't object to moving from your present quarters into the room next to his?''

Eden fought to mask her elation. Downing might have thought he was giving her the equivalent of disciplinary duty. But having as much access to Mark as possible would make her job easier. "I guess that's only fair," she murmured.

Dr. Hubbard's tentative knock terminated the interview. Eden turned to greet him. He was of medium height, with white hair, wire-rimmed spectacles and a rather pasty complexion. The man was only in his midfifties, she knew. Yet his shoulders were slightly stooped, and his years appeared to weigh him down like a heavy cloak. And although he held the same rank as Downing, he seemed to be almost afraid of the chief of station. Did the man have some hold over him?

"Would it be convenient to discuss my assignment now?" she asked after they'd exchanged greetings.

The physician shot a glance at Downing, who nodded imperceptibly. "Yes, I've gotten the patient's records ready for your arrival. Why don't we go down to my office and discuss them."

Five minutes later Eden found herself in a room which could have been a doctor's office in any large military hospital. Shelves full of medical reference books took up most of the wall space. Behind Hubbard's desk hung a diploma from Johns Hopkins Medical School as well as several certificates of merit. Apparently his training had been top rate.

The doctor seemed to undergo a transformation once he reached the comfortable leather chair behind his desk. His shoulders straightened, the slack skin of his face tightened slightly as his jaw molded itself into a firmer line. In this domain, at least, he was the authority. And that gave Eden some cause for hope.

"Well, you certainly come well recommended, Dr. Sommers," he was saying. "The Pentagon personnel office that hired you has been singing your praises for the last week. Lucky for us that you were considering a leave of absence from the Balsinger Clinic."

Leave of absence? Eden thought. She'd been considering no such thing. But the casual remark made her wonder what strings Amherst Gordon had pulled and what subterfuges he'd resorted to in order to get her to Pine Island. The Falcon must have been so sure of her compliance that he'd put his cover story into action before she'd even been contacted.

Graciously she acknowledged the compliment and then asked to see Mark's records.

"By the way, I can have breakfast sent in so we can work while we eat. Would that be satisfactory?" the doctor asked.

"Fine," Eden agreed.

While they drank coffee and ate scrambled eggs and biscuits, Dr. Hubbard seemed almost eager to talk about Mark's case. Eden could see why. As far as the patient's physical condition was concerned, this aging air force physician had practically pulled off a miracle. Up till now there had been no one with whom he could share the success. Probably the only recognition Hubbard had gotten from Downing was increased pressure for treatment that would ensure the patient's cooperation.

As Eden sipped a second cup of coffee and went over Mark's medical records, the doctor leaned forward, awaiting her comments.

"I see the East Germans kept him just barely functioning. There doesn't seem to have been any physical therapy during his initial convalescence. That certainly made your job a lot harder," she said.

Hubbard nodded. "It's nice to be able to talk to someone who can appreciate the problems. Of course, there *is* Sergeant Marshall, and he's been a tremendous help with the physical therapy. But he hasn't been making any of the decisions."

Eden hesitated for a split second. To pretend she hadn't encountered Marshall already would lead to more complications that she'd have to cover up. "Oh, I think I met the sergeant this morning when I got lost on the way to the chief of station's office," she admitted. "I presume he was taking Colonel Bradley to breakfast."

Hubbard looked surprised. "Then you've already seen the patient?"

"Just for a moment. But I'm looking forward to starting my own program with him as soon as possible."

"In that case, you'll want to study the psychological records." Opening his desk drawer, the doctor brought out a sealed folder that was stamped Top Secret.

Eden wanted to reach out for it; instead she let it lie there between them on the desk.

Hubbard's eyes flicked down toward the folder and then back up to her face. "Dr. Sommers," he began slowly, "I'm sure you were told before you came down here that Colonel Bradley was held in a Leipzig hospital after his plane crash. Officially, the air force is worried that they may have gotten the plans of the top secret weapons project out of him. But that's only part of the problem. Actually, there's something so disturbing in this folder that I feel I have to give you some warning rather than letting you read it cold."

Eden met his gaze without faltering. "Go on," she said.

"You know, of course, that reconstructive surgery was necessary. What you don't know is that his air force medical records—including his dental records—have mysteriously disappeared."

Why didn't he just come out with it, whatever it was? Eden wondered. "I don't think I understand," she ventured.

"To put it bluntly, the man we have here at Pine Island may be a doppelgänger—a duplicate, if you will."

Eden gasped. She thought she had been prepared for almost anything. But not that.

"Yes, air force security is afraid the individual 'returned' to us may not be the real Mark Bradley at all, but a cleverly coached, and perhaps very deadly, East German agent."

Eden heard the words, but her mind just couldn't cope with this new revelation. On a personal level it was simply too devastating. Yet her response to Hubbard was couched in much broader terms. "But... but the physical trauma. The broken bones. The burns. Only monsters would do something like that to one of their own men."

Hubbard shrugged. "I don't think we can underestimate their determination."

Mercifully, after delivering his bombshell, the doctor left her alone to go over the top secret records. Amherst Gordon had already shown her most of it. In fact, the Falcon's file was more complete. It had given Mark's Peregrine assignments along with his cover duties for the air force. And it had gone into his boyhood background. She'd learned all sorts of things about Mark that he hadn't gotten around to telling her five years ago—everything from his anchor position on the high school swim team to his long-held interest in collecting historical letters.

The only thing missing from Amherst Gordon's version was the distressing question about the identity of the man in custody at Pine Island.

Had the Falcon's Intelligence sources failed to provide that information? It took only a few moments of reflection to realize that the question really answered itself.

Of course Gordon had known. In fact, he had probably counted her intimate relations with Mark a colossal stroke of good luck. There were undoubtedly a number of therapists who could do just as good a job of mending the patient's battered psyche, assuming the patient really was Mark Bradley. But there was no one else in a better position to determine the identity of the man being held here.

Eden didn't realize she was clenching her teeth until the pain brought her back to the reality of Hubbard's office. She looked around at the walls lined with medical texts as if to orient herself. Then she closed her eyes. Very deliberately, on the screen of her mind, she brought up an image of Mark Bradley's face—first the lover she had known so well and then the patient in the wheelchair this morning. Carefully she examined one and then the other. They were the same, yet different in a dozen subtle and not so subtle ways.

Certainly Mark had changed. But that was to be expected. And hadn't there been a brief moment of recognition in his eyes when he had looked up and seen her? Or was that just wishful thinking? If Dr. Hubbard was right, he could simply be a carefully coached double.

No, she refused to accept that explanation. The man in the wheelchair had to be Mark Bradley. Otherwise, this whole assignment was a farce. Then suddenly another thought struck Eden. If the man upstairs was not Mark, he was playing a very high-risk game. She let her mind elaborate on that scenario. The integrity of a critical U.S. weapons system was at stake. If an impostor had been sent here to compromise it, undoubtedly he would be prepared to kill anyone he suspected could expose him. And he would surely know about Mark Bradley's affair with Eden Sommers. She shuddered as she let her thoughts follow that path to the ultimate conclusion. For her own safety she'd have to proceed very cautiously, no matter what her heart urged.

Getting up briskly, Eden located the doctor once more and asked for a copy of Mark's treatment program. She wanted to study his daily routine with an eye to becoming part of it.

"I'd like to get right down to work," she told Hubbard. "Is there an office I can use?"

"The one next to mine is empty," he replied.

She had turned to leave when she felt his hand on her arm. "Listen," he began. "I didn't say it before, but I'm glad to have you aboard. A lot of responsibility goes with this billet, and I'm relieved to have someone to share it with."

Eden nodded. "Yes. Well, I think we both want to do the best that we can for Colonel Bradley."

A troubled expression flickered in the doctor's eyes for a moment. "Within the limitations of the assignment, of course," he mumbled.

"Limitations of the assignment?"

The doctor clarified. "Considering the circumstances, Colonel Bradley's best interests and those of the U.S. government may not be precisely the same."

"Oh?"

"I would have thought Major Downing had made that clear when you arrived. He certainly made it clear to me that the prime objective of the staff is getting whatever information we can."

"And you agree with Downing?"

"He's my commanding officer. What alternative do I have? Besides, the man we have down here may not even be Bradley."

"I think we have to assume that he is," Eden said with more conviction than she felt. It was hard to mask her disappointment. She'd dared hope she could count on the physician. Apparently he hadn't been thinking of the man in his care as anything more than a damaged machine in need of physical repair. Or did he have some other, more subtle motive?

Hubbard looked uncomfortable. "I'm a thirty-year man who's just dealing with reality."

"I'll remember that."

Once back in her office, Eden fought the temptation to simply sit and brood over Hubbard's words. She wasn't going to allow herself the luxury of wasting any of her energy on him when she had important work to do. Resolutely she got out a pencil and started making notes.

Two hours later a tap on the door startled her from her concentration. It was Dr. Hubbard announcing lunch.

"I'll be along in a second," she told him as she hastily finished up her last few notes.

On her way to the dining room, she mentally ticked off the officers she was likely to meet. Besides Hubbard and Downing, there would be the members of the hot-shot interrogation team, Price and Yolanski.

At the curved entrance to the room, she paused for a moment to study the men who would either be her allies or her adversaries. They were seated at a long, heavily carved table. The table and high-backed chairs looked as though they might once have graced a medieval castle. Downing commanded the far end. The others were arranged along the sides. As though sensing her presence, Downing looked up. "Good afternoon, Dr. Sommers."

"I'm sorry I'm late," Eden murmured as she took the one empty chair. It was opposite Downing.

"Late, but worth waiting for," someone near the end of the table said under his breath.

The chief of station nodded. "As you know, Dr. Sommers will be joining our staff for the next few months. And I'm sure she'd like to sort us all out."

Apparently he wasn't going to be openly antagonistic in front of his staff. When he looked pointedly at the officer on his right, Lieutenant Price introduced himself as a member of the security group.

Gordon had given her a brief description of everyone here but Captain Walker, a powerfully built black man with intelligent dark eyes and a cautious manner. Was he, like herself, a recent arrival to Pine Island? Or was the Falcon lacking some important information about the installation?

The unknown factor was disturbing, but she pushed her concern to the back of her mind and forced herself to make the most of these first moments with the staff. She knew the value of unspoken communications. There was a great deal a trained observer could pick up from body language and eye contact—or lack of it.

As they introduced themselves, she gave what appeared to be polite interest in each. However, she was picking up all sorts of cues ranging from curiosity to nervousness and even well-disguised hostility. Price, who was tall with medium brown close-clipped hair, was the least subtle. Like Downing, he apparently saw her presence as the grounds for a turf battle.

Ramirez had come in to bring her iced tea. And the compact, ruddy-faced Yolanski, who happened to be seated next to her, passed the country-fried steak. He seemed the most easygoing of the group. Price was definitely uptight.

Walker didn't say much, but he was listening to the general conversation and sizing her up.

As the meal drew to a close, Downing made a few announcements. Among other things, Eden learned that the station's original function of testing ocean water samples was still ongoing.

Afterward she walked back to the medical wing with Dr. Hubbard.

"Well, I guess I'm ready to have my first session with the patient now," she announced.

The doctor looked surprised. "Don't you want to spend a bit more time with the background material first?"

"I believe I've gotten about all I can get out of the psychiatric evaluation. It was made when he first got here, and we know what kind of condition he was in then. I need to find out if the situation has changed. The only way I can do that is by working with the colonel."

"That's your department, of course. I'll phone up to Sergeant Marshall and see if Bradley's ready to receive any company."

Eden knew the words were an attempt at humor, but she didn't smile.

Twenty minutes later she was ushered into the small elevator that led to the second floor. Hubbard had explained that it—along with a narrow, twisting stairway that was locked with iron gates at the top and bottom—was the only means of reaching the upper story in the medical wing, since the exit to the other part of the building had been blocked off. The arrangement made the top floor a virtual prison. Suddenly Eden remembered that she'd soon be sleeping in this restricted environment.

As she stepped out of the elevator, the male nurse she'd met that morning came striding down the hall. "We weren't officially introduced," the tall, muscular attendant said. "But I'm Sergeant Wayne Marshall." He held out a large, iron-hard hand.

"Eden Sommers," she returned, breathing a sigh of relief as they clasped hands briefly. His suspicions must not have been aroused by her early-morning wanderings, nor must he have noted her use of his name earlier.

She studied his face, thinking that it could have been stamped out of hardy midwestern stock. His sandy hair was just starting to thin, his brown eyes were wide-set and his teeth were a bit uneven. Like everyone else here, he seemed to be holding back until she proved something to him.

She had felt the vigor in his grip. Lifting incapacitated patients must be a good way to build upper-body strength.

"Do you want me to stay for your interview with Bradley—at least until we see how things are shaping up?" he asked solicitously.

"No. We're going to need privacy so he can talk freely." She didn't bother to add that the Falcon had warned her the sessions could be bugged. She'd just have to make sure that they didn't contain any obvious references to her previous relationship with Mark, or to her real purpose here.

Marshall's brow wrinkled. "Usually he's pretty docile, but a few times he's gotten, shall we say... out of control."

"Well, if I need you, I'll call." Her tone of voice left no room for argument. "Now, where can I find the colonel?"

"There's a small lounge at the end of the hall where he usually spends a few hours in the afternoon recovering from his morning physical therapy session."

"That ought to do."

Now that the moment had arrived, Eden hesitated before pushing open the heavy door. Trust was so fragile. This first private meeting would set the tone for everything that followed, and she desperately wanted it to go well.

The translucent curtains in the room were drawn against the afternoon sun, so that most of the light came from a pole lamp in the corner. The only occupant was sitting in an easy chair against the wall facing a television set, which was turned to a daytime soap opera. The room was large enough to hold only another few chairs, a leather couch and a battered coffee table.

A quick inventory told her that Marshall had indeed prettied up her patient for the occasion. His dark hair had been tamed to a straight line that slanted across his forehead, and his sweat clothes had been exchanged for a white polo shirt and jeans that were looped with a woven belt on the tightest notch. He was sitting up straighter than he had been in the wheelchair. That meant the shoulder strap had simply been a convenience for transporting him around. She hoped the chair itself had been a convenience, too.

Despite her mental preparations, her heart gave a painful lurch. Although he was staring in the direction of the TV screen, his face had the same blank appearance she remembered from that morning. Or was it quite the same?

She took a step closer, studying his expression. It was not like that of other withdrawn patients she had worked with. Somehow, inexplicably, he didn't have the look of a man being helplessly controlled by events—but of a man who was exercising control.

The insight, coupled with her extensive briefings from Amherst Gordon, gave Eden a measure of hope. The Falcon had told her Mark, like his other operatives, had mastered an experimental mental technique for withstanding enemy brainwashing. If he hadn't succumbed to the East Germans, this technique had been what had saved him. And if that was true, he would still be using it in this equally threatening situation at Pine Island, where he had no one to trust and no one to turn to. But now she was here to help him. And she had to get that message across.

Masking her thoughts, she walked to the television and flipped off the program. "I understand that security has been using some weird methods around here, but soap operas seem like cruel and unusual punishment." Her little joke had no apparent effect. Ignoring his lack of response, she continued. "As I told you this morning, I'm Dr. Eden Sommers, and since we'll be working together closely, I'd like to put the relationship on a first-name basis. What do you think about that?"

Still nothing.

Eden knelt down on the floor so that she was in his line of vision. She half expected him to glance away, but instead he seemed to look right through her. Was he deliberately tuning her out? Unfortunately, there were other possibilities that might account for the wall that seemed to separate them—torture-induced psychosis, for example.

"Mark," she tried again, "we can take this slow and easy, but you've got to give it— You've got to give *me* a chance to help you."

She felt his awareness of her come to the surface as though he were a deep-sea diver being forced upward by lack of oxygen.

There was an unexpected flash of anger in his obsidian eyes.

"Get out of here. Leave me alone," he rasped. The gravelly quality of his voice sent a chill up her spine. The Mark Bradley she remembered had spoken in deep and resonant tones. This man could barely whisper. Yet if he had been silent for six months, that made sense.

Despite the sound of the words themselves, Eden was elated. As far as she knew, he had consciously responded to no one since he had been here, even during Downing's tough interrogations. That meant she was even more of a threat to him than the security team was. Would that be possible if she were a total stranger? She doubted it. She held on to that doubt, unwilling to consider the other possibility Dr. Hubbard had suggested.

She was just about to use the opportunity Mark had given her, when she heard a bloodcurdling scream from somewhere else in the building. At the same time, the lights went off, plunging the room into semidarkness. Instinctively, Eden gripped Mark's knees and felt him tense as she struggled to her feet.

"What the hell...?" Sergeant Marshall's voice sounded in the hall. She whirled around just as he flung the door open. The light was dim but she could still make out one riveting feature of the silhouette in the doorway. In his hand was a standard service revolver. And it was pointed directly at Mark Bradley.

# Chapter Four

"All right," the large man ordered. "Stay put until they let me know what's going on."

"I trust that means I'm allowed to sit down," Eden countered with more bravado than she felt.

Marshall nodded tightly. "We can't get downstairs, anyway. Move a chair over by the colonel so I can cover you both." He gestured with a flick of the revolver.

After Eden complied, he eased his muscular form onto a wooden folding chair. From the way his feet were braced against the ground, she knew he was ready to spring up at a moment's notice.

Eden cast a sideways glance at Mark. His shoulders were rigid and he was looking in the sergeant's direction. Otherwise, he hadn't moved. She wanted to reach out and lay a reassuring hand on his arm. Or perhaps she wanted to reassure herself by the physical contact.

"Isn't this carrying things a bit too far?" Eden ventured.

"Security precautions," Marshall snapped. The warning note in his voice signaled Eden to keep the rest of her questions to herself.

She repressed a flash of anger. The situation was bad enough, but this man's attitude made it worse. If he thought this was an escape attempt, she could understand his concern. But he knew perfectly well that Mark was in no shape to go climbing down a second-story drainpipe—if he could have pried the heavy metal bars off the windows.

Was the sergeant simply the kind of man who enjoyed exercising power? Or was he compensating for the job title "male nurse"? She didn't know him well enough yet to go beyond speculation.

Time seemed to crawl by. Eden tried to keep from looking at the gun, which seemed like an extension of Marshall's hand. Every time her gaze encountered the blue-black steel of the weapon, it seemed to have increased in size. Despite the air-conditioning, which was still running, Eden felt a trickle of perspiration slide down her neck and into her collar. She didn't move to wipe it away. In the dim light, she risked another glance at Mark. She could detect tension in the way he was rubbing the pad of his thumb against his ring finger.

Her mind flashed back to information she had found tucked into the back of his file, information that had made her want to bang her fists against the desk. The men she'd met at lunch had systematically subjected Mark to six- and eight-hour inquisitions. They'd taken two-hour shifts. Even though Mark had been in terrible physical condition, they'd denied him sleep and used every trick possible to try to trap him into compromising himself. He hadn't broken.

Was being held at gunpoint just another ploy? Or did it have some unknown sinister meaning?

Finally, after what seemed like an eternity but was probably less than five minutes, the lights flickered on. Marshall looked up approvingly, but he didn't put the gun away.

Now there wasn't any excuse for being treated like this. "I believe the drill is over, Sergeant," she observed, starting to get up.

"We'll wait for official word," he shot back.

Eden sighed and dropped back down in her chair.

Again the minutes dragged by. Below them Eden thought she heard movement and muffled voices. But she couldn't be sure of that, or anything else.

Finally the elevator door wheezed open. Moments later Corporal Blackwell was standing in the doorway.

"You're to come with me right away," he said, looking directly at Eden.

"What's this all about?"

"You'll have to ask Major Downing," Blackwell clipped out.

Eden stood up and faced the nurse. "I assume I'm free to leave?" She was unable to keep the sarcasm out of her voice.

"Naturally, if the security chief wants to see you," he answered blandly before turning to Blackwell. "Is everything secure?"

"Yes."

Only then did Marshall lower his weapon and relax his posture.

Eden repressed a shudder. Staring down a gun barrel had frightened her—and she had masked that fear with anger.

What effect had this little drama had on Mark? She wasn't free to try to find out right now. Instead she followed Blackwell down the hall and into the elevator. Not a word was exchanged between them. Once they reached the first floor, she almost had to run to keep up with the young man's long strides. Eden had the feeling that the concessions she'd won that morning had been wiped away by some unlucky event beyond her control.

As they strode down the hall, another framed poster caught her eye. It showed a marksman riddling the center of a bull's-eye with bullets. "Keep security on target" the message read. Eden felt her lunch curdle. Living with propaganda like this must have affected the way the men down here viewed Mark. He had come to Pine Island labeled "enemy." They seemed determined to prove it.

Downing was conferring with Captain Walker, the new member of the security team, when she entered the room. Immediately the low-pitched conversation stopped and both men looked up in her direction.

"Sit down," the chief of station ordered, gesturing toward a chair opposite the one Walker occupied.

"I think I have a right—"

"Sit down."

Eden sat.

"Thank you." Downing's pale blue eyes never left hers as he reached down and brought out a familiar-looking plastic appliance. One end was blackened and charred.

"Is this your hair dryer?" he asked.

Eden was suddenly even more confused. "Yes. Why do you have it?"

"Because it damned near killed one of my men and shorted out the whole upstairs. Or didn't you notice that the lights were out?"

Her breath caught in her throat. She had certainly noticed the lights. But she still didn't understand what he was talking about.

Both security officers watched her reaction intently.

"Airman Ramirez went to your room to move your belongings to your new quarters," Downing explained. "When he tried to unplug the hair dryer you'd left on the sink, it gave him a rather nasty jolt—and second-degree burns up his arm. Dr. Hubbard's working on him now."

Eden stared at the appliance that had suddenly been transformed into a weapon. "There was nothing wrong when I used it last night," she protested.

Captain Walker's mahogany brow wrinkled. She sensed that this interview was as uncomfortable for him as it was for her. "That may be so," he conceded. "But this afternoon when Ramirez inadvertently switched it on, it certainly wasn't working properly."

"Are you trying to tell me it wasn't an accident?" Eden challenged. And then, from the peculiar way they were looking at her, another idea took hold. "Are you suggesting that I'm responsible?"

Walker's eyes never left her face. "There's a special policy here at Pine Island," he began, apparently ignoring her question. "Every duty station is monitored by at least one other individual." He paused for a moment to let that information sink in. "I've checked with all stations. No one was away from his post at any time today. So if someone tampered with the hair dryer after you left your room in the morning, I don't know when it could have happened."

Eden considered his words. "Yes, but what motive would I have to injure one of your enlisted men? And come to think of it—" she turned to Downing "—you never told me my luggage was going to be moved. I expected to do my own packing." As the implication of her own words sank in, she felt suddenly as though the wind had been knocked out of her. "God, if Ramirez hadn't come in there to move my things, I'm the one who would have been burned," she whispered.

The expression on the faces of the two men sitting across from her gave nothing away. In fact, either one of them could have set the trap.

For several heartbeats, no one spoke. "None of this makes much sense," Downing finally mused. "But I think it's worth noting that the incident coincides with your arrival."

"And what inferences do you draw from that?" Eden managed.

"I never jump to conclusions," the chief of station returned evenly. For a moment they stared at each other. Neither might want to admit it, but they both recognized that the incident had stirred up a bubbling cauldron of possibilities.

It was Eden who finally broke the silent exchange. "While you're making up your mind, I'd like a lock installed on my bedroom door," she said.

"That won't be necessary. The rooms in the medical wing come equipped with locks. Blackwell's already moving your things, except the hair dryer, of course, to the room next to Colonel Bradley's."

His words held a note of dismissal, and Eden was grateful. She wanted to be alone to think about this frightening new development.

EDEN HAD PLANNED to spend the afternoon drawing up a formal schedule for working with Mark. But after returning to the office Dr. Hubbard had given her, she found she couldn't concentrate. Finally she put her papers aside and went back upstairs.

As Blackwell unlocked a door near the end of the hall and handed her the key, she caught him looking at her strangely. Was he holding her responsible for what had happened to Ramirez? Briefly she considered bringing the issue out into the open. But in this case, she decided with a sigh, further discussion would probably do more harm than good.

After closing the door, she looked around the room, trying to focus on something besides the frightening incident that had marred her first day here. To her surprise the large, airy bedroom was a lot more pleasant than the one on the other side of the main house. Apparently the original furnishings had been retained up here. The bureau, double dresser and easy chair were real antique white wicker. The four-poster double bed with its beautifully crocheted spread carried out the theme. It matched the draped swag curtains at the window.

Had Marshall or one of the other enlisted men been moved out of here? Eden wondered with a grin. She could just imagine they'd been quite willing to escape this frankly feminine setting.

One door led to a walk-in closet, the other to a white-tiled bath with both a claw-foot tub and a shower stall. A second door of the bath connected her room to one that was evidently Mark's. Eden stood for a moment looking at his quarters. This bedroom was quite different, with heavy mission oak furniture and a wide-planked pegged-pine floor. But its most distinguishing characteristic was utter lack of personality. She had almost expected to see Mark's air force jacket draped over the valet in the corner, but the valet was bare. The dresser top, too, was completely clear. The barrenness gave her an eerie feeling, as though the man who lived here had no personal possessions whatsoever.

When she stepped back into the bathroom, she realized that, except for a toothbrush, toothpaste and a hair brush, there were none of the usual toilet articles she might expect to find. It seemed they weren't trusting him with a razor.

Even though the quarters were nicely furnished, the environment was claustrophobic. She could leave when she wanted. Mark was locked up every night. How must that make him feel?

She had returned to her own room and begun unpacking when she heard the outer door to Mark's quarters open. With the doors to the bathroom still ajar, Marshall's words floated to her quite clearly.

"I will say you're walking a lot better, when you make the effort. But you're going to have to stop dragging that right leg if you want to compete in a marathon, Colonel," he needled.

There was no reply. But the male nurse must be used to the one-way conversation.

"I understand they're moving Dr. Sommers's things into the room next door," he went on. "She's sure a looker, even if her hips are a little narrow for my taste. But her breasts make up for it, don't you think?" The speaker paused and chuckled. "Just about every guy here would give a month's pay to get into her pants. But then we're a pretty horny bunch."

Eden felt her cheeks burning. It was one thing to sense the reaction to her from the all-male staff. It was quite another to overhear a monologue best suited to a men's locker room.

Marshall was still talking. "So, are you going to find out what turns the good doctor on, now that you've got a connecting room?" he asked, laughing. He answered his own question. "Not likely," he said. "If you ever had what it takes to be a man, you don't anymore."

Eden held her breath, waiting for some reaction. But there was no reply to the crude comment.

When she finally heard Marshall's footsteps fading down the hall, Eden put her hand on the doorknob. Yet her training and experience stopped her from rushing into Mark's room and letting him know that she had overheard. As with any other returnee from hostile captivity, it was imperative to go slowly. What she needed was to establish a bond between them during their therapy sessions before leading him into anything that might be painful.

Turning back to her own room, she forced herself to go on with her unpacking. But while her hands were busy, so was her brain—grappling with everything that had happened since she'd arrived.

Over the next few days nobody mentioned the hair dryer again, and Ramirez appeared back on duty with a bandaged hand but no comment. It was as if the incident had never happened, except that she was now drying her hair with a replacement model Walker had silently handed her one day after lunch.

She couldn't help feeling isolated. Even though Downing had introduced her to the men, the enlisted staff was coolly polite, nothing more. And the officers seemed to guard their words in her presence. More than once she walked into a room and found that conversation had suddenly ceased.

It didn't take Eden long to realize why the duty here was so taxing. The staff members were just as much prisoners as Mark. There was no time off for good behavior. Even on weekends, one day was pretty much like another. And no one could go into town on leave to break the monotony.

During this time, however, she did achieve an important goal—setting up the agreed-upon communication link to the Falcon.

"Would it be possible for me to make a trip to the medical library at Augusta?" she casually asked Downing one morning after breakfast.

"Why?"

"A colleague is about to publish some research that might be important to this case. I'd like to check it out."

"I'm sorry. You can't leave the base." His blue eyes challenged her. "But we can call and have it sent," he added.

Eden hadn't expected the concession, and for a moment she was thrown off-balance. "That could take days. Besides, I'd like to see what else is available." She paused for a moment. "If I had access to a computer terminal, I could get what I need from a medical data base."

"You mean something like the Medlars system Dr. Hubbard uses occasionally?"

Eden marveled. Was he actually taking the bait so easily? "You have a terminal here?"

"Oh, we're not quite as isolated from the outside world as our location would suggest," he said with some pride. "We have a modern communications center with several terminals and over a dozen outside links."

"I'm impressed. Does that mean it would be convenient for me to use the Medlars system periodically?"

"Yes. Dr. Hubbard can handle that. Tell him I've given you clearance."

Eden smiled gratefully and then turned away quickly before the chief of station could see her look of triumph.

The computer terminal was in an alcove off the communications center. As Eden accessed the data base with its up-to-the-minute wealth of medical information, her fingers trembled slightly on the keys. Getting permission to use the computer had been relatively easy. Pulling off this deception was another matter.

She resisted the impulse to glance to her right at the stocky, barrel-chested Captain Yolanski, one of the senior security officers. He was at his own terminal, apparently writing a report. If he got up and strolled in her direction, she didn't want anything suspicious on the screen.

First she did a global search that would pull out references to psychological literature on brainwashing, torture and hostages. After saving the reference material to a file, she began drafting what looked like an innocuous message to the author of one of the articles. However, its destination was an electronic mailbox that could only be accessed from the Aviary.

She and the Falcon had agreed that certain signals would be embedded in the messages. The word *clarification,* for example, would indicate the start of her real communication. Any reference to *treatment* or *treated* would actually refer to herself. The word *patient* would be a code word for Mark.

Eden had put considerable time into composing her initial message. She wanted desperately to ask about Walker. But there were no agreed-upon code words for the purpose.

She began to type.

Dear Dr. Goldstein, I read with interest your discussion of conversion reactions among returning hostages. There are a few points I would appreciate some clarification on:

1. Do any of the subjects you have treated still feel their life is being threatened in bizarre ways?

2. How do you deal with patients who are almost completely uncommunicative?

3. What do you do when treatment time must be limited by major complications?

"Major complications" were, of course, Maj. Ross Downing.

Eden shot a quick glance toward the other computer terminal. Yolanski appeared to be editing his text.

Quickly she risked one final question, knowing that anyone who looked over her shoulder might wonder about the odd capitalization in the text.

4. What are the additional problems involved when a patient is confined to a Wheelchair or needs to use a Walker?

She had no idea whether the Falcon would be able to decipher that last bit of subterfuge. But at least she had to make the attempt.

Eden also wanted to ask what to do when the record—read: Falcon—has omitted certain important facts about the patient's history. But Yolanski had begun stacking his papers. Quickly she keyed in the sequence that would send the message to the Aviary.

Yolanski stood up and ambled in her direction. "Find anything interesting?" While the question was innocuous enough, the look he gave her was assessing.

"Oh, quite a bit. I'm going to ask for the full text on a couple of these," she returned, striving to keep any sign of nervousness out of her voice. "I assume I'll be able to browse through them tomorrow on-line."

As Eden walked back toward the main house, she sighed. Probably she'd gotten her messages across, but she found no satisfaction in the one-way monologue. She longed to be able to discuss her concerns and fears with *someone.* But there was no one here she could trust.

Ross Downing, she knew, would have jumped at the chance to hear her inner debates. But that was simply too dangerous. She couldn't even ask what progress he was making on the damn hair dryer investigation.

The whole incident was making her imagination run wild. Did someone know the real reason why she was on Pine Island? Or was just the eventuality of bringing Mark Bradley out of his unresponsive state so threatening that it called for drastic measures? Had one of the men here actually tried to kill her? Was she simply being warned? Or had someone tried to throw her off-balance so that she wouldn't be able to work effectively with her patient? She wasn't even able to discount the possibility that Walker, under orders from Downing, had lied about the hair dryer in order to observe her reaction.

It didn't help that the coded message she received the next day from the Falcon was disappointing. He simply acknowledged the receipt of her communiqué and mentioned that he'd be sending along draft copies of some pertinent papers over the next few days. There was no mention of Walker.

Eden had hoped for a lot more. She had never felt more alone than when she switched off the terminal for the second time. But she was here for the duration. If she had to rely on her own resources, so be it. She couldn't afford to let uncertainty drive her crazy. So she turned her thoughts and efforts to her primary mission—Mark Bradley.

The patient, however, like everyone else at Pine Island, was doing nothing to make her mission easy. At the first session after Marshall had held them at gunpoint, she'd tried to get some reaction from Mark.

"I was frightened," she began, letting him hear her own vulnerability. "How did it make you feel?"

She saw his lips draw together in a thin line, but he didn't answer.

She tried again. "Have you ever been in a situation like that before?"

She watched as he settled his dark gaze on a point somewhere behind her head. She had the impression that he was tuning her out completely, as though he had mentally switched off a television broadcast.

It was no better at the next session, or the next. Even though she was seeing him twice a day, once before his morning physical therapy and again in the late afternoon, she was making virtually no progress. Techniques that had worked in other cases got her nowhere with Mark. No matter what verbal tack she took, he refused to do more than passively listen. Sometimes there was no indication that he was even aware of her physical presence in the room.

She tried springing random questions on him. "Did you ever have a dog when you were a boy?" she asked one afternoon. Long ago, in another life, they'd talked about their childhood pets. She'd made him laugh with stories about the succession of alley cats she and her brother had adopted. He'd told her about his family's dogs. His favorite, a golden retriever named Ginger, had been run over on the morning of his tenth birthday. He had canceled his party and spent the day at the vet's. In the afternoon he'd helped make the decision to put the animal to sleep. The puppy his father had brought him the next week had never quite replaced Ginger in his heart.

Now his fingers worried at the place where his class ring had been, but beyond that he gave no indication that her question had any personal meaning.

"So what about your friends?" she tried the next morning. "Are there any you wish you could talk to now?" Again she remembered vividly the stories he'd told about Jerry Jennings and the feeling of bucking the crowd the two of them had experienced back at Ohio State. They'd been in ROTC together in the days of campus protests against the war. And it had almost been a relief to graduate and go into the service, where most people had respect for the uniform.

Apparently Mark Bradley didn't want to—or couldn't—share those memories with her. Despite herself his resistance made her angry and frustrated. She had promised Downing a psychological report in ten days. Was she going to have to make the whole thing up?

Maybe she could simply turn in a statement of her own reactions to the patient. She had certainly spent enough time staring at him.

At first the scars and the silver hair at his temples had been a shock. But as she'd become accustomed to the changes, she had to admit that she was fascinated—perhaps obsessed—by the new Mark Bradley. The lingering traces of his injuries only added to the air of danger and mystery that clung to his silent presence. But it was more than that. While he said nothing, it was as though he impelled her to be conscious of him as a man.

She told herself that she was simply looking for evidence to verify his identity. But that really couldn't justify all the time she spent studying the dark eyes fringed with thick lashes, the firm yet cynical line of his lips, the rigid profile, the strong jaw that still threatened to dominate his face.

Outside of therapy hours she continued to be haunted by him, but that shouldn't be surprising. After all, she was living right next door to him. Through the bathroom door she heard Marshall get Mark up in the morning and help him into the shower. Late at night, as she hovered between waking and sleep, the edges of fact and recollection would blur. Her mind would fill with warm memories of an ardent, responsive Mark Bradley, and she would long to feel his arms around her. More than once she awoke from sleep knowing that in her dreams she had crossed the short distance that separated them.

By the end of the week her daytime exasperation made her feel as though she were going to explode. Ironically, she was beginning to understand some of Major Downing's irritation. In a month of concentrated effort, he hadn't been able to pry a thing out of Mark Bradley. And she could see why. The man who sat so calmly in front of her had an iron control over his immediate environment. The harder you pressed him, the more he was able to exercise his will against you.

"What is it going to take to get you to cooperate with me?" she questioned, barely able to keep a very unprofessional edge of annoyance out of her voice. If she were the kind of person who relieved tension by swearing, she would be turning the air blue by now. Jumping up from the chair she had been occupying for the past half hour, she began to pace back and forth. But her patient was too busy playing statue to notice her agitation.

"You're afraid of making contact with another human being, aren't you?" she goaded, aware as she spoke that her words would probably garner no more response than Marshall's taunting gibes. "You don't trust anyone, do you? But you've got to start somewhere or you're going to destroy yourself."

Still the figure in the easy chair remained silent. Eden felt something inside her chest tighten painfully. She wanted to pour out a torrent of assurances that he could trust her. She wanted to explain that the Falcon had sent her here to get him out of this mess. She couldn't offer that frank an explanation yet. There had to be another way to get through to him.

Crossing the room, she knelt before Mark as she had that first day. For a long moment she searched his face. Then, before she could change her mind, she reached out and covered his hand with hers.

His skin was warm and dry. Now that she was so close to him, she was suddenly aware of the clean smell of soap and water mingled with the indefinably masculine scent of his body. All at once she was forced to ask herself whether she had made this contact for her patient or for herself—or for both of them.

Closing her eyes, she stroked her fingers along the back of his hand, feeling the ridge where a line of recently healed scar tissue met normal skin. It was another reminder of the ordeal he had gone through, and how he was coping with the aftermath.

"Mark," she whispered. "Mark, please let me in, let me get through to you." And then, clasping his hand more tightly, she lifted it and pressed it against her cheek. She had told herself she was making a bid for his trust, just as she would with any former captive. But the emotions involved were infinitely more complex.

She hadn't known what would happen, but she hadn't been prepared to feel the hand she held against her cheek tremble slightly. For several heartbeats the man in front of her didn't move, and she sensed some inner struggle raging within him. Then, finally, his fingers began to move against the soft skin of her face. He might have been a blind man memorizing her features, except that the stroking caress held a much more sensual quality.

Eyes still closed against the harsh reality of her surroundings, Eden swayed forward slightly.

"Eden." Her name was the barest of whispers. But she heard, and her heart leapt inside her chest. When two of Mark's fingers found her lips and traced slowly along the upper curve, she trembled with reaction. From someone else, it could have been a small acknowledgment of their past. From this man, it might be everything. Moving her head slightly she kissed his fingertips.

The gesture seemed to bring him back to the here and now. As though the pads of his fingers had been burned by her lips, he snatched his hand away.

At the sudden movement, Eden's eyes snapped open. For a dizzy moment, she found herself trapped in the intensity of Mark Bradley's midnight gaze, and she had to steady herself with one hand on his knee to keep from falling forward. Need, anguish, confusion and anger all seemed to battle in the ebony depths of his eyes. And then, as on that first day in the hall, those eyes seemed to close her off as though a heavy drapery had been drawn across his emotions.


IF THE INCIDENT had been disturbing to Eden, it was far worse for her patient. That night, after Marshall had finally left him alone, his thoughts went back to what had happened in the therapy session that afternoon. In a way he had been waiting an eternity for somebody to come and tell him whether or not he was Lt. Col. Mark Bradley. And now that someone had arrived who might be able to do that, he was terrified.

He fought the emotion with the iron will that had kept him going all these months through the physical agony and the interrogations—and the terrible uncertainty. But it wasn't enough anymore. Before Eden had come to Pine Island, something inside him had been cold and lifeless, as though he were apart from the rest of humanity. A normal man would have felt buried alive. He had simply been relieved that he could cut himself off from the grim reality of his situation. That bastard Downing had brought in all his artillery. But he had held him off. And Marshall's cunning little tortures? He hadn't succumbed to them either. He had them all beat. Until some clever SOB had thought to bring in Eden Sommers.

She had meant something to Mark Bradley. After the initial shock of her arrival, he had tried to tell himself she meant nothing to him. But the very act of denial had been the first chink in his carefully constructed armor. His memories of Eden were too warm, too vivid, too full of longing to be denied.

He squeezed his eyes shut and shook his head violently, as though that would dispel the betraying images from his mind. They were no comfort. Like a rodent circling an exercise wheel, his thoughts kept coming back to a science-fiction movie he had seen called *Blade Runner.* It was about artificial human beings—androids who had been cheated out of both a past and a future by their makers. But one of them, a beautiful young woman named Rachel, had been given synthetic memories of childhood. They were so tangible and vivid that she had thought they were the truth.

In a way he was like Rachel. The memories were there. But did he have a right to them? Did they belong to him—or to a dead man?

# Chapter Five

The day of reckoning had arrived. But judgment would have to wait for Maj. Ross Downing, and he was late.

Though Eden sat quietly across the table from the rest of the security team—Price, Walker and Yolanski—her mind was anything but calm. She had half expected—dreaded, actually—that Dr. Hubbard would be present for her little performance. But luck was apparently on her side. The man who was best able to see through her trumped-up report was conspicuously absent.

To keep from thinking about the trial by fire ahead, she reviewed her assessments of the three men who waited with her. Though she'd kept her dealings with them coolly professional, over the past week and a half she had gotten to know them a bit better.

Lieutenant Price was a yes-man, an extension of his commanding officer. She'd bet that he didn't have a thought—official or otherwise—that hadn't been filtered down through the chain of command. Even his knit polo shirts were the same brand as Downing's. Probably if he'd thought he could get away with dyeing his light brown hair blond, he would have. He seemed to be into physical fitness, Eden noted. Despite the muggy Georgia heat, she'd often seen him doggedly jogging along the beach, or completing lap after lap in the once-elegant swimming pool.

Yolanski was decidedly less athletic. Eden had become accustomed to seeing him relaxing during off-duty hours in the garden with a book from the library in the main house. His reading interests seemed to range from detective fiction and computer manuals to chess puzzles.

Walker, the lone black man at the facility, seemed to fit in least well. She'd sensed his discomfort in the hair dryer inquisition with Downing. The impression had only grown stronger as she'd gotten to know him better. Next to the chief of station, he was probably the most intelligent of the security staff. But Eden noted that he was always quick to defer to the others when a point of discussion came up, even though he didn't seem to approve of this particular assignment.

Eden had learned that he came from a Georgia sharecropper family. Apparently the air force had been a way to escape the poverty of his background. And he wasn't going to take any chances by incurring any demerits on this billet.

Her thoughts were interrupted as Major Downing opened the door and took his seat at the head of the table.

"So what is your psychological evaluation of Colonel Bradley?" he asked, getting right down to business.

Eden had carefully rehearsed her answer to the question. There was no way she was going to discuss the afternoon when she had, for a few minutes, forged a very meaningful bond with Mark. And for that matter, she wasn't going to mention what had happened after that, about the way he had shut her off again. If anything, after that brief but intense encounter, her patient had become even more resistant to her efforts to get through to him. But she had learned to look for subtle clues to his inner feelings in the way he sat, the way he held his hands, the way he handled eye contact. And she could tell that his control was being stretched to the limit. It seemed to take more and more effort for him to remain indifferent.

Opening her notebook, Eden glanced down at the detailed evaluation she'd prepared over the past few days. It sounded plausible, but in actuality it was made up of half-truths, evasions and more than a few prevarications.

In the first place, what Eden thought she'd learned about Mark wasn't verifiable in any measurable sense. She simply had a set of feelings and impressions that wouldn't stand up to close scrutiny. And more important, she didn't want to share with Downing what she had learned about Mark's iron control.

Yet she knew she was walking a tightrope. She had to hold out hope that she could help the security team get what they needed.

"Well, I've identified a number of Colonel Bradley's problems," she began. "He's definitely paranoid, but not entirely without justification. And he's suffering from the severe depression one would expect after an experience like this."

She saw Downing lean imperceptibly forward. Though his face was neutral, a muscle in his face was jumping.

"At first," she went on, tapping the eraser of her pencil against the notepaper, "I was afraid his withdrawal was the result of a severe personality breakdown—actually a catatonic reaction. But after additional observation, I'm convinced it's more treatable." She paused for effect, and watched as three sets of eyes drilled into her. "He seems to be suffering from what used to be called a hysterical reaction—like blindness or paralysis. In other words it's a conversion reaction in which symptoms of some physical malfunction or loss of control appear without any underlying organic pathology. In the colonel's case it's a sort of self-punishment in response to what he sees as a failure on his part."

"Do you mean like what happens to soldiers sometimes when they're terrified of going into combat?" Walker questioned.

"That's one example. It's a way of coping with the stress of war without feeling guilty about not wanting to go into combat."

"So how does this apply to Bradley? Do you mean he feels guilty about spilling his guts to the East Germans?" Yolanski asked bluntly.

Eden hesitated. These professional security specialists obviously weren't stupid. And it was a little unsettling that Walker had zeroed in on the correct page in his abnormal-psych textbook. In fact, the whole security team had probably been put through a good deal of psychological training. But almost certainly their course work had not been oriented toward diagnosing mental illness. And that gave her an edge, especially with Dr. Hubbard absent. Downing might be scornful of the doctor's abilities, but Eden had been impressed with his acute powers of observation. More than once, to her later alarm, Eden had allowed Hubbard to draw her into discussions of Mark's psychological problems. The doctor's perceptions had been surprisingly sharp. But since Downing obviously didn't value his opinions on the subject, he hadn't bothered to voice them.

Eden considered how best to answer Yolanski's question. "Feelings of guilt aren't necessarily in proportion to real wrongdoing," she began. "In Colonel Bradley's case, simply having allowed himself to be captured could be the source of his guilt. Of course, we won't know for sure until his condition improves." It amazed Eden that she was able to discuss these hypothetical symptoms so convincingly.

"But how could he have avoided it?" Walker questioned, obviously ready to follow where she was leading.

"Maybe he thinks he didn't take sufficient security precautions when he left Berlin. For all I know, maybe he didn't. But in any event, you can't assume that he'd be reacting normally."

"And just how do you know all this without having talked to the man?" Price's voice cut through to the heart of the matter like a hot knife through butter.

The chief of station gave his junior officer a sharp look, and Price flushed.

Eden noted the byplay even as she struggled to keep her outward composure. She had gone to great pains not to mention the fact that Mark was still almost completely uncommunicative. But eager-beaver Price had just slipped and let her know what she had been cautioned to assume—her sessions with Mark were being carefully recorded and monitored.

"Experience with dozens of cases like this, Lieutenant. I can tell a lot just from the kind of response he's trying to hide."

"So when do you expect him to improve?" Downing asked.

"That's a fair question. And the answer partly depends on your cooperation. As you know, the colonel has come back from six months of enemy captivity. Other men in his position have been treated like heroes. He, on the other hand, has simply substituted one kind of captivity for another."

"If you're suggesting that we turn him loose, you can forget it," Price said.

Eden gave him a dismissive look and continued. "I believe the first key to getting through to him is opening up his claustrophobic environment. He needs to get outside, away from the constant reminders of his status here." And away from your listening devices, she added silently.

"But our security isn't set up to handle that," Yolanski objected.

Downing looked thoughtful. "Oh, I hardly think the colonel is going to jump into the ocean and swim back to the mainland. Maybe with sufficient safety measures we can give him a little more freedom, if that's what Dr. Sommers thinks he needs."

"Thank you," Eden said, surprised that the chief of station had jumped in to support her. "Conducting my therapy sessions outside ought to help. Once I open a wedge, I think I can widen it. And I'd also like to suggest that Sergeant Marshall take advantage of the swimming pool here for some of the colonel's physical therapy."

Downing gave her a steady look. "I'll think about it."

Eden nodded. Better not press for more concessions.

"Do you think I'm driving you and everybody else so hard because I enjoy seeing Bradley sweat?" the chief of station surprised her by asking.

Eden resisted the urge to say yes.

When she didn't answer, he continued. "Let me remind you that Bradley may have compromised a major U.S. weapons system. We've got to find out what he told the East Germans. You have two more weeks to start getting something out of him. After that we'll have no alternative but to try an experimental drug therapy."

So it was out in the open now.

"What experimental drug therapy?" Eden asked.

"I'm afraid your clearance doesn't give you the need to know that."

But she did know. Amherst Gordon had warned her. Downing was going to try a new "truth serum." The trouble was, it was also an unstable hallucinogen that made LSD look like cotton candy.

A REPORT OF what had happened in the confidential meeting went out later that day.

The contact at Pine Island picked up the phone at the prearranged time.

"What's the news on the hurricane watch?" the man in Washington asked.

"Two tropical storms have potential for trouble."

"Let's have it, then."

"Sommers has made her preliminary diagnosis."

"Go on."

Succinctly, the local observer summarized the meeting between Eden and the security staff.

"Why is she getting two more weeks?" the man in Washington challenged.

"At this stage it should look as if she's been given a real chance to do something." The man hesitated for a moment. "You know, even though she hadn't made any obvious progress, there's something that makes me uneasy about this Dr. Sommers. There may be more to her being here than meets the eye."

"Can you be more specific?"

"No, it's just a bad feeling. Maybe you ought to check your sources and see what you can find out."

"I'll get back to you on that." There was a pause at the other end of the line. "There's one more thing I want to ask. What about *your own* evaluation of the patient? What do you think? Is he really Mark Bradley or not?"

"He's tight as a clam. How the hell am I supposed to know?"

"You're pretty sure Sommers can't get anything out of him, either?"

"For now, anyway."

"But if she does, they're both expendable. Can you take care of that?"

"Yes."

"This won't be like that fiasco with the hair dryer, I trust."

The man at Pine Island flushed. "I've got everything under control now."

"You'd better. Moscow doesn't suffer fools gladly." There was a click, and the red phone went dead.

EDEN COULD have joined the officers in the library or the wardroom after dinner that evening, but as she often did, she went right up to her room instead. There was a good supply of books and magazines on her bedside table. But they were only for show. Mostly she spent the evening thinking—and keeping an ear peeled toward Mark's room.

As she'd settled into the station's monotonous routine, her feeling of isolation had only increased. There were times now when she found herself wishing she could call her father and ask his advice. She missed her family more than she had in years. Bill Sommers had been an air force career man, and because the family had lived all over the United States, their "roots" had been their reliance on each other.

As a child she'd believed her father had all the answers. Even as a young woman, following in his footsteps had seemed the right thing to do. Major Sommers had been proud of her then. But he hadn't understood her need to get out of the service. And though she'd officially discharged her air force obligation, he'd reminded her more than once how much the U.S. government had spent on her "high priced" education.

Though Eden had done her best to soothe his disappointment, relations between them had been strained ever since. And her mother had felt compelled to support her husband's stand, even though she'd had misgivings. Now, maybe because Eden was getting nowhere with Mark, she longed to reach out and restore those older relationships. But that was impossible for the time being. Security on Pine Island precluded unofficial calls or letters to the outside world.

She was daydreaming about the weekend her whole family had come up to Cornell when she'd been awarded her Ph.D. Her younger brother, Billy, had been an undergraduate at Michigan State. He'd tried not to act overawed. But when she'd come down the aisle in that black gown with the special hood and the crimson stripes on the sleeve, she knew he'd been impressed. They'd all been in such good spirits. And it was typical of the many memorable times they'd spent together. That special family feeling she'd had before the rift had enabled her to know what she was looking for in a life partner.

Five years ago she'd thought she'd found it with Mark Bradley. But she'd been wrong. Now she couldn't help wondering if she'd been wrong about a lot of things.

Her thoughts were interrupted when she heard the door of Mark's room open. Marshall was getting his patient ready for bed. She supposed she ought to be grateful for small favors; at least the male nurse had curtailed his sarcastic remarks. Apparently, as soon as he'd realized she had been officially installed, he'd become more circumspect.

After the attendant left, Eden made her own bedtime preparations. The confrontation with Downing and his staff had been exhausting. And she had a busy day ahead, too. Once the lights were out, she heard Mark get out of bed and begin moving around. He did that most evenings. From the muffled grunts and labored breathing she heard, she had to assume that he had started a supplementary exercise program of his own. The knowledge gave her a measure of hope. Even if he was maintaining his unresponsive demeanor with her, he apparently did have some private goal in mind.

Eden had been asleep for several hours when she was startled into instant alertness by a different sound. Glancing at the clock, she saw that it was close to three a.m. What had wakened her? Her heart began to pound. But in the next moment a groan drew her attention toward Mark's room. She hesitated, listening intently. The groan was followed by another—and then a strangled exclamation. Had Downing broken his word and sent for Mark in the middle of the night?

Throwing a light robe over her satin gown, Eden hurried through the connecting bathroom and quickly pushed open Mark's door. After her eyes had adjusted to the dim light, her gaze searched the room for intruders. There were none. But a muttered curse drew her attention to the far wall. There, shafts of moonlight coming in through the barred window cast the bed in stripes of pale light and shadow, and she could make out Mark's restless form. The tangled covers had slipped to one side, and she could see that his body was naked from the waist up. Eden quickly crossed the room, drawn by moans interspersed with words that made no sense.

She watched Mark struggle against the twisted sheet that held him prisoner. There was a sheen of perspiration on his bare torso. Evidently he was in the throes of one of the nightmares Downing had mentioned.

Her heart seemed to turn over in her chest. What torture was he remembering?

"Mark, Mark, you're safe. You're only dreaming," she murmured, sitting down on the edge of the bed and grasping his shoulders to quiet him. The gesture didn't have the calming effect she had hoped for. He was still caught in the grip of the frightening dream. Now that she was closer she could see his features. His teeth were clenched and his eyes tightly shut. The pain written on his scarred countenance was almost too much to bear.

Despite her efforts to hold him down, he began to struggle against her hands with more strength than she would have thought possible, given his supposedly weakened condition.

"Damn it. I don't know. I just don't know," he groaned, flailing out at her with an arm that suddenly twisted free from the restraining sheets. His hand struck Eden's shoulder, almost knocking her off the bed. At the same time, a string of muttered imprecations filled the air.

Under other circumstances she would have taken a moment to nurse the spot on her shoulder that would certainly be a bruise by morning. But that would have to wait.

She tried again. "Mark, it's Eden. I'm here. You're safe with me."

Her words apparently didn't penetrate into whatever hell he was reliving. But he seemed to know there was someone else with him in the room, and his struggles redoubled. One large hand grabbed Eden's wrist and began to shake her arm back and forth as though he were trying to break it. This time her cries of pain mingled with his muttered oaths.

Calming Mark had suddenly taken a back seat to freeing herself from the punishment he was intent on meting out. Changing her position, she maneuvered herself on top of him and tried to clamp his arm to his side. Luckily, his other arm was still tangled in the sheet, so he wasn't able to throw her off. But his body began to twist and turn under hers as though he were desperate to escape the restraining weight.

"Mark," she pleaded. "Wake up. It's Eden. Don't you know me?"

She must have repeated the words half a dozen times before she got any response. His dark eyes snapped open, focused on her at first uncomprehendingly.

"Eden?" She heard her own name gasped, heard the raspy, unused quality in his voice that she had noted before.

"Yes."

At last he seemed to understand, and she felt his body go completely still. Sprawled along the length of his suddenly motionless form, she raised herself up so that she could look down into his face. His dark eyes were wide now and still staring at her. She saw that the fear haunting his dream had not been dispelled. Or was there something different now?

"You were having a nightmare," she whispered, reaching up so that she could stroke his cheek as though comforting a child. "But it's all right now." She waited, almost afraid to breathe.

She could feel her own heart racing—and his, too. She was suddenly very aware of the warmth of his naked chest pressed against her breasts through the thin fabric of her gown. Was he going to push her away? But he didn't seem to have the will to do it.

His tight grip on her wrist shifted, and she winced.

"I've hurt you." His fingers probed lightly against the delicate bones.

"It's not too bad."

"You shouldn't have come in here."

"You needed me."

"No." *God, yes!*

In two weeks of silent fencing, they hadn't exchanged this much dialogue. As a psychologist she might have tried to keep him talking. As a woman she knew that words weren't always the most important form of communication.

His hand slipped up her arm to her shoulder so that he could pull her more tightly against his chest. He had been telling himself that he didn't need her. But he had been longing to hold her like this—no matter how dangerous it might be to his own survival. Despite his own inner warnings, his fingers moved in small circles along the velvety expanse of her back, reveling in the soft, feminine feel of her skin.

Eden shivered with growing awareness. She had calmed other patients who had awakened from terrors in the middle of the night. On those occasions she had offered the simple warmth of human contact. This was much more than that.

She felt his fingers move up to tangle in the soft disarray of her hair, sifting through the strands as though they were spun of the rarest silk.

She moved her head slightly against his hand, increasing the contact. She wanted to touch him, as well—to trace the strong shape of his jaw, to feather her lips along the line of his dark brows, to know again the warmth of his mouth merged with hers. But she dared not. The last time she'd taken the initiative, he'd pulled back and withdrawn even more tightly.

Almost afraid of what she might see in his eyes, she lifted her head and looked down into their onyx depths.

Her lips trembled slightly. She felt his warm breath against her face, as though he were begging her to bridge the small space between them. If they kissed, she might finally know who this man really was. That was what she had been sent here to discover. Yet she realized that whether or not he was Mark Bradley, she cared about him. And suddenly she didn't want to know.

His eyes focused on her lips. To lose himself in the warmth of her caress was infinitely tempting. Surely in the intimacy of that mingling he would know where her allegiance lay. But it was too dangerous. He could already sense his control slipping to the point of no return. Could he resist her, even if he knew she might ultimately be responsible for his death? It was simply too great a risk.

The moment passed.

"You'd better leave."

"Will you be all right?"

His laugh was hollow. "No. But go anyway."

EDEN SLIPPED back into her own bed and pulled the sheets up around her neck. They felt cold against her heated skin. She was torn between duty and desire, anguish and elation. What had just transpired between herself and Mark played back through her mind. She had been a coward. Or had she taken her cue from him? They had both wanted something more to happen. Yet powerful forces had kept them from crossing an imaginary boundary line.

On the other hand, maybe she should count her victories instead of her defeats. For a few brief moments the man in the other room had risked his vulnerability. He obviously wanted to trust her. And that was something to build on.

He had taken a risk. She must do the same. Tomorrow she was going to change the rules between them. It might lead to disaster. But if she didn't seize this opportunity, they might never get another one.

# Chapter Six

Five hundred miles away, at the Aviary, the Falcon tapped on a section of the library wall with his silver-headed cane. The richly polished wood panel slid open to reveal a very modern and efficient-looking office quite out of keeping with the colonial elegance of the rest of the inn. Against the far wall clocks displayed the local time in Hong Kong, Berlin, Moscow and Cairo. Below them Constance McGuire was seated at a computer terminal typing travel orders.

"I've got one of our best operatives lined up for you," she said without turning around. "Michael Rome is on his way to Savannah now to start making contingency plans."

"Excellent." As he spoke, Gordon slowly crossed to a wide mahogany desk piled high with computer printouts and folders—along with a telephone and a crystal decanter of Napoleon brandy. He pulled out the comfortably padded executive chair and eased himself down into it. His damn knee was acting up again. But he supposed he should be grateful that he could walk at all.

"I despise sitting here on the sidelines waiting for something disastrous to happen," he grumbled.

"Maybe you're getting too old for this type of work," his assistant observed dryly.

Her words had the desire effect. "Don't count on it. You'll be the first to know when I've reached senility."

She laughed appreciatively and turned to look at him over the top of her gold-rimmed half glasses. "You're so stubborn you'll probably find a way to run this operation from the grave."

They exchanged warm looks. The gibe was familiar, and so was the rejoinder.

Deliberately Gordon reached over and poured a shot of brandy into the cup of steaming coffee Connie had set out for him. He was thinking about the Roman playwright Plautus and his advocacy of patience. Was it really the best remedy for every trouble? But then Plautus specialized in comedies, not tragedies.

The Falcon took a thoughtful sip of his fortified brew before continuing. "We've played waiting games with the best of them. The trick is being prepared to move when the time is right—and in this case it won't do us a damn bit of good to get Bradley off that island unless Eden is convinced that it's really him—and if it is him, that he hasn't been compromised."

Connie turned back to the computer terminal for a moment, running her fingers lightly across the keyboard. Through it she was tied in to every major information source available to the U.S. government—and a few the government didn't even know about. Yesterday evening one of those contacts had paid off.

"Well, we've got Hans Erlich's name now," she said. "At least Eden can see what effect that has on the colonel."

The Falcon's cane slammed down against the polished mahogany desk top, making the telephone receiver jump in its cradle. "Hans Erlich! God, would I like to get my hands on that sadistic bastard!"

LAST NIGHT Eden's decision had seemed very clear-cut. This morning as she pulled on jeans and a T-shirt rather than her usual daytime garb, she had a few second thoughts. Leveling with her patient was taking a big risk. Yet if she wanted to help him, she had to take the chance.

Sitting down at the small dressing table in her room, she hastily wrote a few words on a small slip of paper torn from her notepad. After folding it in half, she stuffed it into the front pocket of her jeans. She had to restrain the impulse to jam her hand in after it as she headed for the dining hall. Through breakfast, the note seemed to burn a hole in her pocket. She felt almost as though she were carrying around a grenade that was about to go off. And in a way she was.

When it was finally time for her morning session with Mark, she did have to stuff her hands into her pockets to keep them from trembling as she waited for the elevator in the medical wing.

The metal door wheezed open and Dr. Hubbard stepped out. He gave Eden a friendly nod and then peered at her more closely. Despite his vow to remain aloof, he had come to think of Eden Sommers as one of the few bright spots in this uncomfortable assignment.

They'd been forced to work closely together. In less than two weeks he'd gotten to know her pretty well—although he recognized that there were certain compartments of her life that were off-limits. But that was true for him, as well.

Maybe because she saw him as a sort of father figure, she'd shared some glimpses of her childhood. One afternoon when he'd referred to himself as "an old sawbones," they'd discovered they were both *Star Trek* fans. He had watched the original series back in the midsixties. Eden and her younger brother, Billy, had gotten hooked on the reruns ten years later. Hubbard hadn't been able to resist brightening up his days a bit by using Trekkie terminology as a little inside joke between himself and Eden.

"You're looking a little under the weather this morning," he observed now. "If you don't feel better by lunchtime, stop by sick bay and let me or Nurse Chapel take your temperature."

Eden forced a smile. She was too keyed up to enjoy the *Star Trek* patter right now. "I'm sure I'll feel better once I get outside with Colonel Bradley."

"Oh, that's right. Major Downing did mention something about this being the big day."

"Yes."

"Well, I think the patient's up to it. He's been showing a lot of improvement with his walking over the past week."

Hubbard sounded pleased with the way things were going, but still cautious. "If I were you, I think I might take a cane, just in case. We don't want him to fall down and have a setback."

Eden waited while he issued the suggested equipment.

When she opened the door to the therapy room, Mark was in his usual chair. But instead of slippers he was wearing tennis shoes with his blue jeans and T-shirt. Even though she could tell he noted her presence, his eyes avoided hers. Did he want to be sure she wasn't making any presumptions after last night?

There was no time for questioning his motives now. She had to go ahead with what she had planned. "Did Sergeant Marshall tell you we have a little outing scheduled for today?" she asked.

She hadn't expected an answer to that question. It was strictly for the benefit of whoever was listening in.

"I think you're going to enjoy getting outside," she continued, reaching in her pocket and pulling out the piece of paper. Unfolding it, she held it in front of Mark's face.

We are being monitored. Don't ask any questions now. Come outside where we can talk. I have a message for you from the Falcon.

Mark's face jerked upward. His dark eyes seemed to drill into hers. *What the hell!* How had she gotten hold of that name?

Last night he'd made a mistake by letting her past his defenses. But what were you supposed to do when a warm, willing body tempted you beyond endurance? He might have lived through hell, but he wasn't dead yet. The irony of the situation had kept him awake for hours. This morning he had been prepared to redouble his efforts to resist temptation. But now, what did he do with this new piece of information? Eden Sommers could have come by that name by a variety of devious means. To his knowledge she'd never been part of the Peregrine Connection. And his information sources had been quite good. Who was she *really* working for, for Lord's sake? He was going to have to play along, at least until he found out.

She put her finger to her lips. Did she actually think he was stupid enough to say something here? Instead, he nodded.

She visibly relaxed and offered him her arm. "Dr. Hubbard suggested that you might need a cane," she continued, as though the spoken part of the conversation was all that had passed between them.

Mark shot her a contemptuous look and reached for the walking stick. For a moment he simply held it. Then he shifted it back and forth in his hands as though he was testing its weight.

He noted Eden's quizzical look and her raised eyebrow. But reactions could be faked. Methodically he ran his fingers along the smooth wood. Near the bottom there was a barely detectable notch, which he pried up with his nail. Holding the cane out, he showed her the tiny transmitter nestled inside the small cavity.

Eden's eyes widened. Quickly he closed the recess back up and stood.

"Ready?" she asked, trying to sound chipper and enthusiastic. Suddenly the room—and all those hidden ears listening in—seemed to be pressing in against her.

They made slow progress down the hall. And as they passed the physical therapy room, Eden saw Sergeant Marshall scowl in their direction. Evidently the male nurse didn't share the doctor's enthusiasm for taking Mark out.

"You know, Colonel Bradley tires awfully easily," he called out. "Are you sure you don't want me to be nearby in case you run into trouble? After all the progress we've made, I'd hate to see him slip back."

"We'll take it very easy today," Eden promised.

"Just so we understand where the responsibility lies for any setbacks," he mumbled, looking down at the papers on his desk.

"He's a real sweetheart," Eden whispered as they moved farther down the hall. She could have said the same for Price, or almost any of the other men here at Pine Island. Then she looked in horror at the cane.

Mark shot her a warning look.

For the next five minutes she kept her expression neutral and her comments to herself. When they reached the front door she turned to her patient. "The beach certainly looks inviting. Let's walk down that way."

The outside air was hot and moist as usual, but the breeze blowing off the water seemed to cut through the heat. Eden watched as Mark took in several lungfuls of the salty air. It was the first breath of freedom he'd had in months. But she could see him fighting not to show any emotion. Together they threaded down the gravel path through the flower beds where hibiscus and day lilies were still holding their own with the sea grass.

They had progressed a few feet into the sand when she stopped as though a sudden thought had just occurred to her. "You know, that cane seems to be sinking in. I think it's actually making it harder for you to walk. Just drop it here and we'll pick it up on our way back."

Following her cue, Mark pressed the end of the walking stick into the soft sand and twisted it down below the level of the transmitter. She could just picture the little grains wrecking the delicate mechanism. Then he tossed the cane aside.

AT THE MAIN HOUSE there was a burst of static before two separate receivers went dead. At both locations, the malfunction was followed by a string of curses.

"We'll have to take the mobile unit out," Price growled downstairs in the security room.

"Too bad nobody took a course in lip reading," Yolanski quipped. "I'll toss you for the detail. Heads you go. Tails I stay here and man the inoperative equipment."

Price didn't laugh. But then he hardly ever did.

"LEAN ON MY shoulder if you're having trouble walking," Eden suggested as they crossed the deserted beach.

Mark ignored the offer and struck off doggedly by himself. Apparently he wanted to put some distance between himself and the main house before they got down to business. Eden noted he was walking now with just the barest trace of a limp. Though his body was still thin and angular, he had gained a bit of weight since her arrival, and his muscle tone had improved considerably. His shoulders were back and his head was up as though the fresh air was having a strong reviving effect.

Eden glanced back over her shoulder. Yolanski, who was ambling down the garden path in their direction, had also decided to take a stroll. He had on what looked like a jogger's radio. Of course, after the cane incident, she could believe that might be some sort of receiver, too.

Mark headed toward the breakwater, where a wall of piled stones separated one part of the beach from the other. As they approached the line of crashing surf, the noise level increased. Eden hid a smile. He knew what he was doing. They were going to have trouble hearing each other talk, and it would be next to impossible for someone else to pick up their conversation.

"Sergeant Marshall's right. You don't want to overdo it. Maybe we've gone far enough," she observed, watching as Mark shaded his eyes against the glare of the morning sun on the water. They were as close as they could get to the crashing surf without becoming wet from the waves rolling up the beach. He stood for a moment looking at a flock of gulls circle over the water. The breeze from the ocean whipped his dark hair back off his forehead. And in the bright sunlight the scar tissue on his face and neck was painfully apparent.

The last time they had been on a beach together, he had looked different—carefree and happy. That had been on Cape Cod, where the two of them had spent a long Columbus Day weekend. The water had been too cold for swimming, but neither of them had minded. They'd spent hours walking along the sand, arms around each other to ward off the nip of autumn in the air.

She longed to put her arm around him the same way now. Instead she sighed and sat down. After a long moment he lowered himself a bit stiffly to the sand beside her. She watched as he dug his fingers into the soft grains and then let them cascade through his fingers. The gesture made her vividly aware once again that this was the first time he'd been out of close confinement in months. She would have liked to let him enjoy the freedom. But there was so little time.

"Do you know who planted the bug in the cane?" she finally asked.

He hesitated. He had kept his own council for so long that it was hard to share even obvious information. "Downing at least," he finally replied in the raspy voice that was already becoming familiar. "Who knows who else might be listening in."

Eden shuddered, yet at the same time she couldn't suppress a surge of joy. Now that they were away from prying ears, he was actually going to talk to her. There were so many questions she wanted to ask. But he didn't give her the chance.

"All right, let's have it. What's the Falcon to you?" he challenged.

"He sent me here to help you."

"Convince me."

Eden looked at him blankly for a moment. She'd hoped the Falcon's code name would be sufficient password. Apparently Mark needed more. "How do I do that?"

"Let's see how you answer a few questions. What's the Falcon's name?"

"Amherst Gordon."

"And what about Karen McGuire?"

"Constance McGuire, his assistant," she corrected.

"And his valet Cicero."

She had to laugh at that one. "His parrot, you mean."

"And where is their operation?"

"The Aviary is in Berryville, Virginia."

"I still can't be sure whether you've met him or you've been carefully coached."

The matter-of-fact statement made her review their exchange in another light. Suddenly she realized the same could be true for the man who was quizzing her. He might have been trying to trip her up. Or he might have been verifying crucial facts. If he wasn't Col. Mark Bradley, she'd probably just confirmed Intelligence information that was only supposition in some East German file.

A shiver went through her body, and it wasn't from the wind blowing off the ocean.

For endless moments they sat in the sand looking at each other searchingly. In the intensity of the exchange, Eden had forgotten all about the crashing of the breakers against the rocks. Now they sounded like a symphony of dissonant percussion instruments. The tide was creeping in and the waves were getting closer. Overhead a gull circled.

The expression on the face of the man across from her was unreadable. But doubt and hope fought for control of Eden's countenance. She had anticipated so much from this first private meeting. But it wasn't going the way she had expected.

It was her perplexed vulnerability that triggered his decision. He might be a fool to trust her. But even if she really wasn't on his side, he reminded himself, he might be able to use her. "All right," he relented. "I'll assume that you're an ally until you prove otherwise."

She hadn't known she was holding her breath. Now it came out in an audible sigh of relief. "Mark, I have to make another report to Downing in a few days. And I've got to show some evidence that he's going to be able to get what he wants out of you."

"He's never going to get what he wants out of me!"

She shuddered at the vehemence in his voice. But all the resolve in the world wouldn't help him against what Downing had planned. "Do you know what RL2957 is?"

"No." But he did, although he thought the Joint Chief of Staff had scrapped that particular project.

"It's an experimental truth serum—with some devastating side effects like acid trips that last forever. Downing has the okay to use it on you."

"When?"

"He's given me two weeks to change his mind. That's why you've got to help me convince him that my therapy is working."

"So what was your diagnosis of the patient?"

Quickly she summarized yesterday's exchange with the security team.

When she was finished, he laughed hollowly. "Is that what you think about me?"

"No." *I still don't know what to think.* She reached over and touched his wrist. She could feel the heat of the sun on his skin. With those scars and his incarceration, he was probably going to burn. Next time she'd try to remember to bring some lotion.

"Please trust me," she whispered.

"I want to." *God, if only I could.*

A strong incoming wave suddenly lapped at their clothing and they both jumped up.

Eden turned to see Yolanski standing fifty yards away up on the rock wall. He was looking intently down at them, all pretense of a morning stroll abandoned.

"Enough sun for today, I think," Eden said. Together they turned and made their way slowly back toward the house.


"WELL, WHAT DO YOU think?" Major Downing leaned back in his chair and looked at the other members of the security team.

"A disaster," Price spoke up. "We don't have a thing on the tape but crashing surf and birdcalls."

"Maybe we could sell it to one of those sound effect companies," Yolanski suggested.

Price shot him a withering look. Walker repressed a grin.

"I don't think it's all that bad," Downing cut in. "In the first place, I'm going to insist that Dr. Sommers conduct her afternoon sessions upstairs in the usual room. That way we'll be getting half of what they're saying. But even if we lost them this morning, I'm encouraged. Bradley *looked* different when he came back from that outing. Did you notice it?"

"Yes," Walker agreed. "There was something more open about his expression. And his eyes didn't look quite so empty."

"He looked more guarded than vacant," Yolanski agreed.

"What do you think she was *doing* to breathe life into him out there?" Price broke in.

Downing waved his arm in a dismissive gesture. "I don't care if she was giving him mouth-to-crotch resuscitation—just so long as it gets results."

There was a chorus of male laughter around the table.

"So that's why you moved her into the room next to his," Yolanski joked.

"As a matter of fact, more than one soldier has been brought back from the dead by a good-looking woman. Never underestimate the power of healing passion." He paused for a moment. "So I had nothing to lose by giving the good doctor a chance to see if that's where her inclinations lay."

There were more snickers around the table. "And I thought you had been getting ready to try your luck with her yourself," Yolanski said.

"Business before pleasure," Downing mused philosophically.

THAT AFTERNOON Eden hesitated for a moment as she pulled open the door to the therapy room. Until her discussion with Downing after lunch, she had assumed she and Mark would have another private session. Now they'd be back to playing games. Only the stakes were higher. She was going to have to show some progress. But maybe there was a way to accomplish her purpose and his, too.

Mark looked up expectantly when she walked in.

"There's been a change in plans. Major Downing is concerned that you might overexert yourself. So he's asked us to stay inside for our afternoon sessions."

Her patient's features were immediately guarded. Was she lying? Was this some new trick?

"But I don't want to lose the momentum we established this morning," she continued.

He waited.

Eden took a deep breath. Even with this setback, she wasn't going to allow them to regress to square one again. "With similar cases I've found it useful to start by talking through what happened before the trauma took place. Your folder has given me some idea of what happened during the time period before your accident. Let's see if we can bring it into focus."

Mark shook his head vehemently from side to side.

"Don't be alarmed. I'll do most of the talking. You just have to answer yes or no. And if a question is too painful, we can come back to that point later."

The closed expression that she had first seen on Mark's face was starting to settle over his features like a papier mâché mask hardening into place.

Instinctively she reached out for his hands and squeezed them so hard that her nails dug into the flesh of his palms. Anger flashed briefly in his eyes.

"Trust me," she mouthed without saying the words aloud.

When she let go, just a bit of tension went out of his shoulders.

"Why don't you lie down on the couch?" she suggested. "I think you'll be more comfortable."

"You mean so that you can play headshrinker?" There was a raw edge to his voice.

Eden shook her head. "No. I'm not going to sit behind you. I'll be right where we can see each other." Turning, she pulled a wooden chair over toward the couch. She didn't look around, but she heard Mark get up and follow her.

She offered him a pillow and waited until he seemed comfortably settled.

"Are you ready?"

He nodded curtly.

"Fine. Then let's start with a few facts for the record," she began. *And let's hope you'll tell me what the Falcon needs to know about whether you completed your assignment for him.* "I do hold an Alpha clearance. So you don't have to worry about compromising national security." *Or your own security.*

Their eyes met. Could he read between the lines? Did he realize she wouldn't do anything to endanger him? "Your name is Mark David Bradley and you hold the rank of lieutenant colonel in the air force. Is that correct?"

"Yes."

"Your last duty assignment for the air force was project Orion."

"Yes." Of course, Mark Bradley had also been on special assignment for the Peregrine Connection. But she'd been careful to specify air force. He looked up at her in acknowledgment, and she nodded.

"You had been sent on TDY to Berlin in September?"

"No, October."

She went on. "You were there to coordinate engineering specs with our West German allies."

"Yes."

"October is a lively time in Berlin. Did you get a chance to take in the Octoberfest?"

His eyes questioned her. What was she getting at?

She just smiled and gestured with her hands, palms upward. *Let Downing make what he would of that.*

"Yes."

"You also accomplished your mission?"

He hesitated. "Yes."

"Did you renew any old military or air force acquaintances?"

"Not really."

"Make any new friends?" The question slipped out and Eden realized suddenly that it was strictly for her personal information. Had he been seriously involved with anyone else since their affair?

He looked her straight in the eye as if reading her thoughts. "No."

"You found out what you needed to know?"

Again he seemed to make a decision. "Yes."

*And what did you do with that information, Mark?* she desperately wanted to ask. *Is it safe?* But that would have to wait—until they were alone and he trusted her more.

"You were hitching a ride back on a cargo plane from the U.S. facility at Tegel Air Base?"

"Yes." His voice was a whisper, as if the very mention of that place had brought back terrible memories.

"The preflight procedures were perfectly routine?"

"Yes." Again he barely mouthed the syllable.

Eden reached out and laid her hand over his reassuringly for a moment. "An engine caught fire on takeoff?" she guessed. No one really did know what had happened, except that the plane had crashed almost immediately on East German soil.

"No. A bomb." His eyes closed tightly as though to shut out the horror. But it was too late. He had shied away for so long from what had been done to him. Now suddenly here was someone offering to share the burden. For a moment he didn't even know whether the story was true or whether he'd simply memorized the script. It didn't matter; his anguish was real.

"The bomb was planted under my assigned seat. But I'd decided to nap instead of look out the window. So I was in the back, where it was dark. I think we'd just started our climb when the bomb went off. The explosion was deafening." He put his hands over his ears, and his face contorted with remembered agony. He wanted desperately to stop, but the words kept pouring out. "It tore a hole the size of a garage door in the side of the plane. I was strapped in or I would have been sucked out. But maybe a clean death would have been better. We lost altitude right away. There was fire everywhere. God, it was a flying inferno, and there wasn't a damn thing I could do about it." Perspiration beaded on his forehead.

"Mark," she called, but he didn't seem to hear. And when she reached for his hand again, he clutched her fingers in a death grip. But it might have been the arm of his airplane seat. He wasn't on Pine Island anymore. He was in the middle of hell.

It was as though a logjam of denied memories had broken loose. His tight control had finally snapped. Eden had thought the remembering would be therapeutic. She hadn't been prepared for him to let go like this so quickly. Suddenly she was afraid of what he might say, and who might hear it.

"Fire everywhere. The smell of burning flesh, and it's your own."

She heard him suck great gasps of air into his lungs as though he were still trapped in that fire and fighting for each breath.

"God, then the impact," he choked out. "It must have thrown me out of the plane. I don't remember. I don't remember anything else." But there was suddenly something else that was burning like a brand on the backs of his closed eyelids. It was a number: 002-72-52. He had no idea what it meant. It could have been a combination lock, a bank account, his patient I.D. number. The significance was beyond his grasp. But he knew it was important—and deadly.

Despite himself he whispered the digits aloud.

"What?" Eden prompted.

He groaned and pulled his free hand up over his eyes, but not before she saw the moisture trickling from behind the closed lids. Her own face was damp, too.

"Mark. It's all over. It's all over," she said soothingly, her hand gently stroking his. He didn't immediately open his eyes. But she was sure he was aware of his surroundings again. His breathing had begun to steady, and the deeply etched lines of stress in his face softened slightly.

Eden leaned over and gently pressed her cheek against his. His arm came up to clasp her shoulder. And for a moment he seemed to accept the comfort that she offered. His head turned slightly and she wondered fleetingly if he might be going to kiss her. Instead his lips made the barest sound next to her ear. ''Someone here wants to make sure it's not over.''

# Chapter Seven

Under other circumstances Eden would have felt elated by Major Downing's change in attitude when he approached her that evening after dinner. In one sense, anything would have been an improvement over the imperious way he'd been acting. Ever since she'd arrived, he'd hovered in the background like a silent tiger stalking her and Mark. Now that she had begun to make some "progress," the chief of station was suddenly less assured. Officially she wasn't supposed to know he was listening in on the sessions upstairs in the medical wing. So he couldn't come right out and ask what she'd done to change the status quo, but curiosity was written all over his face.

"Colonel Bradley certainly looked remarkably improved after that walk you took on the beach this morning," Downing said, fishing.

"Yes, the sea air seems to have done him a world of good," Eden returned with a smile.

"Can't you tell me if anything significant happened out there?"

"You'll be the first to know."

He gnawed on his lower lip. He knew she was making astounding progress. He'd heard her afternoon session himself. Why didn't she want to talk about it?

Eden watched his expression. In a way it gave her a great deal of satisfaction to play dumb and watch the major beg for table scraps like a hungry mongrel, but maybe teasing

Downing was simply too dangerous. In fact, if she gave him no satisfaction, he might start coming to his own conclusions; and they could be too close to the truth.

"I consider my sessions with Colonel Bradley confidential, but I did make an exciting breakthrough this morning that I'd like to share with you," she offered.

"Go on."

"One of the articles I accessed from the Medlars system suggested trying hypnosis on recalcitrant cases like our patient. I was afraid he'd resist the approach, but down on the beach with the rhythmic crashing of the waves, it was easy to put him under."

"And?" Downing couldn't keep the eagerness out of his voice.

"He started talking. With the right encouragement, I think he may let me take him back through his experiences of the last eight months."

Downing looked thoughtful. His burning curiosity satisfied, he was quickly reverting to type. "That's good news. Now that Bradley's dropped the silent act, we might be able to get somewhere with the interrogation team."

"That's rather shortsighted," Eden shot back.

"Oh?"

"We've only crossed the first barrier in the hundred-meter hurdles, Major. If you step in with the interrogation team, we're never going to finish the race," Eden cautioned. "I've just earned Colonel Bradley's trust, and the bond is fragile—and so is his recovery at this point."

Downing's jaw muscles clenched. "Don't forget, winning that race of yours isn't our main mission. I'm willing to bet that Bradley's memory is selective. If he's not giving you what I need, we'll have to fall back on other measures."

It wasn't an idle threat. Even though Downing was biding his time for the moment, he held the real power here. Eden was still going to have to walk the thin line between returning Mark to normal and satisfying the chief of station's demands.

ALTHOUGH MARSHALL pointedly left the cane beside the door the next morning, Mark just as pointedly ignored it. He'd spilled his guts to Eden yesterday, he thought in self-disgust. God knows what she'd be able to get out of him today.

For months he'd treated his memories like a man locked up with a canister of poison gas. In German it would be called *Gift Gas,* and the irony didn't escape him. It was the Leipzig legacy still controlling him four thousand miles away. Uncorking that German canister might well be a death sentence, for himself and maybe for others.

Until Eden had arrived, his inner resources had kept the seal on that lethal container intact. He'd fooled himself into thinking that the pressure wasn't building to the bursting point, but he no longer had those illusions. Day after day he'd had to fight his reaction to the new member of the staff at Pine Island. It wasn't just her perceptive blue eyes that seemed to penetrate to his very soul. It was the growing conviction that she sincerely wanted to help him; and, dammit, it was his awareness of her as a woman.

But maybe that was precisely the problem. He hadn't just bottled up his memories, he'd bottled up his emotions, as well. In fact, turning himself into an automaton had been all that had saved him from Downing's security team so far. But Eden Sommers had succeeded where the major and his minions had failed. That bastard Marshall hadn't been the only one who'd noticed how Dr. Sommers filled out her clinging knit tops, or how her jeans hugged the round curve of her bottom, but he was a lot more tuned to Eden than a clod like Marshall ever could be. From behind his emotionless mask, he'd made a study of her. He knew the graceful way she moved, the stormy look that came into her eyes when she was exasperated, the way her long, tapered fingers felt in his when she was trying to comfort him.

The night she'd come into his room to quiet his nightmares, he'd sent her away, but the memory of her warm body covering his had haunted him ever since. He'd played that scene over and over again in his mind, and in his fantasies he hadn't let her go. More than once he'd been helpless to stop the intimacy from reaching its logical conclusion. Achieving physical release had vented only a little of the pressure. What he craved was the warm, living, breathing reality of Eden Sommers. He wanted to bury himself in her softness and shut out for a few moments all the forces that were trying to destroy him.

The question on her lips when she entered the recreation room was too perceptive for comfort. "How did you sleep last night?"

"Badly."

The acerbic tone brought a look of compassion to her face. "That was a tough session yesterday afternoon."

He didn't reply.

"Would you like to get out for a walk again this morning?"

"Yes."

This time she also ignored the cane. When they were out of the shadow of the main house, Mark paused and took a deep breath, filling his lungs once again with the salty air. He wasn't going to admit it, but breaking his confinement had made a tremendous difference. Today he gained the line of the breakers more quickly. Instead of sitting down when they reached the stretch of beach beyond the stone wall, he kept walking. Here the hard-packed sand was strewn with colorful shells. Stopping for a moment, Eden picked up one that was shaped like a delicate coil. Mark didn't wait.

Eden straightened and then hurried to catch up. For a few minutes she kept pace with him in silence. Then she cleared her throat. "Let's not overdo it."

"I think I've recovered sufficient strength for a stroll on the beach."

"Mark, what's the matter?"

"What a question." His foot kicked at a little pile of seaweed on the sand.

She laughed. "Where would you like to start?"

He turned and faced her. "Don't try to take me back to East Germany." In the hot August sunlight, beads of perspiration stood out on his upper lip.

"But you've got to confront what happened."

"No."

"Listen, maybe you're not tired, but *I'm* not used to conducting peripatetic therapy sessions. Could we sit down?"

Mark looked back toward the rock wall. It was a good hundred yards behind them. If someone had planted a particularly sensitive microphone there in anticipation of his quarry's return, he was going to be disappointed. Mark shrugged inwardly. He didn't intend to say anything important this morning, but you never knew what the loquacious Dr. Sommers was going to come up with.

When he sat, it was with his body angled away from her, his eyes fixed on the ebbing and flowing surf. Eden knew that closed, guarded expression all too well. She had miscalculated yesterday and pushed too hard. What she had gotten from Mark hadn't been worth it, because now she had lost him again.

She looked down at the tube of suntan cream in her shirt pocket. She'd brought it along to smooth on Mark's face to protect his skin from the sun. Now she knew that her touch would definitely not be welcome.

THE CHIEF of station's face registered his disdain. "This isn't grand rounds at the hospital, Doctor. I just want a simple medical opinion about giving Bradley the RL2957. Answer yes or no."

Dr. Hubbard cleared his throat. "It's not as simple as yes or no."

"Why not?"

"Because a thousand things could go wrong."

"Like what?"

"You've read the case studies. Bradley's cardiovascular system may not be able to withstand the dose you're proposing. His brain may be irreparably damaged. This information he gives you when he's under has only a seventy-five percent chance of being accurate."

Downing waved his arm dismissively. He didn't want to let this has-been physician interfere with what he had to do.

Yet it was incumbent on him to make a show of asking for a consultation—for the record, in case anybody decided to sift back through the Pine Island logs. Considering what was riding on this assignment, he had a pretty good suspicion that might turn out to be the case.

"A *medical* opinion, Doctor," he said now. "I just want a medical opinion. The stuff arrived yesterday, and I want to know if Bradley's body can withstand its effects."

Dr. Hubbard shifted uncomfortably in his seat. Downing had been treating him like a two-bit veterinarian ever since he'd arrived here—and he hadn't exactly protested. He'd decided a long time ago that it was safer to go with the flow. Now he thought of the performance appraisal the major would be writing on him at the end of this tour. He'd already been passed over for promotion twice now. If it happened again, he'd had it as far as the air force was concerned. What would become of his wife then? She needed round-the-clock nursing care, and that cost money. If he were forced out of the service, he'd be scraping for cash, and he'd be of use to no one. The thought made him set his jaw. The worst wasn't going to happen, he assured himself.

Then he thought about Eden Sommers and the dedication she'd brought to this case. Before she'd arrived, he'd been able to convince himself that Mark Bradley was just an unfortunate son of a bitch caught in a web of circumstances. Now it wasn't so easy to remain detached.

"I thought you were going to give Dr. Sommers two weeks," he ventured.

"She's stalled again. If something positive doesn't happen by the end of the week, all bets are off."

"Are you going to tell her that?"

"No, and I want this conversation kept completely confidential. Do you understand?"

The doctor bit back the scathing remark on the tip of his tongue. "Yes."

THE EXCHANGE between Downing and Hubbard would have chilled Eden to the bone, had she known about it. Instead she was simply left to ponder her own assessment of Mark's condition. Physically he was much better. The scars on his face had blended in with his normal skin. Now that he had gained a little weight, his features had almost the old harmony she remembered. From the strength of his uncompromising jaw to his aquiline nose, he was once more a handsome man. When he walked, he held himself straight and tall. And almost all trace of his limp was gone. Since his hair was wet when she came in for their afternoon sessions, she had to assume he was being allowed to use the pool as she had suggested, but he didn't say anything about the new concession to her.

Although she tried a number of conversational gambits during the next two days, she met with no better success than she had on the beach. The bond she'd begun to establish had just been too fragile. Mark didn't really trust her enough to share his fears. With another patient there would have been no question about pulling back. It would be much more effective to let the healing process unfold naturally in its own good time, but time was one of the luxuries Pine Island lacked. She had to keep fighting.

Though Eden knew nothing definite about Downing's plans, she was good at picking up vibrations. She didn't like the assessing looks the chief of station and Price were giving her. More than once she thought Dr. Hubbard was about to confide some privileged piece of information, but he always turned away before he could get the words out.

However, the long-awaited message from the Falcon tipped the balance. She had been depressed after her fourth unsuccessful session with Mark and had almost decided to lie down before dinner instead of checking in with the Medlars data base, but some sixth sense had urged her to log on.

The communication she had been waiting for was embedded in the text of a letter from "Dr. Goldstein." It looked like four lines which had been garbled in transmission, but the seemingly meaningless character sets could be easily decoded using a simple key; and that key was found in one of the standard psychology textbooks Eden had brought to Pine Island. A duplicate volume was on Constance McGuire's desk back at the Aviary. Gordon's assistant had simply used the date at the top of the letter as a page number in the book and encoded her message using alphabetical substitutions keyed into the first eight letters of the top line of that page. To read the message, Eden had to check the date and turn to the same page so she could reconvert those substitutions to the letters of the plain text. Without the psychology book as a reference, the code was virtually unbreakable by anyone else without a computer powerful enough to test every possible letter combination.

It was basically a simple system, but following through with the plan did involve some risk. If someone noticed the garbled lines on her printout of the letter from "Dr. Goldstein" they might get curious; and in fact, she did have a bad moment when Lieutenant Price walked by just as she was tearing the sheet out of the printer.

"Is your terminal acting up?" he asked as he glanced at the less-than-perfect page.

Eden's heart lurched. As a member of the security team, Price would be on the lookout for any unusual communications. Yet he might be more than just an air force officer doing his job, she reminded herself. He could be a spy sent here to keep tabs on Mark Bradley. If that were the case, he certainly wouldn't let her know he had any special interest in the message she'd just received.

She looked down at the letter and pretended to see the garbled lines for the first time. "Darn! Wouldn't you know it. The only material I need has its bits scrambled, but maybe I can get the gist of it from the rest of the text."

Price seemed to accept the explanation, and Eden didn't know whether to be relieved or not.

However, he didn't miss the opportunity to lecture her on procedures. "If you see it happening again, you'd better report it to the Comms Center."

"Thanks, I will," she said, tucking the letter into a folder.

After signing off the Medlars system, she wanted to rush back to her room. Instead, she made the effort to walk slowly through the garden as though she simply had a few minutes to kill before the evening meal.

Once she'd closed the door to her room, however, she set to work feverishly decoding the message. Connie had made the process sound simple, but Eden had never done anything like this before. The first time she tried to carry out the set of instructions, she only got more garbage. So she started from the beginning again and worked more carefully. This time her efforts paid off.

Gordon's message was succinct and to the point. Like Downing, he was pressing for signs of progress. But he'd also given her an important piece of information—a weapon that might help her breach Mark's defenses. It was a name from Mark Bradley's recent past, and she was sure he would react to it. The trouble was, that reaction might be quite violent.

AT LEAST MARK was still willing to go outside with her, Eden reflected the next morning as the two of them headed for the beach again. This session with her patient had to be private.

When they reached a stretch of sand that was hidden from view of the main house, she looked back over her shoulder. Since that first time when Yolanski had coordinated his morning constitutional with her session, they had been left alone, but she didn't take anything for granted anymore.

"Let's sit down," she suggested, spreading out the blanket that she'd gotten in the habit of carrying along on their walks. She'd seen Marshall give her a speculative glance when he thought she wasn't looking, but frankly she hadn't cared what he thought she and Mark were doing in private.

Her patient shrugged as she spread out the navy blue rectangle. Again as he lowered himself to it, he angled his body away from her; but this morning, the sun glinting off the water seemed to be in his eyes.

"You might be more comfortable if you turned this way," she hinted.

He shifted his position imperceptibly, but his eyes still avoided hers. Eden watched him for a moment. Getting out in the sun had improved his color, even with the scars, and as the breeze off the water blew his hair back from his face, she noted how vibrant and thick it looked. Even the streaks of gray in his dark locks had taken on a silver sheen.

It made her heart turn over to see him regaining the appearance of vitality, because in Mark's case appearances were deceiving. Something was still eating him up inside, something he was unwilling to share with her. If pulling him into her arms and holding him close could make a difference, she was willing to offer him everything a woman could offer a man—but she'd already tried that and had been rejected.

He wasn't emotionally ready for intimacy, but maybe she could reach him with Gordon's new information. Of course, probing his psyche might be the equivalent of stabbing a raw wound. With one stroke she might wipe away all the progress he'd been able to make, but he had given her no other choice. She was going to have to chance it. Eden took a deep breath and let it out slowly, as though to center her own emotions before pressing ahead. "You remember when we first came out to the beach?" she began.

He didn't appear to be listening. Instead, his index finger was tracing a random pattern in the sand at the edge of the blanket.

"I told you we didn't have much time," she continued. "And we have even less now."

"So?"

"So we've got to make some progress, even if it's painful for you."

His senses seemed to sharpen like those of a boxer waiting to dodge a lethal right hook.

She'd have to hit him now before he could raise any more defenses. "Let's talk about Hans Erlich."

The fingers that had been sifting through the sand convulsively clutched for a handful of the tiny grains.

"Hans Erlich," she repeated. "Tell me about Dr. Erlich."

His face had turned ashen and she glimpsed fear in the depths of his soul. "Satan come to life." The words were torn from him in a haunted whisper. He didn't say anything else, but the power of that name had propelled him into a maelstrom of nightmare images. He saw a hard, uncompromising face with blond hair curled across the forehead. A dark, prominent mole stood out on the right cheek. The eyes were watery blue, with colorless lashes. The intelligence that gleamed from them had belonged to a genius—or a madman. The memories were jumbled, indistinct, but he knew one thing. Erlich had been his lifeline, his salvation, his link to reality, and the key to his destruction.

*"You are Mark Bradley. You are my creation."*

His mind echoed the words that had been drummed into him with the force of a sledgehammer.

*"No,"* came his answering silent denial.

*"You are a means to an end."*

*"No."*

*"You will bend to my will."*

*"No."*

*"Mark Bradley belongs to me . . . to me . . . to me . . . You will remember the importance of 002-72-52, 002-72-52, 002-72-52 . . . But when you try to recall anything else about our conversations, the pain in your head will be intolerable."*

Suddenly even that snatch of memory was gone, and he felt like a man bashing his head against a brick wall. The veins in his temples stood out. His face had taken on the flush of fever; and all at once Eden was afraid at what she'd unleashed. She didn't want to go on with this, but there was no other way. "What did he do to you?" she persisted. "Try to remember."

For a moment, it looked as though he were trying to answer her question. "He . . . Oh, God— Day after day— Week after week . . ." The effort to get out each word was a silver spike of pain in his head. His hands clawed at his temples as though he could somehow pull those spikes out, but it was no good.

He was gasping for breath now, his skin cold and clammy.

She tried to bring him back to the present. "Mark!" But it was obvious that he was beyond her reach.

A spasm hit him, and then another, and then, in slow motion, he collapsed sideways onto the blanket, his knees curled up to his chest.

Eden watched in horror. Erlich was the doctor who had interrogated Mark. The techniques he had used must have been unspeakable. No wonder Mark had tried to lock away the terrifying experience.

She put her hand on his shoulder, but he was too withdrawn now to even shrug away her touch. His eyes were glazed over and each breath was a painful gasp. She grabbed his icy hands, chafing them between her fingers. "It's all right. He can't hurt you here," she repeated over and over.

*You're wrong,* his mind shouted. *You don't know what he can do, what power he can exercise.* But the words were frozen in his throat.

It was only slowly that he came back to the reality of Pine Island. He was aware first of the sun's healing warmth and then the waves pounding against the shore. When his eyes snapped open, he saw Eden's tense face hovering above his. "Mark, forgive me. I didn't know it would be that bad." Her fingers brushed back the dark hair that clung damply to his forehead.

"Eden, hold me," he whispered.

Until now, he hadn't asked for what she so desperately wanted to give. There was a sad joy in her heart as she stretched out beside him on the blanket and pulled him into her arms. For long moments, she held him against her body, rocking him back and forth, and this time he didn't fight the comfort of her embrace. His arms went around her shoulders to pull her even closer. The seconds that ticked by were beats of his heart. She couldn't be sure what had happened. She only knew that by bringing him pain, she had broken through to him again.

By slow degrees, she felt some of the tension go out of his body.

He drew in a ragged breath. "That plane crash in Berlin should have been the end of Mark Bradley."

"No!"

"You don't know. You can't understand."

"Mark, you think this is something unique, but you're wrong. I've worked with people who've been through what you have. I've helped them."

Been through what he had. He doubted it.

"I can help you," she repeated, shifting slightly so she could look down into his face. "Breaking the lock on those memories was the worst part, but you've got to go back more than once, Mark, if you want to be whole again."

He shuddered. "I can't. When I try, I feel as though the pain in my head is going to shatter my skull."

"I didn't know." So that's what Erlich had done. He had locked up Mark's mind with barbed wire fence, and when his victim pressed against the barrier, the twisted metal tines dug into his flesh. Erlich was counting on the pain to block Mark's recovery. She had to hope that the worst part would be crossing that barrier the first time. After that, it would be easier.

She squeezed his hand reassuringly. "It tears me up inside to put you through this, but you've got to make that journey, Mark. Nothing less than your survival is at stake."

"I guess I've always known that, too. That's why it's so bad. There's nothing solid to go back to. It's only fleeting images, incoherent memories—and the damn pain in my head that threatens to explode every time I try to piece things together."

She recognized what admitting that had cost him. "Bringing that out into the open is a tremendous step," she assured.

"Or a dead end."

"No."

"Suppose you're wrong?"

"Trust me. We'll solve the puzzle together, piece by piece. From now on, whenever you have an image or a memory, no matter how fuzzy or fleeting, bring it to me and we'll work with it.''

His arms tightened around her again. He was afraid to accept what she was offering. But he was more afraid not to.

# Chapter Eight

"You idiot, I told you not to call me here," the man in Washington hissed.

"This is an emergency."

"It'd better be."

"Sommers is on the verge of getting results."

There was an instant alertness on the other end of the phone line punctuated by a low curse.

"Did you get that information on her?"

"There's a hold on her file. But my contact in the administrator's office has promised to make me a copy tonight."

"So I should be ready to move as soon as you give the word."

"Yes. And make it look like an accident."

"That shouldn't be too hard. You step off this island in the wrong place and the undertow will do the rest."

"I'll get back to you tomorrow."

There was a click and the line went dead. The operative on Pine Island looked at the receiver and then set it down with a jolt. He was doing all the dirty work down here, and that jerk in Washington would keep his hands clean. He'd gotten into the spy business for the money. Somewhere along the line the money had stopped being enough. It didn't make up for the risks he was being forced to take. Briefly he'd thought about turning himself in. But that was madness. They'd get to him somehow. There simply wasn't any way to resign from this job and live to tell about it. So he'd just have to follow instructions and make sure everything went as planned.

MARK STOOD NEXT to his bed, clad only in jeans. He'd been in the act of undressing for the night—Marshall, to his relief, was now letting him do that for himself—when an image had flickered through his mind. It was of a room with institutional green walls and sparse furnishings in sterile white enamel. A hospital room. And he had occupied it. He could almost feel the coarse sheets against the naked skin of his back. The tactile memory made his skin crawl.

Then he felt the old fear gnawing in his gut. This was where it had happened—whatever it was.

He slammed his fist into the palm of his hand. He wasn't going to run away this time. When the image faded, he tried to call it back. But it was like trying to dig his fingernails into a cloud. The effort made his head throb again the way it had this afternoon, and he eased himself down the edge of the bed. Eyes closed, he leaned forward, cradling his forehead in his palms as he struggled to calm his breathing.

In a moment the pain passed, to be replaced by frustration. It was the same stone wall he had come up against again and again. There was something here he wanted to understand, had to understand. The pain and the memories of those six months were tied together in a way he couldn't explain. But maybe Eden was right, maybe he didn't have to do it by himself. All at once he realized he wanted to talk to her about it. That knowledge made him feel as though someone had just lifted an enormous weight from his chest.

Quickly he glanced toward the bathroom door, where his room connected to Eden's. There was only dim light coming from underneath. She must be in her room with the door open. That meant she was still awake.

Crossing his room, he turned the knob and stepped onto the tile floor. Then he realized his assumption had been mistaken. Eden was standing in front of the bathroom mirror brushing her golden brown hair in the half-light that filtered in from her room.

Mark's breath caught in his throat. Every detail of the scene was instantly impressed upon his senses. She was wearing a sleeveless satin gown that tantalizingly cupped her breasts, narrowed in to emphasize her slender waist, and descended in graceful folds around her legs. Her hair cascaded around her head like a burnished halo. Her blue eyes were wide with surprise as they met his in the mirror.

Neither one of them spoke. They simply stood there looking at each other.

"What is it, Mark?" she finally whispered.

"I wanted to talk to you about something—a piece to the puzzle."

But now that he was here, seeing her like this, what had brought him to her was no longer important. A wave of intense longing washed over him, threatening to drown him. He wanted her with all his being, yet he was still afraid of what he might discover about himself in her arms. Without even knowing that he was crossing the tile floor, he came forward and put his hands on her shoulders.

In the mirror he saw her lips part, as though she might be going to ask another question, but the words remained unspoken. Her eyes never left his, and he felt her shiver as his fingers began to stroke the vibrant warmth of her skin. He had never felt anything quite so sensual. After weeks of denial, he gave in to the luxury of nuzzling his face against her hair, letting the scent of almonds and exotic spice envelop him. He heard her sigh with pleasure, felt her arch against him.

When his eyes asked a silent question, her reflection answered. With fingers that were far from steady, he slipped the straps of her gown down her arms and watched as the satin bodice followed their downward progress. He held his breath again as the tops of her breasts were bared. All at once the fine material lost the battle with gravity and came to rest around her waist.

In the dim light her breasts were alabaster, her nipples dusky pink. Even as he watched, they puckered and hardened. He had never seen anything so beautiful in his life.

Eden swayed backward against him, her arms trapped at her sides by the satin straps of her gown, her very being trapped in an invisible net of silken threads. She felt the intensity of Mark's gaze like a burning caress. She longed to feel the sweet reality of his touch.

"Please." The word was a whispered supplication.

"Oh, Eden. If I touch you now, I won't be able to stop."

"I don't want you to stop."

In slow motion, his hands slipped from her shoulders to graze her breasts. Then he was cupping them, feeling their weight in his hands, gliding his thumbs across the taut nipples.

She closed her eyes and arched her back, straining to increase the contact. The pleasure of it was a raw ache deep inside her.

Answering an elemental need to give as well as receive, she turned in his arms, her mouth seeking his. Their lips fused together in a searing kiss that finally proclaimed all the pent-up needs and longings that neither of them had been able to banish.

He reveled in the taste of her sweet mouth, the feel of her soft breasts pressed against his naked chest, the sensual response of her body to his.

He felt her struggle impatiently with the straps that held her arms. Free of the restraints at last, her hands came up to knead the muscle and sinew of his shoulders and tangle possessively in the dark hair at the back of his head.

When their mouths finally drew apart, they were both breathless—yet burning for more.

"Come to my bed," she murmured.

"Yes."

She pushed the gown down over her hips and let it pool around her feet. Stepping gracefully out of it, she took his hand and led him through the door. The room was a landscape of unreality. They had eyes for each other alone.

"You have too many clothes on." The words were spoken as her lips hungrily nibbled at his bare neck and shoulder. And then her fingers were unashamedly fumbling with the button at his waistband. He stepped away slightly so that she could help him out of his jeans and briefs. Then he was pulling her against the taut, naked length of his body.

"You're so damn soft," he marveled.

"And you're so hard." Her hand closed around him, her fingers clasping him as her body soon would. There was nothing tentative or unsure about the gesture.

The intimacy of the touch brought a gasp of pleasure to his lips. How many times had he dreamed about her caressing him like this? The certain knowledge that she had shared his longings seemed to shatter the last barrier between them.

They were on the bed then, holding and touching and tasting each other with an urgency that was almost frightening in its insatiability.

For Eden, two weeks of living together—yet apart—made this more intense than anything she had experienced in the past. But there was an underlying familiarity that made her heart race with joy. He knew her body, knew what pleased her, knew what drove her to a frenzy of wanting. And that was exactly what he was doing as he slipped his finger inside her and then out again in a tantalizing rhythm.

"Mark, please . . ."

He looked down at her. Her hair was in erotic disarray, her lips slightly swollen from his kisses, her eyes begging him not to wait any longer for the final joining. She didn't have to beg. He was powerless to deny her.

His mouth sought hers, even as he covered her body with his. There was no hesitation. In one powerfully satisfying stroke he was deep inside her. She felt like a tight, hot cocoon, pulling him deeper into her velvet warmth.

Every stroke bound him to her until there was nothing in the universe but Eden. He felt her trembling beneath him. She called out his name again and again, as the spasms of her ecstasy contracted around him. And then they became his own.

There was no thought of muffling the shout of satisfaction that started deep in his throat.

They were both out of breath. For several heartbeats he simply held her close. Then she felt him stir.

She clasped his shoulders more tightly. "Don't leave me yet. I don't want it to be over."

He caressed her cheek with his and hugged her fiercely.

She felt a warm glow surge through her. This was the Mark Bradley she remembered. She smiled up at him. "It is really you, isn't it?"

The tenderness went out of his face, to be replaced by pain and then a cold expression that gave her a sudden chill. "You're dead wrong, Eden. I'm not the Mark Bradley you used to know."

He rolled off her and turned away, his back rigid.

The grating words made all Eden's old doubts rush back. Had she just made love to an impostor? In fact, had she surrendered to the enemy? The thoughts made her want to cringe away toward the other side of the bed.

She forced her rational thinking processes to push away blind fear. If this man were an impostor, surely he would be all too happy to let her go on thinking that he was Mark Bradley. No, in this case it was Mark's own uncertainties that had prompted his words. He must be motivated by an inner hopelessness, not from a desire to hurt her. And she was trained to deal with that.

That thought gave her the courage to put a questioning hand on his shoulder.

"Leave me alone." The words were a savage growl.

She stared at his unyielding back. "Don't shut me out. Not now."

The plea in her voice pierced through to his heart. God, how he wanted to be the man that she remembered. A moment ago when they had made love, he had been able to catch hold of flashes of his old identity. But they were little more than disconnected fragments.

Yet what had he expected, after the things that had been done to him in that "hospital" in Leipzig? Making love with Eden could only be a moment out of time. And yet, she was right. He owed her some explanation.

"Eden, it can't work for us. I must have been crazy to have let this happen."

"Mark, you're not making sense."

He turned back to face her, his face an angry mask. "What do you want from me?"

"The truth."

Before he could respond, a floorboard in the hall creaked. They both froze.

Mark was instantly alert, their personal differences forgotten, as his years of Peregrine training took over. He put a finger to his lips and shook his head vigorously.

She nodded her understanding. They waited in silence. This time the sound of a foot being carefully placed was almost imperceptible. But they heard.

Mark sat up. He looked toward the door, then back at her. "I'm going to take a shower. Want to join me?"

For a moment she was completely confused. Then she realized the running water would serve the same purpose as the waves pounding the shore. They would be able to speak without being overheard.

She recognized the ploy. "That sounds like a good idea." Her words were calm, but inside she was battling with equal parts of fear and outrage. Someone had been listening outside her door while she and Mark had been making love.

Taking her hand reassuringly, he led her back to the bathroom. Neither of them spoke until he had turned on the water full force.

"Who?" she whispered.

"I don't know. The elevator and the stairs are locked. The door to the next wing is bolted. No one could get up here—unless they have a key." As he spoke, he stepped under the hot water and pulled her in after him. Then he closed the curtain.

Her arms went around his shoulders and she clung to him, feeling the hot water pounding down against them.

The water made his skin slick. As her hands slid over his back and shoulders, she was more aware than ever of the uneven ridges of scar tissue. She thought again about the horrible burns and shuddered.

He mistook the reaction for present fear and held her tightly, his cheek pressed against hers. The urge to comfort and protect her almost overwhelmed him. But he had to think, not just react.

Names were spinning in his head. Downing, Price, Hubbard, Yolanski, Walker, Marshall—even the other enlisted men. At least one of the crew here was working for someone besides the U.S. Air Force.

There hadn't been much for Mark to do except study their personalities and resist their interrogation. He'd had to assume the Russians had sent someone to Pine Island to protect their man in the Pentagon. In the two months since arriving here, he'd been speculating about who it might be.

Almost any of them could use the money. But somehow he couldn't see that as a motive for Downing. He was obviously acting from the strength of his convictions, whatever they were. On the other hand, Hubbard was such a weakling that he might be easy prey for an enemy blackmail scheme. Walker, Ramirez and Yolanski might be bitter about the American dream turned sour for minorities. And what about Price and Marshall? They were both after status in their own way. Warm appreciation from the Soviets and a chance to feel important might go a long way with men like that.

There was suddenly so much to talk about—and so little time.

"You wouldn't have hit me with Erlich's name if you were on their side," he finally murmured.

She felt his body tense. It cost him a lot just to say that name.

"I wanted so much for you to believe I was here to help you, but I just couldn't spell it out."

He hugged her fiercely. "They don't want me to know what happened in East Germany."

"Can you tell me anything more about it?" It wasn't safe to speak above a whisper.

He took a deep, shuddering breath. "Eden, I'm not the same man who went to West Berlin for the Falcon. I don't even feel as though this patched-up body is really mine."

"Oh, Mark." Her hands traced over his shoulder and down his side, feeling again the scar tissue from the skin grafts. Then she reached up and delicately touched the line between nose and mouth. It owed a great deal to the plastic surgeon's art. How would it be to look in the mirror every morning and know you weren't seeing quite the face you had been born with, to see scars that would never entirely fade? Her heart went out to him at the thought. Yet it didn't matter to her that his exterior was somehow different. The important thing was that his body was whole and well again and he was getting his strength back.

But he wasn't finished. "Eden, that's not the worst. It's what's inside that's driving me crazy. They've done something to my mind. And I don't know what. I may be some kind of time bomb. I may hurt you. Destroy the Peregrine Connection. Compromise national security by betraying the Orion project. In fact, I may have already done it." He had finally voiced the fear that had been gnawing at him for what seemed like an eternity.

"You couldn't!"

"Don't be too sure."

"We'll take care of whatever it is."

"That might be impossible."

"Mark, Gordon told me you had learned some sort of self-hypnosis technique—a protection against interrogation."

"Yes. But not against Hans Erlich." Again she felt his frustration and his torment. If just the mention of the doctor's name was so destructive, what had the man himself been able to do?

"He may be trained to hurt. I'm trained to heal."

"Oh, God, Eden. You don't know. You can't know."

They clung together for long silent moments, letting the hot water pound against them. Finally he shifted his body so their eyes could meet.

"We can't stay in here forever."

She tried to laugh.

He bent to lick droplets of water off her shoulder. It seemed a familiar gesture to him. Had he done this before?

She smiled. "You always did like to do that."

"I still do."

It was tempting to give in to the sensuality of the moment. But there were still issues to settle. "I need to know some things."

She nodded.

"That first morning when the lights went out. Tell me what happened."

She quickly filled him in on the hair dryer incident.

He swore. "Someone tried to kill you!"

"Or warn me."

"You're in worse danger now. If someone is sneaking around in the hall, he must be desperate."

"An East German agent?"

"No. They've spent a lot of time and money patching me up, because they want something from me. They wouldn't waste their investment by killing me."

The casual way he spoke made her shiver, even under the warm, pounding water.

"It's got to be the Russians," he continued. "They're the ones with the mole in the Pentagon. If I can nail him, the guy's had it."

"Can you?"

"Yes. But he's so high up, no one will believe me without proof."

"You have it?"

"Yes. In a safe place—I hope." His jaw firmed. "We've got to get out of here."

"How?"

"Swim maybe."

"Impossible. It's too far."

"I was a high school champion freestyler." She heard the doubt in his voice even as he tried to sound confident for her sake.

"But you're out of shape," she reminded him gently.

"I'd rather die trying to get away than get it in the back here."

Their eyes met and held. He squeezed her arm reassuringly. "We'll make it. Can you get an emergency message to the Falcon?"

"Yes."

"Do it. Tell him the situation."

A new thought struck her. "I'm the one who put you in danger. As long as the agent down here thought Downing wasn't getting anywhere, you were safe."

"No. It was only a matter of time, if he was planning to use that drug."

"But—"

"Don't." Mark stepped back and looked at the shower head. "I've got to turn off the water or somebody's going to come find out why we're spending the night in here. You understand it won't be safe to talk."

She nodded in frustration. He was right, yet she knew he was also deliberately cutting the discussion off.

"We've got to behave as though we don't know we're being stalked."

"I know."

Reaching out, he turned the knobs and the water subsided. Then he pulled her into his arms. His lips found hers in a hungry kiss. To her surprise, despite the danger, or maybe because of it, she found herself responding with equal passion.

THEY PARTED before dawn, to any observer, lovers with nothing on their minds but each other. Yet as they'd lain in one another's arms in the early hours of the morning, each had been silently assessing the critical elements that would have to come together if they were going to make good their escape.

The first item on Eden's agenda was tapping into the Medlars network. But as it turned out, the Falcon had already initiated a communication.

At breakfast Ramirez brought her a folded sheet of paper. She was aware of Downing's and Price's eyes on her as she opened the printed message.

Dr. Goldstein can comply with your request for a teleconferencing session today at 9:00 a.m.

"Problems?" Downing inquired.

"No. That doctor who's been doing research in our patient's area has agreed to a consultation."

"You know that the details of this case are classified."

"I'm aware of that." Her voice was crisp. But inside she was full of dark anxiety. The Falcon was breaking his own rules. He wouldn't be doing it unless the situation had deteriorated substantially.

"Then you'll act accordingly," Downing reminded her.

"Most of the information will be coming from Goldstein. I'm only going to talk about my case in the broadest general terms."

At the appointed hour Eden reported to the communications center and logged on to the medical system.

"Dr. Goldstein" was on the line and ready to transmit as soon as she connected. She hadn't known exactly how this thing was going to work, but it soon became clear. On the surface, they conducted a perfectly normal question and answer session in which he used their agreed-upon conventions to quiz her about Mark. As best she could, she filled him in on her certainty about Mark's identity. But she held back Mark's own doubts about what might have been done to him in Leipzig. She knew that was not telling Gordon the whole truth. But then, how truthful had he been with her in the beginning?

There was, however, another purpose to the communication, as well. The Falcon had some important information for her, which he once again encoded in the last line of each page of their dialogue. While they conducted their "professional" interchange, Eden hastily copied down the scrambled text. It took twenty minutes to get four lines. And by the time she had signed off, Eden felt as though her insides had turned to jelly. She had to decode this quickly before her morning session with Mark on the beach, because that would be her only opportunity to speak privately with him all day.

This time, luckily, she was more familiar with the procedure. But as the words emerged from the garbled text, she knew the blood had drained from her face. Her worst fears had been realized.

EDEN WAS LATE for her session with Mark, and she could see the tension on his face.

"I'm sorry I was delayed," she said, trying to put all the empathy she felt for him into her face. "Let's go out and get some sun. Maybe you'll even be up to wading in the waves today."

He shot her a questioning look, but she shook her head. She couldn't say more now.

Outside he headed directly for the breakers. And as soon as he reached the water's edge, he turned to her.

"Something's happened."

"Yes. The Falcon sent me an emergency message this morning. Somebody's been riffling through my air force personnel file in Washington."

"Then your cover's been blown. Whoever reads it will see we were together at Griffiss."

She nodded. "The Falcon's pulling us off."

"Then he's taking a chance on Mark Bradley."

"I vouched for Mark Bradley."

The conviction in her voice brought him a brief, bittersweet satisfaction. Staying on the island now was unthinkable. But leaving it wasn't going to be a picnic, either.

"Tell me the plan."

She laughed. "Could I interest you in a moonlight swim?"

"All the way to the Georgia coast?"

"No. Someone is going to pick us up in the water about a mile from here, either tonight or tomorrow night, whichever we can manage. Do you think you can make it that far?"

"I guess I'll have to." He was thoughtful for a moment. "But how is the guy with the boat going to find us?"

"It seems that the antique pin I brought in with my luggage is a transmitter, and my manicure instruments turn out to be burglary tools. Gordon says you'll know how to use them to get past the lock at the stairway."

A half smile played around his lips. She could see that his mind was already focusing on the escape itself. It must be exhilarating to be able to finally act after months of ineffective waiting.

"So all we can do till tonight is sit tight."

"I guess so."

THAT PREDICTION didn't prove to be correct. After lunch, the chief of station called Eden into his office. There was an ominous chill in the air as he asked her to sit down.

"Dr. Sommers," he began. "I'm not satisfied with the progress you've been making. So you won't be having your afternoon session with Colonel Bradley today."

Eden stared at him, forcing herself not to betray the heavy thudding of her heat. "Why not?"

"As ordered from Washington, I'm going to go ahead with the drug therapy we discussed last week."

Somehow she had known what he was going to say, but the casually spoken words still hit her like a wrecking ball. *Oh, God, not today.* "I think that's a mistake," she countered.

"It doesn't matter what you think anymore. Bradley is my responsibility in the end."

"And if you destroy his mind without getting what you want?"

"As I said, I'll take that responsibility."

She wanted to scream. She wanted to shout out her defiance. But she kept her composure. It wouldn't do any good to argue with the man. Downing had made up his mind. And the only thing she could accomplish by continuing the discussion would be to arouse his suspicions.

Automatically she stood up. "Thank you for telling me, Major."

"Not at all."

# Chapter Nine

Eden clamped her teeth together and marched grimly toward the medical wing. Her first thought was to find the supply of RL2957 and destroy it. If the chief of station used it on Mark this afternoon, there was no telling what the outcome might be. Downing could be the Russian agent. And if he was, Mark would probably never leave that session alive. A convenient overdose of an unstable drug—who would question that? Even if Downing weren't operating with a hidden agenda, a session with that deadly compound could turn Mark's mind into raw hamburger meat. The possibilities made her fight down the panic that rose like bile in her throat.

But when she reached the other side of the house and saw Blackwell sitting at his desk, the flimsiness of her half-formed plan hit her. That drug was locked up, either here or in Downing's office. She couldn't get to it.

Blackwell looked up from the file sheets he was counting and she turned away. She had to think, and think sensibly. Then it hit her. Maybe Dr. Hubbard could do something—if he wasn't the enemy agent.

God, she was getting paranoid. But who wouldn't be? Someone down here had almost certainly tried to kill her. Was it one of the obvious people like Downing, Price, or Marshall, who had shown their animosity? Or was it someone much more unlikely—Walker the quiet observer, or Yolanski the smart aleck. Ramirez could even have arranged that accident for himself to divert suspicion. She didn't have a clue who the enemy might be. But if she read the Falcon correctly, he or they were getting ready to try something again.

But that didn't eliminate the danger for Mark. If she was going to abort the chief of station's plans for the afternoon, she needed the doctor's cooperation, even though she was taking a terrible risk in asking for anyone's help. If Hubbard couldn't buy her some time, the whole game was up right now, just when she'd dared to hope that she and Mark were going to get out of this alive.

When she came into his office, Hubbard put down the medical journal he was studying and smiled. "I thought you'd be getting ready for your afternoon session with our patient."

"Do you have a moment?"

"Certainly." He took in her pale complexion. "What's the problem?"

"Major Downing has just informed me he's going to use that experimental truth serum on Colonel Bradley this afternoon."

The doctor sighed. "I knew it had arrived. He wouldn't tell me when he was planning to use it."

*You knew and you didn't tell me,* she wanted to shout. But she bit back the accusation. "You can't let him do it," she said instead.

"You and I both know there's nothing I can do to stop the major when he has his mind made up."

"Dr. Hubbard, I'm on the verge of getting something from Colonel Bradley, quite possibly today. If Major Downing gets his chance with him first, I may not be able to pick up the pieces."

Hubbard nodded. He'd read the reports on what that drug had done, and the effects weren't pretty.

"You've got to put the major off at least until tomorrow," Eden insisted.

The doctor studied her tense features. What was it about this woman that made him want to help her, despite the personal cost? "Why is one more day so important to you?"

Could she risk telling him? No. "It just is. Please."

"Downing's made it clear that he doesn't want to hear my opinion unless there's some medical problem involved."

"Could there be one in this case? Something. Anything."

Hubbard pursed his lips. "I've been reading up on the literature. Most clinicians recommend administering the drug on an empty stomach because it sometimes causes nausea. And in the patient's drugged state, he could aspirate vomitus."

"And choke to death?"

"It's not likely but it could happen. Maybe I can insist that Downing keep the colonel on a liquid diet for twenty-four hours before he goes ahead."

"Would he listen?"

"I don't know."

Eden glanced at her watch. "Downing's preempting my therapy session at 1500 hours. That's less than two hours from now."

"All right," the doctor said resignedly, pushing himself up out of his chair. "I'll talk to him now."

"I'll wait here for you."

Hubbard nodded, suddenly remembering all the *Star Trek* banter he and Eden had exchanged. Right now he felt a little like Captain Kirk preparing to beam aboard a Klingon warship. But then hadn't Kirk always beaten the odds? As he left the room, he gave Eden's shoulder a reassuring squeeze.

In response she found herself offering up a silent prayer.

She tried to relax. But there was no way she could keep her glance from flicking to the large clock on the wall, which gave a whir and a click every time the second hand passed twelve. Five minutes, ten minutes, fifteen minutes. Downing must be arguing with Hubbard. She gnawed on her lip, imagining the scene, imagining the chief of station's biting displeasure, the doctor buckling under and giving in.

For a long time, she realized, she had felt like a rabbit caught in the talons of a falcon. Amherst Gordon had snatched her from her safe surroundings and dropped her here. But he wasn't the only bird of prey who had her—and Mark—in his clutches. Hans Erlich was hovering in the background like a vulture waiting to feed on the terrible uncertainties he had planted in Mark's mind. And on Pine Island, Ross Downing had the power to terminate her mission just as effectively as an eagle suddenly dropping its victim to the rocky floor of a canyon.

When the door of Hubbard's office finally opened again, she jumped and then anxiously inspected the physician's features. His face was gray, but his jaw was set.

"Tell me," Eden demanded.

"He didn't like it."

"Then he . . . ?"

"He agreed to think about it."

"What does that mean?"

The doctor sank wearily back into his chair. "I told him I wouldn't certify the patient as medically ready until tomorrow afternoon, and that my failure to do so could raise serious procedural questions back in Washington. That worried him."

"When do I find out?" Eden couldn't keep the tension out of her voice.

"At your afternoon therapy session. Bradley will either be there—or he won't."

Eden had thought waiting for the doctor to come back was unbearable. It was nothing compared to what she suffered during the next hour and a half. She had done what little she could. Now there was no way she could sit still. After thanking Hubbard for his efforts, she slipped out of the house and wandered down to the beach. She looked for the lines of footprints in the sand where she and Mark had walked earlier as they had discussed their escape plans. Seeing that the waves had obliterated their tracks brought a lump to her throat. This morning she had been so confident of getting out of this hellhole. Now the wide expanse of beach seemed claustrophobic, as though someone had dropped an impenetrable plastic dome over the whole island. She and Mark might never be able to claw their way out of here now.

A little before 1500 hours she turned and made her way back to the main house. She didn't notice the speculative look Blackwell gave her from the desk by the elevator, or the exasperated expression on Marshall's face as she crossed in front of the physical therapy room. All her attention was focused on the closed door to the room where she and Mark had been working together. What if Downing had just wiped away all the real progress they had made? Her hand hesitated on the knob. She was afraid to open the door.

When she stepped into the room, her eyes flicked to the chair where Mark usually sat. It was empty. Her heart gave a lurch inside her chest. And then she saw him standing with his hands behind his back looking out the window. He turned as he heard her close the door.

"I saw you walking on the beach."

She couldn't answer. All the control she had been holding on to so tightly finally snapped. In a second she was across the room throwing herself against his chest. Automatically his arms came up to steady her.

"Eden, don't," he whispered against her ear.

She didn't speak. Instead he felt her body shaking. She was crying, muffling her sobs against the cotton knit of his shirt.

He could only stand there, trying to soothe her, his hands stroking her back, his lips against her hair. The frustration building inside him felt like a pressure cooker on high. He was the kind of person who had always taken action rather than sitting around waiting for things to happen. Now, because of those prying microphones in the room, he couldn't even comfort Eden properly.

He had a damn good idea what the problem was. Eden might have thought she could stall Downing forever, but he was a realist. The knowing look on Marshall's face at lunch—and the way he'd rushed him through the meal—

had sent up a red flag. Mark had started mentally preparing himself for a struggle if the security team came to get him. They were going to be surprised at how much of his muscle tone he had back. He'd faced two-to-one odds before and come out on top. The question was, how many men would they call in to restrain him?

But the plans had changed abruptly, and he didn't know why. He could only guess that Eden had spent the morning moving heaven and earth to buy this reprieve. But he had to assume the stay of execution was temporary. That meant he and Eden had to get out tonight.

He continued to hold and stroke her, waiting for the storm to pass. Finally he felt her quieting. Stepping back, he looked questioningly into her eyes, and she seemed to draw strength from that exchange.

"Do you want to sit down?"

She nodded.

He led her to the couch and handed her the box of tissues. Despite the grimness of the situation, the simple gesture made her smile. A box of tissues was standard issue for therapy sessions. But they were usually for the convenience of the patient, not the therapist.

She blew her nose. "Thanks."

He put his finger under her chin and tipped her face up so that their eyes could meet again. *I know.* He mouthed the words. And then, *Don't worry.* For a moment he held her hand between his larger ones before settling back on the couch.

"What do you want to hit me with this afternoon, Doctor?"

The rest of the session would have won a pair of Academy Awards for Best Performance Under Duress.

SERGEANT MARSHALL knocked on the door to the security conference room and shifted his weight imperceptibly from one foot to the other. The last thing in the world he had been anticipating was this summons. But then, the past twenty-four hours had been full of surprises, not the least of which were Downing's orders and subsequent counter-orders for Bradley.

When he stepped into the room, there were three other men present besides the chief of station: Yolanski, Price and Walker.

"Have a seat, Sergeant." Downing waved his hand in the direction of an empty chair. Then, without preamble, he began. "I've called you all here for a strategy session."

Marshall looked around the room. This was the first time he'd been invited to sit in on a planning meeting with the Pine Island inner circle. He couldn't help being flattered yet also a little wary.

"This seems like a good time to check in with each other and pool some information," Downing continued. *And make a reassessment of your strengths and weaknesses,* he added silently.

"Let's start with the Comms Center." He turned to Price, who was in charge of monitoring the security logs for that facility. "Has there been any unusual activity?"

Yolanski was glad the chief of station's eyes were not on him at that moment. He'd made a few unauthorized connections, the most innocuous to a dirty-joke bulletin board at Berkeley. But he was pretty sure he'd covered his tracks.

He wasn't the only one in the room bothered by the question. Price looked uncomfortable. Those logs piled up every day. And going through them was worse than proof-reading the phone book. Did he lie to Downing and say nothing had happened? Or did he admit he'd scribbled his name at the bottom of every third page without reading it? Suddenly the conversation over Eden's garbled message popped into his mind. At the time he'd chosen not to raise any alarms. But had someone been looking over his shoulder?

"Come to think of it, I was curious about activity on line number seven," he said. "But I have to go back and review my records." He was going to be up till midnight checking the blasted backup tapes.

Next the chief of station turned to Marshall. "You're right in the hub of activity in the medical wing. Have you picked up any suspicious—" he hesitated as though searching for the right word "—vibrations?"

"What do you mean, sir?"

"I mean, I have the feeling that something fishy is going on over there. It looks to me as though Sommers has subverted Hubbard. Or maybe she's just using him for some private purpose of her own. Do you have any impressions that might help me form an opinion?"

What a question. And what the hell was the best answer? Marshall played for time. "Sir, I'd rather not make accusations about superior officers."

"Sergeant Marshall, your loyalty is commendable. But let me remind you that your first duty is to your commanding officer, not Doctors Hubbard or Sommers."

The nurse remained silent, and the chief of station drummed his fingers against the uncluttered surface of the conference table. Downing was thinking that perhaps he had been arrogant in placing too much faith in locks and security systems, even if they were the best that money could buy. If Bradley escaped, it was Maj. Ross Downing's head that would be on the chopping block. But he wasn't going to share the insight.

"Starting today, I'd like the four of you to rotate evening duty in the medical wing. The man who draws the assignment will sleep in one of the infirmary beds. That way he can report any suspicious nighttime activity to me."

"Might I ask what you're expecting, sir?" Walker asked. Things were taking an unexpected turn, and one he didn't much like.

The chief of station shook his head. "I simply don't want to take any chances." Downing concluded the meeting with a general pep talk about security precautions.

After the major left, Price shook his head. "What do you suppose has gotten into him?" he asked, addressing no one in particular.

"His ego is all wrapped up around this job," Yolanski observed dryly.

Price started to redirect the blame. "Yeah, well maybe if you were a little more on top of things..." He wasn't the only one who'd been derelict in his duties. Yolanski was a positive slob about paperwork. Why hadn't Downing asked *him* about the duty station reports, for example? He had a suspicion that Yolanski simply faked them.

"Knock it off," Walker broke in. "We're all on edge. But this can't go on forever." From where he sat it looked as though things were going to break soon. He just hoped that one of the flying pieces didn't land on him.

Marshall observed the byplay from his seat in the corner. They were officers. He was an enlisted man. And he'd better not overstep any boundaries.

"Okay, let's flip a coin to see who draws the new duty first," Walker suggested.

Price won—or rather, lost. With a sinking feeling he wondered how he was going to go through those Comms Center tapes and logs if he had to spend the evening babysitting the medical wing.

The group broke up, but one of the other men remained behind. "Listen, I get the feeling you'd rather not take that duty tonight."

"What choice do I have?"

"I don't mind taking it. You can do me a favor sometime."

Price looked genuinely appreciative. "Thanks, I owe you one."

IT WAS AN EFFORT for Eden to go about the rest of the day's activities with some semblance of normality. She was thankful that she had established the pattern of going to her room soon after dinner. Tonight, however, on her way to the medical wing, she made a stop in the kitchen. She knew that Mark had been put on a liquid diet and must be hungry. So she fixed him a thick roast beef sandwich and added a scoop of the cook's excellent potato salad and a glass of ice tea.

Blackwell, who had the duty station at the end of the hall, commented on the tray as she waited to go up in the elevator.

"Sometimes I get hungry after you lock us in," she explained casually. "And I'm not taking any chances tonight."

Blackwell sympathized. "I know what you mean about midnight snacks." He paused for a minute. "Dr. Sommers, if you're going up now, would you mind if I made my room inspection and lock check early?"

He had made the request before and Eden had always agreed. She knew that after the elevator and the gates at the top and bottom of the stairs were secure, he was free to go. And she hadn't minded building up a little goodwill by letting him off early. Tonight it suited her purposes perfectly.

In her quarters, Eden set down her tray on the desk and sat in the chair by the window while Blackwell made his inspection. It took only a few minutes. But she allowed several more minutes before getting up and changing her clothes. Instead of underwear she put on a light swimsuit that fit like a second skin. Over that went casual attire.

Mark was in his room. He looked up in welcome when she opened the connecting door and stepped across the threshold. Like her he was dressed in jeans and a dark T-shirt.

She came bearing gifts. Besides the tray of food, she also had the ornate pin and the manicure kit. Mark accepted the food gratefully. While he ate, they examined the equipment. There was a glint of approval in his dark eyes as he inspected the burglary tools. Next he held the pin up to the light and, with one of the instruments he'd just examined, turned an almost invisible dial in the back. Apparently that was how the transmitter was activated. Then he pinned it securely to her T-shirt.

She pulled a pad and pencil from her pocket.

He nodded.

*We're being picked up at 1:00 a.m.* she wrote.

He grinned, and she caught the excitement that simmered below the surface of his controlled manner. She was trying to hold her terror at bay, while he was actually thriving on the danger. But then why not? After months of being at other people's mercy he was taking control of his own fate. She could believe what he'd said about getting out of this place or dying in the attempt.

*We'd better sit tight until after midnight.*

She glanced at her watch. They had three hours—an eternity. She could imagine spending that time in his arms. She wanted his lovemaking to help her forget the knot of fear growing tighter in her abdomen. And she knew her expression told him that.

He reached out and stroked her cheek regretfully.

She turned her face so that her lips brushed his fingertips. Weeks ago he had snatched his hand away at the same gesture. Now he moved his fingers against her lips as though sealing the promise that there would be time later for the intimacy they both wanted.

It was strange, she thought, how their roles had reversed. When she'd first come here, she was the strong one. She had used the force of her will to pull Mark out of his depression. Now she was way out of her depth, and he had taken charge. If they got out of this alive, it would be due to his efforts, not hers.

Mark turned to the paper again. *You lie down and get some rest. I'll stand guard.*

She glanced questioningly back toward her own room. He shook his head and pointed toward his bed.

She understood. He needed her close by just as much as she needed to stay with him. Slipping out of her shoes, she lay down. Mark crossed the room, unfolded the cover at the end of the bed and tucked it around her. He had planned to go back to his post at the window. Instead he sat down on the edge of the mattress.

She looked up at him trustingly, and he reached out to smooth a wayward strand of hair back from her forehead.

When they'd been lovers five years ago, he'd glimpsed many of the special qualities in her, but he'd never known the depths of her courage. She'd risked her career to come down here and help him. She'd held her own in dealing with the gang of brigands who ran this place. Now she was putting her life on the line to help him get away.

He remembered how leaving her before had torn him into a thousand aching pieces. But he had taken the coward's way out and simply disappeared from her life because he hadn't been able to ask her to share the crazy existence he led. After what had happened to him in Leipzig, a future for them together seemed even more impossible.

She could quote any textbook psychological theory she wanted, but he knew in his gut he was damaged goods. If he didn't want to hurt her any more, the smartest thing he could do once they got out of here—if they got out of here—would be to put as much distance between the two of them as possible. It might be hard to make her understand that. But she'd be better off without him.

"Try to sleep," he whispered against her ear. The warmth in her eyes almost made him turn away in despair.

*Only if you kiss me good night.*

He complied, but it was the gentlest of kisses.

When he got up, Eden closed her eyes, moving her head against the pillow. It smelled of the clean scent of Mark's body. She could almost imagine that he was still here beside her. She wouldn't have thought that she could sleep, but the emotional turmoil of the day had taken its toll in exhaustion. The next thing she was aware of was Mark's hand shaking her shoulder.

He covered her mouth with his fingers when she might have given a startled exclamation. From the expression on his face, she knew it was time to leave.

Mark opened the door and looked into the hall. Stepping silently out, he motioned for her to follow. They were careful to walk lightly, but they drew a few inevitable squeaks from the worn boards. However, when they stopped and listened, there seemed to be no response.

At the locked stairway, Mark pulled out the manicure set. One of the tools turned out to be a miniature infrared light, which he handed to her. Then he began to work on the padlock. Of course it wasn't a standard lock, any more than Pine Island was a standard installation. The mechanism was sophisticated. And he realized at once that without the high-tech tools the Falcon had provided, they might as well have gone to bed and waited for Downing to come in the morning. As it was, he was beginning to wonder if he'd lost his touch, but eventually the mechanism yielded.

At the bottom of the stairs Mark repeated the procedure. Before he'd tackled the first lock, he'd been afraid there might be a guard down here. Now he understood why the chief of station hadn't bothered with something so fallible as a human watchdog.

There was still one more door at the end of the medical-wing hall. He studied it from several angles. When Eden reached for the knob, he pulled her hand back and pointed to the vibration sensor she had never noticed beside the glass panel. Mark bent to the floor and felt for the connector. In a quick maneuver she couldn't see, he rendered the alarm ineffective.

It was then Eden thought she heard a noise from one of the unlit rooms off the hall. She put a warning hand on Mark's shoulder, and for a moment they both held their breath and listened. But there was nothing except the wheeze of the air conditioner. Mark gestured for her to follow, and they stepped outside.

The warm night air had never felt so good, Eden thought as they crossed the threshold. She wanted to shout for joy. They had actually made it out of the building. Although she wasn't looking forward to a long swim, she couldn't help feeling that in one sense the hardest part was over.

Silently she followed Mark across the garden. Moonlight silvered the foliage and crumbling statues, but under the circumstances the effect was an eerie beauty. She half expected figures to emerge from behind every shadow.

Once past the garden, Mark avoided the stretch of beach that had become their own and struck out instead for the other side of the island, where a wide bay separated them from the mainland.

It wasn't until they were about a quarter of a mile from the house that he slowed his pace.

"Let me see your watch."

She turned the illuminated dial in his direction.

"I'd be happier if the guy with the boat were going to be here a half hour earlier, but we're just going to have to start swimming, anyway. The sooner we get off this hellhole, the better."

Eden heard the undercurrent of fury in his voice. Now that he was free from captivity, he was beginning to admit just how awful this experience had been. She reached down and twined her fingers with his. "We're going to make it," she whispered.

A dark grove of pines guarded the bay. Eden had to repress the wild notion that something—or more precisely, someone—might be lurking there to block their escape. Mark sensed her hesitation. This time it was he who offered reassurance.

"Almost there," he told her.

They threaded their way quickly through the pines and emerged about fifty feet from a rocky beach. The waves here were much gentler than those on the ocean side of the island. At least they wouldn't be swimming through huge swells. Mark let go of her hand. "Wait here while I check out the shoreline."

She pressed her back against one of the pine trees. The rough bark at her back was somehow reassuring. In the moonlight she strained to make out Mark's figure. When he disappeared momentarily, she had to force herself to keep breathing normally.

"All clear," Mark called out.

She took several steps out onto the beach and then began to remove her shirt, revealing the maillot underneath.

She was bending down to retrieve the pin from her T-shirt when something closed painfully around her arm.

It was a hand as large and hard as an anvil.

She screamed, and Mark whirled around.

"What is it?" he called out urgently, running back in her direction.

Eden didn't answer because the hand was now clamped over her mouth. And she could feel the butt of a gun pressed against the small of her back.

"That's right. Over here. Hurry up," a sharp voice commanded. "Or your girlfriend is dead."

# Chapter Ten

Eden didn't have to turn in the moonlight. She knew who it was, and that made her redouble her struggles. *Run, Mark,* her mind screamed. *He'll just get you, too.* But he was oblivious to the silent entreaty.

"Let go of her, you bastard."

Sergeant Wayne Marshall laughed. "You're not in any position to be giving orders, Colonel," he gibed. "Just hold it right there while I secure your chick." The gun that had been in Eden's back was now pointed at Mark.

As Marshall spoke, he maneuvered Eden toward one of the pines. She heard the clink of metal, and then one cold bracelet of a handcuff set was snapped around her right wrist. Marshall looped the connecting chain over a branch and secured the other cuff to her left wrist. She was effectively immobilized with her arms pulled up over her head. The position was painful. She knew it would get worse.

She could see the tension in Mark's body. He was looking for a chance to spring, but Marshall didn't give him one. "Now it's your turn, Bradley," he spat out.

Mark struggled to hold himself in check. All his emotions urged him to charge, even if it meant suicide, but his training told him not to argue with a gun. He didn't care about himself, but if he were dead, Eden wouldn't have a chance.

The sergeant smiled, his eyes flicking momentarily to the neighboring trees and then settling on one about ten feet from Eden. "I think this will do nicely—close enough for you to see the action but too far away to do a damn thing about it."

He gestured with the gun. "Over there."

Mark had no choice. He complied—and then backed up to the tree and reached around it as Marshall had ordered. With a few swift but professional strokes Marshall secured his captive's wrists and ankles with rough cord.

"I want you to know that this little show will be for your benefit as much as mine, Colonel," Marshall taunted as he stuffed a handkerchief in his captive's mouth and secured it with tape. "Think of it as a repayment for all the hours I've played nursemaid, lugging you around, spoon-feeding you—all on orders from Moscow." The raw bitterness in his voice matched the malice in his eyes.

When Marshall turned back toward Eden, Mark tested the bonds. They were tight. He moved his arms as far as he could up and down the tree trunk and then felt a stab of hope. Marshall hadn't noticed, but there was a sharp metal projection in the bark above his wrists—a nail or a marker. Given time, he might be able to saw himself loose. But time might be in very short supply.

He shuddered as Marshall reached out and put a hand on Eden's breast. She kicked him in the leg, and he cried out in pain, taking a quick step backward.

"That wasn't very smart," he observed, regaining his composure. "Let me show you what that gets you." He crossed back to Mark and hit him with several hard jabs to the stomach. Mark groaned and doubled over, sagging against the bonds that held his arms.

"Now, you wouldn't want that to happen again, would you?" Marshall asked, turning back to Eden.

She shook her head frantically. In the shadowy darkness he towered over her like an apparition.

"Would you?" he asked again, a threatening edge in his voice.

"No."

While Marshall fumbled with the button at her waistband and unzipped her jeans, she forced herself to stand rigid. He pulled the denim pants down her legs, leaving them pooled around her calves and ankles. "Get a good look, Colonel. It may be your last chance."

Marshall tossed the gun casually down on the ground and reached into his pocket. Eden heard a click. A moment later a long switchblade knife was in his hand, its sharp edge glittering in the moonlight. She held her breath as he pressed the point against the fabric at the top of her bathing suit. Was he going to kill her now? Instead he ran the razor-sharp blade down the front of the suit.

Mark strained against his bonds. Watching the knife slit Eden's suit was like feeling his own flesh cut. He had been tortured mentally and physically for months, yet this was worse. Seeing Eden helpless in the hands of this madman and being powerless to save her made him seethe. He redoubled his efforts on the rope, heedless of the way the rough bark scraped his wrists.

Eden heard a deep guttural growl of protest and knew it came from Mark. *God, Mark!* This had to be as bad for him as it was for her. He was helpless to stop whatever might happen. She tried to cancel that last thought. She didn't want to contemplate what Marshall might have planned for her, but she was too well trained.

Even in her terror, her mind was racing—remembering what she had overheard when she'd been unpacking in the room next to Mark's. Marshall had been taunting Mark about her proximity, insinuating his patient might be impotent. All at once it came to her. Maybe the male nurse had been projecting his own anxieties. Maybe he had been talking about himself.

Was *Marshall* impotent when it came to normal sexual relations? The question didn't give her any comfort. She could imagine the frustration and rage building up inside the man and forced herself not to think about the possibilities. She had to play for time, and maybe that wouldn't be so difficult. It was clear now Marshall was the enemy agent who had been watching Mark. He had achieved considerable success in his covert role, but there had been no one with whom he could share his victories.

"So you have us where you want us," she forced herself to remark, surprised at the matter-of-fact tone of her voice.

"Yes."

"I can't help feeling some admiration for your achievement—in a purely intellectual way, you understand."

He laughed, his eyes raking over her body. "You mean as one covert operative to another—although you're strictly in the amateur class, and I'm a trained professional. That's why you're hanging from that tree limb."

She forced herself not to look away.

He grinned. "I've had this whole place bugged for months—the security room, Downing's office, even your bathroom," he went on. "That cane was the best that Downing could come up with. But I've got transmitters that are light bulb filaments, chair casters, even toilet paper holders!"

Across the small clearing she caught Mark's eye momentarily before he looked meaningfully down at the gun on the ground. He knew what she was doing. And more important, his arms were moving in back of the tree trunk. Maybe he could free himself. But she had to keep Marshall's attention on her, away from Mark.

"Your pitiful little performance won't make any difference in the end," the sergeant was saying.

"I understand, but can't you at least tell me how you did it?" Her arms were aching now, but she ignored the pain as she focused on her adversary.

She saw the glint in Marshall's eye. Perhaps he couldn't resist the opportunity to brag some more, after all.

"The hair dryer, how did you manage the bit with the hair dryer?" she prompted.

"Oh, that. Rewiring it was easy. It was getting over there to the room without being seen that was the real trick."

She waited, holding her breath as he took a step closer to her again.

"You know the upstairs door that separates the medical wing from the rest of the house?—well I can unbolt it," he went on in a conversational voice. "That's how I got over to your old room while I was supposed to be on duty, and that's how I got into your hallway the night before last when the two of you were going at it with each other." The last words were a snarl. She knew she had probably guessed right about Marshall's problem. She had to get him off that subject.

"And you did it all alone. I'll bet the people in Moscow don't even appreciate your achievements."

"You're right. A Russian agent who's burrowed into the Pentagon gets all the credit." He began to touch her again, invading her in ways that made her want to scream.

"While I was waiting on good old Colonel Bradley hand and foot, I could have slipped him a lethal overdose of medication," he continued. "But Moscow wanted to make sure he hadn't talked." The last words were punctuated with a jab of his finger into her resisting flesh. Then he gave her a direct look. "I know what you've been doing, Dr. Sommers—stalling for time. But time is up—first for you, then for the Colonel. He's going to watch me have some more fun with you, and then he's going to watch you die. And the whole thing is going to look like he went berserk and killed you and then killed himself." A malevolent look shone in his eyes now as his hand found her again. She couldn't prevent herself from wimpering.

"All right, hands in the air," another voice from the shadows advised.

Marshall whirled as Dr. Hubbard stepped out from under the trees. His face was grim. The service revolver he held was leveled at the sergeant's stomach.

"I caught them trying to escape," Marshall tried.

"He's going to kill us," Eden cut in urgently.

"Don't worry, I've heard enough to know whose side I'm on," the doctor said. Hubbard took several more steps forward. "Drop the knife now."

The sergeant tossed the blade to the doctor's right. Hubbard stooped and picked it up. Then he glanced at Eden, his eyes focusing for a moment on the ruined suit that gaped open. His jaw was set in an angry line. "Are you all right?"

She drew in a deep, shuddering breath. "Yes." Her head swam in confusion. The doctor was the last person she would have expected to come to their rescue tonight. "How...how did you know to come here?"

Hubbard edged toward Mark, his gun still pointed in Marshall's direction. "Followed my esteemed colleague following you. He was in the infirmary—supposedly on guard duty. Eden, I'm sorry, I could have saved you some of this. But I wanted to be sure what was going on before I jumped in."

As he spoke, he pulled the tape off Mark's mouth and removed the gag.

"Thanks."

Hubbard moved to the back of the tree, intending to cut Mark's bonds. It was the chance Marshall had been waiting for. The big man dived for the revolver he'd tossed on the ground earlier. Without bothering to take careful aim, he fired off several shots in the direction of the tree. At such close range, the explosions were deafening.

Eden screamed as a bullet struck inches from Mark's head, and wood splinters filled the air. The second round was closer to Hubbard's crouched form. An answering volley flashed from the doctor's gun.

One of the doctor's shots hit Marshall in the chest and the nurse doubled over in pain, his hand still clutching the pistol.

All the stiffening seemed to drain out of Hubbard's spine as he got shakily to his feet. He looked as though he had aged twenty years in the last minute.

"I'd better see if this traitor's still alive," the physician muttered to himself, crossing to Marshall. As he turned the heavy form over, the sergeant's eyes flew open.

"You're dead," Marshall said. Drawing on some inner strength, he pulled the trigger on his own revolver one last time and shot Hubbard at point-blank range.

Eden screamed again. Incapable of rational thought, she thrashed wildly back and forth trying to free her hands. Both Hubbard and Marshall lay unmoving on the ground in front of her, and she was still caught like a victim in a medieval torture chamber.

Mark's reaction was quite different. All his senses were sharpened now, his efforts bent toward freeing himself and Eden. On the ground Marshall moaned and stirred. The bastard was still alive. What if he got the strength to sit up? He was sure to finish them off.

Desperately, Mark sawed and pulled at the ropes. His wrists were on fire, and then all at once the cord gave. He had done it!

Eden didn't hear Mark's shout of triumph as he finally freed himself, didn't see the mingled victory and relief on his face. She didn't know that he had lifted the doctor off Marshall and was quickly checking the male nurse's pockets for the key to the handcuffs.

Marshall stirred again and Mark gave him a quick, reflexive right to the jaw. He would have liked to finish him off, but the U.S. government would want to interrogate him. Mark had never hit a wounded man before, but he had never seen a woman tortured like that, either. No, not just a woman—Eden. The thought made his guts twist again. He was astounded at the way she had been able to keep Marshall talking. It would have been so much easier for her simply to give in to hysterics, but she had bought him the time he needed to free himself.

When he reached her side with the key, he put his arms around her, trying to calm her. "God, Mark! Oh, God," she sobbed.

"I'll get you down," he murmured. When she could finally lower her arms, she collapsed against him.

"It's over," he said soothingly. "It's over."

Eden struggled to pull herself together. It took an immense effort of will.

"Dr. Hubbard," she finally gasped. Kicking off the jeans that trapped her legs, she hurried to the doctor's side. He was still breathing, but the wound in his chest told her that he wouldn't be alive for long.

"Eden."

She could barely hear the faint whisper.

"Eden."

She grasped his hand. "I'm here."

He seemed to be gathering his strength. "Bradley?"

"Right here."

"Forgive me . . ."

"You saved us."

"I should have . . ." He never finished the sentence.

Mark gave Eden a moment to close the doctor's eyes. Then he touched her arm. "We've got to go. Someone may have heard the shots."

THREE MILES OFFSHORE, Michael Rome sat in the cabin of a small, high-speed cruiser staring at the radar screen on his receiver. He was a tall, angular man with the close-cropped brown hair and no-nonsense manner of a seasoned police officer. That was no accident. He was, in fact, an undercover agent, assigned to drug enforcement. He was also a long-time Peregrine operative.

His gray eyes narrowed as he watched the tiny green blinking dot on the radar screen. Was it his overactive imagination, or had that dot moved? The transmitter had leapt to life four hours ago. For the first three, the blinking dot had remained stationary, and he'd assumed Bradley and Sommers were waiting to make their escape. Then he'd followed their progress across the island.

But the blip had stopped moving an hour ago and he had started to get worried. From the distance covered, he supposed they'd reached the shoreline, but why were they waiting? Had they been intercepted? Had the transmitter gotten lost or started malfunctioning? Or was Mark too weak after all to make it to the boat?

Michael shook his head. If anybody had tried to tell him he'd be bailing out Mark Bradley, he would have laughed. Mark was indestructible. Or that's how he'd always thought about his old friend.

On a rescue operation, he wasn't usually given more than he needed to know, but when he'd found out the name of the man he was going to pick up in the water off Pine Island, he'd pressed the Falcon for details. He'd watched the old buzzard do a mental tap dance and then capitulate and break his own rules.

When Michael had been a raw recruit fresh out of counterinsurgency training, Mark Bradley had almost single-handedly brought him and a handpicked team of covert operatives back alive. They'd volunteered to try to spring a group of American "advisers" from the clutches of the Khmer Rouge in war-torn Cambodia. But the enemy had somehow gotten wind of the operation and had been waiting with a full-blown reception committee. The whole rescue squad would have ended up as numbers on a fatality sheet if Mark hadn't somehow held the panicked squad together and gotten almost all of them out of there.

They'd learned when they'd returned to headquarters that the prisoners had been moved a week before their planned raid. So the whole operation had been doomed before it started. The brass had been duped. The only hero as far as he was concerned was Mark Bradley. After that the two of them had worked together a number of times. In fact, they'd been surprised to find they'd both been recruited by the old buzzard, Amherst Gordon, himself. The Falcon had always recognized talent when he'd seen it. Maybe that was why he had bent the rules to explain the full picture now. The horror of what had been done to Mark set Michael's teeth on edge, and he was going to do his damnedest to get his old friend out of here.

Right now he wanted to move in closer to shore. His hand reached impatiently for the throttle and then moved away again. Damn! Making for shore was expressly against the Falcon's orders. And he knew why. Besides the security devices, the island was ringed with sandbars. He could end up stuck on one and turn into a sitting duck, and that meant nobody would get out of here alive.

He glanced at his watch and then back at the screen. The green dot had moved. It wasn't just wishful thinking. They were on their way.

THE WATER WAS A cool shock against Eden's skin. It also felt cleansing—as though it were washing away the inva-

sion of Marshall's hands. She tried not to think about what
might have happened. She couldn't allow herself to dwell
on any of that now—mere survival was still too much in
question. She half expected to see armed men running toward the beach at any second. It seemed impossible that the
gunshots weren't heard by the security staff in the main
house, but perhaps because of the distance the noise hadn't
reached them.

She could see Mark ahead of her, making surprisingly
fast progress in a steady crawl through the water. His
swimmer's body seemed to be in its element. She herself
was a good swimmer, but she'd never gone in for long dis-
tances, and she was definitely out of practice.

Except for the moonlight, there was no illumination. The
water was black and eerie, and now and again a salty wave
hit her in the face. Thank God the bay is calm tonight, she
thought, as they pressed on in silence. They were two figures alone in an ebony sea, swimming because their lives
depended on it.

Time seemed to pass in strokes of her arms. She knew she
shouldn't expect to see their contact yet, but she couldn't
help looking for the outline of a boat or straining her ears
for the sound of a motor. Her feet hit a sandbar and she
looked up to see Mark standing shoulder deep in the water.

She could hear his breathing. It was beginning to be labored.

"Let's rest," she suggested.

"For a few minutes," he agreed. "But I want to put
some distance between us and them." They both turned and
looked back toward Pine Island. It was a low dark shape
without intrinsic meaning, but the recent memories belied
the calm image. Involuntarily, Eden shuddered, and Mark
clasped her shoulder. They stood in silence for a while.

"Let's go," he finally prompted.

"Could we slow the pace a bit?" Eden suggested, as
much for herself as for Mark.

He nodded and then struck out again toward the Georgia coast. They swam on, but Eden found she was tiring

fast. It was almost too much of an effort to lift one arm and then the other. The episode with Marshall had already stretched her muscles painfully. Now she was suffering from the effects.

"Mark," she called.

He was at her side almost instantly. "What is it?"

"My arms. I just can't..."

"We'll tread water here."

She was grateful for the respite. "I thought you were the one who wasn't up to the marathon swim," she gasped.

"I wasn't trussed up with my arms above my head. Besides, I need another rest, too."

They were both silent then, saving their strength. Were they far enough from the island? Or would they have to strike out again in a few moments? Eden didn't know how much farther she could go.

"Please, Lord, let that boat get here."

She didn't know that she had spoken aloud until Mark replied, "It looks as though your prayers have been answered."

In the next moment she heard the throb of a motor.

"Over here," Mark called.

The motor cut to quarter power, and then a dark shape was looming beside them. A light flashed briefly.

"Water taxi service," a pleasant baritone called out. The words were light and joking, but Eden caught the undertone of profound relief.

"Michael Rome, is that you?" Mark questioned eagerly.

"That's right. Just paying back an old debt," the voice replied. A hand appeared over the side of the boat.

Mark reached out and grasped it. "I wasn't keeping score, but I'm damn glad to see you."

Eden sensed the bond between these two men. They must have been in tight spots together before.

Mark hauled himself up on the rope that had been thrown over the side. Minutes later he pulled Eden up to the deck and folded a thick terry robe around her. It matched the one he was already wearing. Now that the immediate danger was over, she could see that he was quickly giving in to the fatigue he felt.

"I was worried," the man called Michael Rome admitted gruffly, "when you were stalled on the beach."

"Tell you about it later."

"The two of you stretch out down in the cabin," Michael advised. "I've got coffee, brandy, angel dust, pot, hash, coke."

"You're kidding," Eden said.

"Yeah, except about the brandy and the coffee or sandwiches. Help yourselves."

"He's a narcotics agent," Mark explained as they descended the stairs. "Warped sense of humor."

Again Eden sensed the easy camaraderie between these two. On the surface things seemed almost back to normal. But she knew the terrors of what Mark had been through, and what they had been through together would take months, years, maybe a lifetime to heal.

Michael revved up the engine. "We've got an appointment with an old bird named the Falcon ASAP," he called out over the noise.

"Knowing him, he probably heard that," Eden pointed out.

"He won't lose any sleep over it. He'll probably just chop off the little finger of my left hand when we get back to the Aviary."

"You've been reading too many macho adventure stories," Mark advised.

"Could be, buddy. Could be."

## Chapter Eleven

Amherst Gordon settled back in his petit point Queen Anne chair and riffled through the written transcript of Eden's midnight debriefing. "You seem to have omitted some important information when you were reporting from Pine Island."

She shrugged. "That makes us even."

It was midafternoon and they were sitting on either side of a leather-topped library table in the Falcon's private study.

Gordon had the grace to give a little self-deprecating cough. "That's all past history. What concerns me now is the state of Colonel Bradley's mental health."

"He's going to be all right. I know it. But he needs time—and therapy"

"Unfortunately, those are luxuries we can't afford. We still have to plug up the Russian leak in the Orion defense system—quickly. Too much is riding on this."

Eden's eyes flashed. She was back in the colonial ambience of the Aviary, yet the situation didn't seem so very different from that on Pine Island. It was simply a matter of degree. Amherst Gordon could never be as raw edged as Ross Downing, yet they were both determined men who knew what they wanted and went after it with single-mindedness. "Mark's been through enough. Can't someone else do your dirty work?"

"No. I've had a session with Bradley, too. After he told me where he hid that evidence, I sent another operative to try to get it. But it's locked up tighter than the crown jewels."

"Then it will keep," Eden shot back.

"Negative. It's going to go up in smoke ten days from now, and there's not a damn thing we can do about it without Bradley."

"You'd better fill me in on the details."

"He was able to make two microdots of the evidence he obtained—which, by the way, is a preliminary program specification for Orion. The work was done in ten highly classified compartments. Each group knew only its own part. There was no cross information. Do you understand what I mean?"

"Yes, but someone in the Defense Department had to oversee the project and put it all together."

"Precisely. Three very senior individuals were working on it. And to put it bluntly, since the preliminary specifications have ended up in Russian hands, we know one of those three is a traitor. I don't need to tell you, the further the projects progress, the more costly the damage will be."

"But can't you bring them all in for interrogation?"

"These are very highly placed people. That would be impossible. Besides, we don't want to tip off the mole. But when I get my hands on those specs, it's going to be obvious. Each of them was marked with a secret code to determine whose copy it was."

"You mean in invisible ink?" Eden's voice was almost sarcastic.

"Something much more sophisticated than that. But until we're ready to show our hand, we want the culprit to think he's still in the clear. Obviously, he's not working alone. The placement of Wayne Marshall on Pine Island confirms that. There may be dozens of others like him. We need to get them all."

A chill went down Eden's spine. She still couldn't be rational about Wayne Marshall and what he had done to her. It wasn't just that he had thought nothing of killing to

protect his position; it was the way he had enjoyed subju-
gating and humiliating both her and Mark. Even though
she was trained to understand that kind of mind, the experience had left its mark on her.

"Thank God you got him," she murmured.

"I'm sorry. We haven't got him."

Eden's eyes widened. "What are you talking about?"

"I'm afraid my Intelligence reports place Marshall in a
very favorable position. He says you and Hubbard were
working together to spring Colonel Bradley, and he was
trying to foil the escape."

"And they believe him?"

"Hubbard's dead, and you've flown the coop."

"Then Mark and I are fugitives."

"Unfortunately, yes, but that's not the worst of my
problems. I have an agent who is absolutely integral to the
success of project Orion, and every time I try to debrief
him, he gets something that makes a migraine headache
look like fun. How the hell am I supposed to know what
those bastards in Leipzig did to him? I'm no psychologist,
but I'm willing to bet those headaches are meant to prevent him from examining his memories, and if they did *that*
to him, what other damage did they do?"

Eden took a deep breath, willing herself to sound coolly
professional. "I know about the headaches, but I think
there's a way to find out exactly what Erlich did to him."

He shot her an appraising look. "What?"

"Something risky," she said. "Something I'm still
thinking through, but if Mark trusts me, it will work."

The Falcon sighed. "There's an important piece of information you don't know. Colonel Bradley has asked me
to take you off his case."

"Is that why he's been avoiding me?" She had been
afraid to ask. Now at least it would be out in the open.

"Yes."

"Will you give me a chance to see if I can get through to
him again?"

"Against his wishes?"

Eden felt the knot of tension in her stomach tighten. "Twenty-four hours from now if he still wants me to leave, I'll call it quits."

"That's about all the time I can give you. Pine Island is a top-security installation—so Marshall's version of what happened down there hasn't even reached the FBI yet. But when it does, the security net is going to be so tight that Bradley won't be able to step out of the Aviary without being arrested, much less get out of the country."

IT WAS AFTER TEN that evening, and the mansion was quiet. In the upstairs guest quarters, Eden had showered and washed her hair with the same almond and herb shampoo she'd used at Pine Island and then slipped into a soft orchid-colored dressing gown she'd found in the closet in her room. But now, standing before the mirror drying her hair, she couldn't keep herself from trembling slightly. She had spoken to the Falcon with more assurance than she felt—because she didn't know if she was capable of battering down the new wall Mark had constructed between them.

She thought she understood his motives, given his doubts about himself. He must be trying to protect her. But that was the last thing she needed. What she hadn't told the Falcon was that she had to get through to Mark again for *herself*—as much as for the Peregrine Connection.

They had been through a terrible experience together. She could only speculate on what it had done to him, but she knew it had left her own emotions raw. The sensitive, feminine part of her psyche had been injured in a very fundamental way. Under other circumstances she would have sought out another professional as part of the healing process, but there was no time for that now. The only person at the Aviary who could help her was Mark Bradley. And in asking for his help she hoped she could make him realize that their relationship was a two-way street—that each of them could give as well as receive.

Eden took a deep breath and tried to calm her pounding heart. She had better act quickly, before she lost her nerve.

She knew Mark's room was across the wide central hall from hers. When she tapped lightly on his door, he didn't answer at first. She tried again more loudly.

"Who is it?" There was an edge of annoyance in his voice.

"Eden."

"Can't it wait until tomorrow?"

"No." Without being invited, she turned the handle and stepped inside, closing the mahogany door behind her.

The only illumination in the opulent room, with its four-poster bed and heavy drapes, was from the lamp on the Queen Anne table. Mark was in bed. The lower half of his body was under the covers, but he was naked from the waist up. He had propped several pillows behind his head and was reading what appeared to be some sort of thick report.

He laid the computer printouts down with an impatient thump. The lines of his face were hard edged as he looked over at her. "Are you in the habit of simply walking into men's bedrooms?" he asked, knowing that he had to send her away no matter what his real feelings. Back on Pine Island he had warned himself that for her own good there was no way Eden could stay in his life. Now that the emergency was over and she was safe, he had been preparing himself to stick with that resolve. But that would become twice as difficult if he took her in his arms and made love to her tonight the way he wanted to.

"I have to talk to you."

"I'm afraid I'm busy."

She took several more steps into the room. At this hour of the evening the air-conditioning was at its most effective, and the polished oak floorboards were cold against her bare feet. She wished she'd thought to put on slippers.

"Can't you spare me a few minutes?" She knew there was a tremor in her voice.

"No."

The single syllable shredded her confidence. Yet she had come too far to turn back now.

"I need some help." A whisper was all she could manage. Had she misjudged his feelings for her, after all?

"Surely someone else can take care of it."

Eden swallowed convulsively. The knot in her stomach had become a giant fist. "Mark, I . . . I tried to talk to Connie. I couldn't." That was the truth.

"All right. Tell me what you came to say so I can get back to work on these damn papers."

She could no longer meet his eyes. She was feeling it all again—the full force of what had happened to her. "Wayne Marshall. I came to talk about how Wayne Marshall made me feel," she finally managed to say.

She didn't see the flash of anger in the depths of Mark's dark eyes.

When she had imagined this conversation with Mark, she had pictured herself in his arms, sheltered and protected. But the comfort of his embrace seemed a lifetime away. Now her only wish was to finish what she had come to say so she could escape. "When Marshall put his hands on me—it made me feel . . . defiled. The only thing I could do was turn myself to stone, and I don't know if I can ever..."

She couldn't finish the sentence. She had thought she could keep this in perspective, but once she'd let the raw emotions out, there was no way to contain them. It simply hurt too much, and she didn't want him to see what it was doing to her. She swung away blindly, fumbling for the doorknob.

"Oh, God, Eden." He was across the room in a few quick strides and pulling her into his arms. He was wearing only a pair of low-slung navy briefs. Under other circumstances the heat from his body would have enveloped her. Now she was too chilled inside to feel the warmth.

She could hold the tears back no longer. "Let me go."

He didn't answer. Instead his arms tightened around her. He lifted her up and carried her the short distance to his bed.

She was struggling against him now, but he wasn't going to let her.

Even as his hands restrained her, they stroked and caressed. His lips were against her hair, her face, her neck. "Eden, forgive me. Please. Let me hold you. Don't push me away. I'm sorry." The words ran together. What an insensitive bastard he'd been.

But finally his display of concern for her began to penetrate her misery. She struggled to bring herself under control.

Sensing the change, he settled her more comfortably into the warmth of the covers and the protection of his arms.

For a long time after she had stopped crying, neither one of them spoke.

"You needed me, and I was trying my damnedest to send you away," he finally whispered.

"It was terrible."

He pulled her closer. "I know that. Eden, when I saw you standing in the doorway, I wanted to take you in my arms and make love to you, and damn the consequences. But I knew that wouldn't be fair. I've been nothing but trouble for you."

"You mean you were going to take the coward's way out again—the way you did five years ago."

"Yes," he admitted.

She moved slightly away so that she could look into his eyes. "Mark, the worst thing that can happen to two people who care about each other is that they don't communicate their true feelings. When you were shutting me out, a thousand horrible reasons flashed through my mind. I thought you didn't care about me. Or maybe you were so repelled by seeing Marshall manhandle me that you had transferred the blame to me."

"No!"

"But there are men who would react that way."

"Don't think *that* of me."

His words were reassuring; the pressure of his embrace was soothing. She took a deep breath and went on. "Marshall did something to me . . . to the way I feel about myself as a woman." She shuddered. "I've helped people who have been in similar situations, but I don't know how to help myself." The admission almost cost her self-control again.

"You came to my room because you trusted me to help you."

She nodded against his chest.

"What is it that you're most afraid of?"

It was hard to say the words, but she forced herself. "That when someone I care about touches me, I won't be able to keep from flashing back to that scene with Wayne Marshall." *Someone I care about. You, Mark.*

Suddenly he understood how she must feel. He drew in a ragged breath. "I didn't really understand."

"Mark, I still have the fears I came in here with."

"Then we'll conquer the fears one at a time together—if you can still trust me."

"I trust you."

"To make love to you?"

There was a moment of silence. "I don't know."

He looked down at her tenderly, his fingers beginning to comb gently through her silky hair. "Can we find out together?"

She nodded, not confident enough to speak.

"And you'll tell me if *anything* is frightening you?"

"Yes."

He wrapped a tendril of hair around his finger and brought it to his lips. "You used the same shampoo."

"I knew you liked it."

"I do. But there are other things I like, too. Not the window dressing—just you. Eden, you're brave, caring—and so beautiful."

His words and the look in his eyes made her feel as though she were. Yet even though he had already begun to weave his soft web of sensuality around her, she was still afraid.

He sensed the tension coiled inside her. This wasn't going to be easy, for either of them. He would have to win her back by slow degrees, even if the process drove him crazy. He had known from the moment she stepped inside his room that if he touched her he would have to love her.

Now, with the merest feather stroke his finger traced the line of her eyebrows, the bridge of her nose, the outline of her lips. At the same time, he smiled down at her reassuringly.

"Your beauty is more than skin deep. But I like what I see—what I touch—very, very much," he murmured, bending to nuzzle his lips against the smooth, white column of her neck.

His soft words and gentle contact sent a ripple along her nerve endings. But when his fingers went to the topmost button of her robe, her body stiffened. "Mark." There was an edge of panic in her voice.

"It's all right. I told you, I won't do anything you're not ready for."

Instead he picked up one of her hands. "Your wrists are so tiny—but I know they're strong," he murmured. "And your fingers . . . so long and graceful."

As he spoke, he began to kiss each fingertip in turn, and then his tongue flicked out to taste the same territory. He couldn't resist tracing the outline of each ivory finger. And he felt her shiver slightly in reaction.

Was she slowly melting, or was the shiver one of apprehension?

His tongue found her wrist. He could feel her pulse quicken. When he drew back slightly, she pressed forward to increase the contact.

"That's nice," she whispered.

His heart leapt at the small victory. "I'd like you to return the favor."

They both knew that the request was more than casual lover's talk. She had admitted her fears of initiating anything.

Now, however, she took his hand and raised it to her lips. As he had done, she traced his fingertips with her tongue. His index finger slipped gently inside her mouth to caress the insides of her lips. He held his breath, but she didn't reject the entry. Instead, she softly nibbled at the finger with her teeth.

"That's nice, too," he encouraged, his breath warm against her ear. A wave of awareness shivered through her.

With his free hand he grazed a butterfly-light caress along the underside of her breasts through the thin fabric of her robe.

Her body tensed again, and she shut her eyes. It was almost as though present pleasure and past pain were fighting a war within her for dominance.

He looked down at her tight, closed expression. "Open your eyes," he whispered. "I want you to know who's touching you. I want you to see how it makes me feel."

She obeyed, and almost drowned in the passion that smoldered in the ebony depths of his eyes. Passion alone might not have swayed her, but in that timeless moment she knew how much he cared. It was written on his soul for her to see.

When his fingers stroked upward to caress the sides of her breasts she found herself responding. He sensed the shattering of another barrier. With light strokes he began to circle inward toward her nipples. When he felt them harden under his fingers, his breath caught in his throat.

"Mark, oh, Mark."

He murmured little endearments and words of praise in her ear, and this time when his fingers sought the buttons of her robe, she didn't resist. He didn't hurry with the fastenings; instead, as he slid each one open, he cherished her with his lips and hands. When he had helped her out of the robe, he continued to stroke and caress her—sliding his fingers along the flat plane of her abdomen, tracing the gentle curve of her hip, the silky flesh of her inner thigh. He sensed her body quickening to his touch.

"Ah, Eden." The words escaped his lips on a sigh.

"That feels so good."

They had unlocked another door. She found that she could let him increase the intimacy of the caress. Now she was actually arching into the pleasure of his stroking fingers.

He felt her body's readiness. He didn't know what mental impediments might still make the final step impossible for her. "Are you ready to feel me inside you?" he questioned, his voice husky with his own yearning for her.

Was she? She couldn't suppress a little shiver of fear at the thought of what that total vulnerability would mean. She looked into his eyes again, seeing the smoldering desire there. Through his briefs she could feel the heat and hardness of him pressed against her. It was obvious how much he wanted her. Yet she knew he would never impose himself upon her. All this time he had been thinking only of her—of soothing away her hurt and giving her pleasure.

"It's all right," he whispered, his cheek caressing hers. "If you can't go any farther now, I'll understand."

More than anything, she wanted to give something back to him, not just take. She had loved him for such a long time, but that emotion had never brought her any lasting happiness. She didn't know what the future would hold for Mark and herself, or even if they had any future together. But though she couldn't burden him with her love, she could warm him with it for this short time that they had together. Her arms came up to encircle his waist and clasp him tightly against her. "Please, yes, now."

"Eden, love."

After a moment, he drew back so that he could slip out of his briefs. Then he was holding her body softly to the taut length of his.

"You're still frightened, aren't you?"

"Only a little."

"We can still stop."

She didn't answer him with words. Instead she parted her thighs and reached down to clasp and stroke him with her hand.

She heard his exclamation of pleasure and satisfaction, even as she guided him to her. Then he was inside her, filling her, and she knew it was going to be all right—more than all right.

He smiled down at her. "Eden, you feel so warm and welcoming."

"Because it's you."

Tenderness for her welled up inside him. He wanted at that moment to tell her how much he loved her. Yet he knew he still wasn't free to speak those words—not with the uncertainty he faced. But if he couldn't tell her how he felt, he could show her.

Slowly he began to move inside her, each stroke an endearment he couldn't confess. Each motion heightened all his senses, and her little moans of pleasure were like an aphrodisiac. The effort to hold himself back and wait for her to reach the edge of readiness was almost impossible. But somehow he managed it, and the reward was worth the self-denial.

She arched against him, even as he felt her first shudders of gratification. His lips sought hers, drinking in her cries of ecstasy. And all at once she was pulling him over the edge to join her in a rapture of pure sensation.

Eden clung to him, feeling the storm sweep over her. The physical intensity was overwhelming, but there was more, too. When she had told Mark she was afraid, she hadn't been able to tell him what she dreaded most—that she would be incapable of responding completely, even to the man she loved most in the world. But now, together, they had swept away her doubts.

The crest of the high wave had passed, but they each strove to catch the after-ripples of delight. Eden sighed his name as his lips nibbled her cheeks and forehead.

"Thank you," she whispered.

"My pleasure."

They clung together, neither one of them willing to break apart. There were still too many things they couldn't express in any other way. Shadows loomed beyond the circle of light from the bedside lamp. Shadows that wouldn't vanish with daybreak, because they weren't just in this room alone. They were ominous charcoal streaks across the face of the world. Destiny beckoned—no, commanded—Mark's presence halfway across the world. And the only thing Eden knew for sure at this moment was that she wasn't going to let him go alone.

# Chapter Twelve

Constance McGuire set down the tray of fresh fruit, croissants and coffee on the glass-topped table in the solarium. Once again, they would have to combine the amenities of breakfast in this warm and tropical setting with the necessity of doing business.

She glanced over at Eden and Mark, who were sitting close together at the other side of the table. She could still see the effects of their recent experiences. Yet this morning there was a noticeable difference that gave her a certain maternal satisfaction. All of yesterday she had felt the raw edge of tension every time they had been in the same room.

Their estrangement hadn't been quite so apparent when they'd first arrived. Eden hadn't been capable of much emotion. She had been close to exhaustion and functioning on a very basic level. But as she had begun to reach out to Mark, for her sake as much as his own, he had shut her off—purposefully avoided her.

From the intimacy of the warm looks they slanted each other this morning, she could see that something had definitely changed for the better. Connie felt certain it was something that Eden had initiated. Mark was too stubborn to bridge the gap himself. She knew that men in the Intelligence business were an independent breed, used to going it alone. The last eight months could only have confirmed the wisdom of that philosophy for Col. Mark Bradley. It would take a strong woman to make him change his mind. But it seemed that Eden Sommers might be such a woman.

The door opened and they all looked up as the tap of a cane on the slate floor announced the Falcon's entrance. Michael Rome was right behind him. Connie knew they'd been going over some of the strategy for the afternoon's departure.

Cicero flapped to his master's shoulder, and the Falcon paused to offer him a cracker.

To the casual observer Amherst Gordon might look like a rich eccentric without a care in the world. But Connie could read the worry lines in his face. Project Orion was a problem. But it wasn't the only thing on her boss's mind. He was directing half a dozen worldwide operations, and not all of them were running smoothly. The situation in Madrid, for example, was also becoming critical. While the chief of the Peregrine Connection was arranging to slip Mark and Eden into Europe, he was also working on contingency plans to smuggle out another operative codenamed the Raven.

Yet as Amherst Gordon sat down at the table, he permitted himself the small luxury of not getting right to business.

He let them wait while he stirred cream into his coffee and buttered a croissant. It gave him a certain gratification to know that he had the complete attention of everyone else in the room. In fact, they seemed fascinated by the action of his butter knife.

He finally relented. "I think I'll let Michael tell you the latest," he said.

Rome straightened in his chair. He looked around the table, his eyes settling for a moment on Eden.

She gave him a quick smile. Yesterday, when Mark had begun to avoid her, their rescuer had tried to compensate by making her feel included. He'd even sought her out and tried to reassure her. It turned out he'd been through a particularly bad time on one of his assignments and could empathize with Mark's withdrawal. He told her how difficult it had been to get back to something approaching normal—but he'd finally done it. He was confident Mark could, too. Yesterday she wasn't sure she agreed. Now she was beginning to hope it might be true.

He began the briefing. "As you probably know, your little swim has instituted a very quiet East Coast manhunt."

"Actually, I've been waiting for someone to shoot a hole through the No Vacancy sign hanging out by the road," Mark quipped.

But Eden caught the underlying tension in his voice. Below the table she reached out and captured his hand. Last night she had been so wrapped up with her own problems that she hadn't fully understood what she was asking of him. Now she realized that when she had needed him, he had put his own anxieties on hold.

"No one's coming here," Gordon said. "But if we don't move fast, I couldn't get you across an airport concourse even if I shaved your head and put you in a saffron-colored robe."

Mark laughed. "So what are your plans for getting me to Berlin?" he asked.

"You mean us," Eden corrected.

Mark opened his mouth to protest. But the Falcon didn't give him a chance. "She's right. This operation necessarily includes the two of you."

"I don't want Eden involved in this any further," Mark snapped. "Michael and I have worked together before. Can't you send him to nursemaid me?"

She heard the self-derision in his voice. Evidently the simple fact that he couldn't be trusted on his own was almost unbearable.

"Mark, let's be realistic," Gordon answered. "I know you're anxious to even the score. But you may be your own worst enemy, and Michael isn't trained to deal with that."

She heard Mark curse under his breath.

"We don't have time to argue about it," Gordon continued. "If I don't send Eden with you, I don't send you at all. And if I don't send you, we know what the consequences are."

As the two men stared at each other, Eden was reminded of wrestlers sizing each other up, each looking for a point of weakness to press his own advantage. But in this situation, Mark was smart enough to recognize that the Falcon had fixed the match. The only way he could win was by cooperating.

"All right," he conceded reluctantly. "Just what do you have in mind?"

"We're getting you through airport security as part of a bank director's tour of Ireland."

"Ireland!"

"Nobody's going to think to look for you there. It's the far northwestern corner of Europe. But that makes it a great staging ground. You'll leave the tour in Shannon and be taken to a safe house somewhere in Connemara, where your closest neighbors will be sheep and donkeys. Eden is going to continue your therapy sessions there." *God knows, you need it,* he thought to himself. The riskiest part of this whole operation, as far as he was concerned, was sending Mark off without knowing just how dangerous he was to himself—or other people. Unfortunately, the time factor was too critical to arrange other plans. Eden didn't know it yet, but he was prepared to scrub the mission up until the moment they left for Berlin, if Mark was unable to keep himself from helping the enemy.

They went on to discuss more details, then separated for final preparations. Appearances had to be altered and scars hidden before their passport photos were taken and the actual documents forged.

But the Falcon had even more pressing reasons for separating Mark and Eden. He wanted to give her additional instructions and make damn sure she understood her role in all this. Misrepresenting Mark's condition on her Pine Island reports was one thing—he understood why she'd done it. But turning a blind eye to even the tiniest of the colonel's German-precision-manufactured defects could be fatal.

CONSTANCE MCGUIRE handled the details of their departure in her usual efficient manner. In the Aviary's underground complex, Eden began to get a better idea of just how well equipped the Peregrine Connection really was. In the basement under the mansion were labs set up to do everything from manufacturing instant passports to altering equipment like the manicure kit she'd taken to Pine Island. Staff was on call on an as-needed basis, and the wardrobe inventory was enough to supply a men's and women's specialty shop.

When Eden and Mark were united again in the upstairs solarium, they each had two well-traveled American Tourister bags and outfits that spoke of casual upper-middleclass comfort. Mark was wearing a lightweight navy blazer and gray slacks. Although it didn't show, around his waist was a money belt full of gold coins—a necessity for efficient clandestine travel through a number of different countries.

Eden had selected an orchid-colored shirtwaist dress. When she had seen it hanging on the rack, the color had brought to mind last night with Mark.

When Mark saw her standing there in the same color that she had worn to his room, a flash of responsive memory flared. He knew she had deliberately wanted to remind him she was the same woman, even if on the surface she was different. Her honey brown hair had been cut in a softly layered style that framed her face. Artfully added blond highlights provided a glow that he found warmly appealing—even with the makeup job that gave her oval face a more angular look.

As a finishing touch she wore oversize tortoiseshell glasses with the initials N. M. in the corner of one lens. For the next fifteen hours she and Mark would be traveling as Mr. and Mrs. Frank McKay.

Eden returned Mark's appraising stare. His appearance was even more noticeably changed than hers. The Aviary makeup technician—or the Master of Disguises, as he was fondly known—had decided to age Mark more than a decade. His hair was now a vibrant silver, and the scars on his face were hidden behind dark makeup.

Although his new look was at first unsettling, Eden found it attractive. This was how Mark might look in twenty years. Would they still be together? Her heart gave a little tug of sadness. There was simply no way to speculate about the future until they solved the uncertainties of the past and the present.

"Will I do?" he questioned.

She was startled by the richness and confidence in his voice—remembering how different he had sounded that first day on Pine Island. He was back in his element again, finally in a position to make things happen. That alone was cause for exhilaration.

"You'll do," she said warmly.

Michael drove them to Dulles International Airport. From the back seat Eden studied his profile. She'd known him a little more than two days. But she'd quickly come to admire his loyalty and his reliability. She could bet that he and Mark had made a good team when they had worked together. And she couldn't help wishing that he was going farther than to the airport with them.

As they pulled into the unloading zone, he reminded them of the Falcon's final instructions. "Get in the left-hand line for international flight clearance. Our guy will be on duty there." He looked at Eden in the rearview mirror. "Try to look excited—like you're going on a holiday. Not like you have a date with the executioner."

She forced a smile, but inside she was trembling. These two men had years of training and experience behind them. She was a rank amateur in the high-risk world of international espionage. Even though she had insisted upon being included on Mark's assignment, she couldn't help feeling uncertain. She only hoped she could carry off this new masquerade as well as she had the last. But she'd been playing herself then. Now she had a new name, a forged passport, and a man at her side she knew so well and yet didn't know at all.

After a quick hug for Eden and a solid handshake and "Good hunting" for Mark, Michael left them on their own. Eden looked at Mark and smiled nervously. "You know how petrified I am about flying, Frank."

He grinned. "You could always stay home."

She gave him a meaningful look. "Not after you've already paid for the tickets, dear."

Checking in kept them occupied for the first few minutes. But after they had cleared airport security and were waiting in the departure lounge, Eden found herself reading the same page of her paperback novel over and over again.

When their flight was held up for half an hour, Mark put a soothing hand on her trembling arm. "I hate these delays too, honey," he admitted. "But it happens all the time. Don't let it get to you."

When flight 580 was finally called for boarding, there was another bad moment. They followed instructions and got in the left-hand line. But just as they were approaching the barrier, the uniformed official checking passports was called away and replaced by another. Had the man who was supposed to pass them through just left, or was he the man coming on duty? Eden glanced back questioningly at Mark. He gave her an imperceptible push forward. They couldn't both step out of the line now without looking suspicious.

"Are you traveling for business or pleasure?"

Mark had heard this question often enough to summon up an automatic response.

"Pleasure," he said, looking as though he meant it.

Eden took her cue from him. Ten minutes later they were finding their seats on flight 580. She couldn't suppress a sigh of relief. So far, so good.

Once they were in the air, she leaned her head against Mark's shoulder. Even with his problems, his basic strength was something she could cling to. He had been through an experience that would have destroyed most individuals. Almost anyone else would have been damn glad to get out with his life. But the man beside her was volunteering—no, demanding—to go back and finish the job.

"Why don't you try to get some sleep," he suggested.

Neither one of them had gotten much last night—or the two nights before, for that matter.

"How about you?"

"Maybe later." *I'd rather look at you.*

She closed her eyes and snuggled against him. He didn't wake her when the flight attendants came around with drinks and the usual processed food. But he ordered himself a double Scotch and sat sipping it. There was a lot he had to think about.

When Eden awoke, his face came into focus, and she blinked. It took a moment for her to remember their transformation.

He grinned. "You go to sleep for an hour and wake up next to Rip Van Winkle."

"You must have spent the whole time I was napping coming up with that line," she said.

"Guilty as charged." He had anticipated her reaction and had come up with the perfect rejoinder. But it had been the one amusing note in a grim succession of thoughts. Despite his reply to the airport official, this wasn't going to be any pleasure trip. He squeezed Eden's hand. "I'm glad you're here," he whispered. It was true, but her presence was still causing him more than a few twinges of guilt.

She seemed to understand. "I'm here because I *want* to be with you," she assured him again.


THE MAN IN Washington put down the summary report from Major Downing at Pine Island. Behind the solid oak door of his private office, he was looking a bit green around the gills. The report was bad news, very bad news. Suddenly he had to fight to keep the panic in his chest from bubbling up and making a mess all over the glass-covered mahogany desk.

For a crazy moment he considered simply walking out of his office and not coming back. In a matter of hours he could be on a flight to Bern, and from there to Moscow. But he had a feeling the Kremlin wasn't going to welcome him with open arms. Things were too critical with project Orion.

He sighed heavily. He was going to have to deliver, or else. But at least, he consoled himself, he had access to these highly confidential reports through regular U.S. military channels. He'd worked hard for fifteen years to maneuver himself into the right place. And he'd been smart about it. Otherwise he'd have been in deep kimchi long ago.

Even now, there was a measure of luck on his side. Downing had accepted Marshall's version of recent events. It could still turn out that the FBI would catch Bradley and Sommers and nail them for murder.

He found his usually logical thoughts scattering in a dozen different directions—and his mood swinging from optimism to despair and back again. Maybe he was indulging in wishful thinking, after all. It was beginning to look as though they'd gotten away. If so, someone had helped them. He wished he knew who.

Bradley on the loose was a threat to everything he'd so carefully set up in the Pentagon. Right now the colonel was probably slipping out of the country. The logical mode of transportation for someone in Bradley's shoes was a slow freighter to Tierra del Fuego. But somehow he didn't think Bradley was South America-bound. He'd bet his Senior Executive Service bonus that the man in question was on his way to Berlin.

The thought made him reach into his desk for the bottle of tranquilizers that he'd sworn he wasn't going to touch again.

He had to get a message to Moscow—fast. And that meant he couldn't wait for his biweekly drop at the National Gallery of Art concerts. He was going to have to risk an international call to his contact in Lisbon. But then, what was the risk, really? If Bradley picked up that incriminating evidence in Berlin, he might as well measure himself for a pair of cement shoes.

Maybe a long lunch was in order—one where he could make that phone call. As he pushed back his chair, he was already starting to compose the message.

"I'm afraid your prize German shepherd has gotten out of the kennel and is on the loose with his mate. I know it's a disappointment, but you can get another one just like him in Berlin—or maybe sooner if you act immediately."

THE LISBON CONTACT dutifully set an international search in motion. Luckily, the Falcon had chosen well when he'd decided to send Mark and Eden via Shannon. They landed a good two hours before word had even reached the agent assigned to keep an eye out for them. After collecting their luggage and clearing customs, they slipped away from the rest of the tour group and headed across the airport to the Emerald Rent-a-Car counter.

The request for the car reserved for Mr. and Mrs. Frank McKay brought an instant alertness to the young clerk.

"If you'll wait out there, our driver will fetch you in a moment," she said, pointing toward a covered pickup area.

Almost as soon as they'd set their bags down by the curb, a dark sedan pulled up in front of them. The driver was a rough sort who looked as though he might have stepped right out of an IRA brigade—even though they were far from Northern Ireland. Eden gave Mark a questioning look. But he didn't seem worried.

"How's the weather been up the coast?" Mark asked.

"Misty as usual," the driver replied in a lilting brogue that she found a bit hard to understand until she caught the rhythm of the cadences.

"Perhaps it will change."

"I wouldn't bet a bottle of Guinness on it," came the good-humored reply.

To any eavesdropper the exchange would have seemed casual enough. But Eden suspected that if each word had not been precise, Mark would never have opened the door of the car and the young man would never have started stowing their luggage in the boot. His name, she learned, was Ryan O'Connor.

There were a lot of things that surprised Eden about the ride. It was disorienting driving on the left side of the road—and zipping right past the Emerald Rent-a-Car building to head for the countryside. In almost no time at all, they were barreling along a two-lane road at speeds more appropriate for a superhighway. Ryan apparently took great delight in driving like a lunatic. Eden hung on to the door and tried to think about the scenery instead of the probability of crashing into one of the low stone walls that hemmed in the narrow road.

The land was incredibly green. But the open fields were strewn with rocks and boulders. Eden knew where the building material for all those walls had come from.

Only a few kilometers from the airport they were forced to stop and wait for a herd of sheep being ushered across the road. To Eden's amazement the fleece on their backs looked as though it had been marked with a patch of red spray paint. Other flocks she saw in the distance were similarly adorned in blue.

The donkeys Gordon had promised were also a prominent part of the rural scene. And more than once she saw a wayward cow being guided back to its herd by a farmer riding a bicycle.

She had plenty of time to take in the scenery. The men were sitting in front, and their low-pitched conversation didn't include her. She might have found this annoying if she had not realized that Mark was cultivating their local contact. By the time they had pulled up in front of a stone cottage with a traditional thatched roof, the two men were on easy terms.

The house, which sat well back from the road, was nestled against a small hill, with green fields spreading down toward the coast. In the distance she could see the jagged shoreline and the blue-gray of the ocean.

In the side yard was a neat pile of what looked somewhat like dark bricks. Eden eyed it questioningly.

"Peat," Ryan explained. "I'll wager this place is a bit more primitive than you're used to. But at least you've got running water inside."

"Just so it's private," Mark said.

Ryan grinned. "Oh, we use this cottage when lads from the battle up north need somewhere to lick their wounds."

So she'd been right about this fellow all along, Eden thought. Apparently the Falcon had friends in all sorts of unlikely places.

The young man carried their luggage inside. "The larder's stocked with a fortnight's provisions," he advised Eden. "I'll show you how to use the stove. And if you want a wood fire in the evening, there are split logs out back."

When he had finished with the domestic explanations, he turned to Mark. "You'll feel safer with this," he advised, pulling a rather formidable-looking revolver out of a kitchen drawer. "I assume you know how to use it?"

Mark nodded and inspected the weapon, noting the well-oiled condition. "Thanks."

When Ryan had finally driven off, Eden turned to Mark. "Surely out here we're not going to need that gun."

"I hope not, but it's always best to be prepared. We'll move it to the bedroom so it will be close by, just in case."

Eden watched him look for a new hiding place for the gun. Finally he settled on a drawer in the bedside table. She was glad he hadn't felt it necessary to put it under the pillow. The idea of sleeping so close to a deadly weapon unnerved her. She hadn't fired a revolver since her air force basic training, and she hoped she wouldn't have to do so any time in the future.

Mark put their bags in the bedroom wardrobe. There was only one bed, she noted, with rope stretchers and what she guessed was not an innerspring mattress.

She had to swallow a lump in her throat as she followed Mark back into the tiny living room with its fireplace wall and country furniture. The isolation in these beautiful green hills and the primitive setting held a certain fascination for her. She could imagine having come here to spend her honeymoon with this man.

"Regrets already?" he asked, joining her by the window.

She straightened her shoulders. "No. I was just thinking about what I'm going to put you through for the next few days."

He tried to make a joke of it. "That bad?"

"You know it will be."

Time was crucial. If there was any possible way to do it, she had to make him remember what had happened in East Germany.

The next day, somewhat recovered from the frantic departure preparations at the Aviary—as well as from their jet lag—they got down to work right after breakfast.

"If the rocks aren't bugged, there's no reason why we can't talk outside," Eden said. A sunny day was unusual for Ireland, and she felt they should take advantage of it.

"Whatever you say." He tossed off the comment lightly, but inside he still felt that familiar tightening in his chest. He watched as Eden spread a thick wool blanket on a level spot on the grassy meadow. Although the air was cool, the sun was warming, and the fisherman's knit sweaters and jeans from the Peregrine boutique were just the right weight.

He lay on his back, his hands behind his head. She rolled onto her stomach and looked down at him. The silver still concealed his vibrant dark hair color. But he had washed off the heavy makeup—and with it the ten years that had lined his face. Now his scars stood out again—even more so in this natural light. God, he had been through so much. And she hated to put him through any more pain. With anyone else she would have taken months, maybe even years, to work through the trauma of East Germany. They simply didn't have that luxury. Yet she wanted to make it as easy as possible for him.

"Despite what I said, we'll start slowly."

She could see the relief in his eyes.

"Why don't you tell me about that evidence? How did you get it and where is it?"

"There's an agent in Madrid who's helped Gordon out on more than one occasion. He's a Russian and his code name is the Raven. Apparently he's pretty highly placed. I think if he could have gotten the goods on this guy in Washington himself, he would have. But he has to be very careful of his moves right now, so as not to jeopardize his own position. Gordon had gotten word to him about what

I was looking for, and through a contact in Berlin he gave me a pretty good lead on where to start.''

"And where was that?''

"Eden, the less you know about this, the better. Let's just say it arrived in East Berlin in a Soviet diplomatic pouch, and a copy was smuggled out to me. I hope the guy who accepted my money lived to spend it. Double-crossing the Russians does put one at high risk.''

"But how do you know he was reliable?'' Eden questioned.

"I don't. My only choice was to trust him.''

Suddenly the warmth of the quiet Irish meadow had turned bone-chillingly cold.

"What is it?'' Eden whispered tensely, watching Mark's expression change.

He didn't answer immediately. He hadn't thought about any of this in months—he'd been too busy coping with Downing's interrogations. Now his mind needed a moment to assimilate the information it had just processed. A part of the picture had just fallen into place like a missing puzzle piece.

The bomb on the plane. The disappearance of the letter he'd sent to the Falcon. Even Marshall's presence at Pine Island to make sure he never got off that island alive. The Russians had been tipped off. The man he'd been forced to trust in Berlin must have been working both sides of a very dangerous game.

So the Russians knew all about Berlin, and they were probably waiting for him there now, as were the East Germans. Lord! He was going to have to keep Eden safe here in Ireland somehow—even if it meant tying her to the bedpost and slipping away in the middle of the night.

"What is it?'' Eden repeated.

"Nothing important,'' he lied.

## Chapter Thirteen

Maj. Ross Downing, who had been sitting with his chair tipped backward against the wall, let the front legs fall forward to the floor with a resounding thump. His usually immaculate desk was awash with an assortment of manila folders, some spilling their contents onto the polished wood surface. He was still playing chief of station at Pine Island, although the station's mission had evaporated with the disappearance of Col. Mark Bradley. At the moment, he was commanding a pretty dispirited bunch of men, and he couldn't pretend he felt much like keeping their morale up.

Nothing like this had ever happened to him before. He'd always done things by the book. Even his plans to give Bradley the RL2957 had come from someone pretty high up in Washington—he wouldn't have taken a step like that on his own. Until now, playing it straight had paid off, but not this time. This time he'd gotten a dressing down from air force security.

Yet the reprimand wasn't what rankled the most. This was his first failure, and since he'd found Marshall and Hubbard on the beach, he'd been trying to figure out what had gone wrong.

There were so many things that didn't add up. Hubbard's presence on the other side of the island, for example. He'd always had a keen sense of people's strengths and weaknesses, and he'd written the doctor off as a wimp. He still couldn't picture Hubbard as a spy. He couldn't even imagine him getting involved. So what had he really been doing on that beach with a gun in his hand?

And for that matter, he couldn't imagine Eden Sommers as a spy—although, in retrospect, there was something fishy about the way she had turned up here. Parts of her records had been sanitized before he'd gotten them. He had assumed the deletions were for clearance purposes. But after the escape, when he'd demanded and gotten the unedited version, the previous association between her and Bradley was there to read. Who had intervened? It must have been someone pretty powerful, someone he didn't even know about.

But there were plenty of other leads to follow. Marshall, for example. The way *he* had turned up here wasn't exactly legitimate, either. Someone in Washington had pulled strings to get him the assignment. That source was now pushing Marshall's version of the escape. Had the same person sent both Sommers and Marshall? Or were two powerful forces working against each other—with Pine Island and Mark Bradley in the middle? The possibilities were mind-boggling.

And what about Bradley himself? Downing had been told this was a national security problem involving the Orion weapons project. But was that the real issue? Over the past few days he'd made himself throw out all his carefully nurtured preconceptions about Bradley and consider his own observations.

He'd been led to believe the man was mentally ill, but Sommers had gotten through to him pretty fast—damn fast. In hindsight, he could believe Bradley was a man with something so important to conceal that he couldn't trust anyone—least of all a ham-handed security chief named Ross Downing. Or was he just conjuring these possibilities up because he wanted to find a scapegoat for what had happened?

Damn! He'd bungled this. He hadn't even figured out who had rewired the hair dryer. And he was a man who didn't like to see things half done.

This time he would go with his hunches. He'd be willing to bet Bradley would end up sooner or later in Berlin, where all this had started.

Downing snapped his fingers. He had a few strings he could pull at the Pentagon himself, and there were some people in NATO who owed him, as well. He wanted to finish this, and he was determined to secure the chance to try to do it.

"MARK, I'M NOT buying that," Eden objected.

The urgency in her voice brought him back to the Irish meadow where they were lying. He reached up to touch her hair, allowing himself a moment to comb his fingers through the newly shortened strands. He had to bury his new doubts so deeply that Eden would never find them. Yet, with her training, that wasn't going to be easy.

"The important thing is that the information was the real McCoy."

She studied his face. He was keeping something back. Should she go after it or press on? She made a mental note to come back to this later. "So what did you do with the evidence?"

He grinned, partly from relief that she was going to let him off the hook, and partly at the memory of his own ingenuity. "Well, you remember that I was always interested in military letters and memorabilia?"

She nodded, recalling the first time he'd invited her to see his collection. She'd thought it was a ploy. But she'd ended up being impressed with his locked cabinet full of historical letters, orders and diaries.

"While I was in Berlin, I visited some estate sales and was able to pick up the three-volume journal of General Ludendorf's administrative aide. It was written before Ludendorf got to be supreme commander, and it would really only be of interest to a collector like me."

She waited to find out where all this was leading. What did a World War I German diary have to do with the evidence that would uncover a mole in the Pentagon?

"I only had the project Orion specs for a few hours," Mark continued. "The contract had to put them back before they were missed. So I photographed them and then had a lab reduce them to two microdots. One was in my briefcase. The other is still dotting an *i* in that German diary, and I'm the only one who knows what page it's on—I hope."

Eden still looked confused. "So where is the diary and why can't you simply go get it?" she questioned.

He sat up and looked away toward the distant shoreline. "I couldn't go rent a safe-deposit box in Berlin. What was I supposed to do, rent another box for the key? So I left the diaries where I knew they would be safe—with the city's most reputable dealer in historical books and papers, Schultz and Stein. But I couldn't sell the diaries to them and I couldn't just deposit them there forever. So I agreed to have them auctioned off if I didn't come back to collect them within nine months—with the proceeds going to me. That seemed like a safe enough bet at the time. I had the other copy, after all. If I didn't make it, I had sent a letter to the Falcon telling him where to get the material. It was a double fail-safe plan. The trouble is, I didn't make it back and neither did the letter."

Eden stared at the rigid line of his back. "I know what happened to you, but what about the letter?" she whispered.

He shook his head. "That's the sixty-four-thousand-dollar question." He thought he knew, but he was going to keep that information to himself. Despite his careful precautions, the Russian agent he'd dealt with must have had him under twenty-four-hour surveillance—undoubtedly by several men, so he wouldn't have known he was being followed. One of them had gotten that letter out of the mail box right after he'd dropped it in.

They talked for the rest of the morning about Mark's last few hours in Berlin. Now she had a much better idea of what had happened just before that plane exploded. But they still had the crucial issue of his time with Hans Erlich to deal with.

That afternoon the weather turned nasty. As the heavy rain pounded on the thatched roof, Mark made a fire and they got to work again, but the depressing weather turned out to be an omen. Though she tried to help him get in touch with the memories of his captivity, he simply couldn't do it. She watched as he broke out in a cold sweat, his face deathly white and teeth clamped together. She knew that trying to pierce the protective shell around that time had brought back one of the terrible headaches she remembered from Pine Island.

They progressed no better the next day, or the next. In fact, it was worse. The knowledge that she was putting him through such agony tore Eden apart. She felt that one of them was going to break and she didn't know which.

Maybe that was why every evening they ended up in each other's arms, each seeking comfort from the other and returning it with a desperation neither could hide.

By the fourth morning, as she woke up in the double bed beside him, Eden pressed her forehead against Mark's shoulder and knew that something radical must happen to break the intolerable stalemate. She had told the Falcon she had a plan to crack the shell around Mark's buried experiences, but she'd known the risk it would entail. She'd tried every other way. Now she was left with this one dangerous strategy. It might well help Mark, but it could also destroy their relationship.

He stirred slightly in the warmth of the bed they shared, and she closed her eyes again, hoping he wouldn't awaken yet. She wanted to put the reckoning hour off as long as possible.

But when his eyes opened and looked into hers, he knew without a word passing between them that things were going to be different today.

Her fingers groped for his under the covers, and they twined together. He waited for the guillotine blade to fall.

"Mark, we have to shatter the mental wall you've built around that Leipzig clinic, no matter what the cost."

His fingers tightened painfully on hers.

"We're going to have to use hypnosis."

It was almost a relief for him to hear those words. "I can't be hypnotized."

She shook her head. "Not by anyone else. But while we were at the Aviary, I studied the reports on the self-hypnosis methods you learned as an interrogation protection. I think I can do the same thing to you that you did to yourself."

"You'll use those techniques to take me back?"

"We have to do more than that. We don't have time to gather up fragments and piece them together. The only way you're going to know what happened is by interacting with Erlich again."

"But that's impossible."

"No. Remember, I'm talking about hypnosis. I'm going to be Erlich and you're going to believe it."

The old fear clawed at his soul again like a raging tiger. Erlich. The man's name brought back terror, but the deepest fear stemmed from more than that. Now that his strength had returned, Mark knew that he'd kill Erlich or die in the attempt rather than let him infiltrate his mind again. And Eden had just promised to make him believe she was Erlich.

"The hell you will. You haven't the vaguest idea of what you're asking to get into."

"Yes I do, Mark."

"If you really hypnotize me into thinking you're that bastard, I could kill you, Eden."

She didn't doubt what he said, but she had just as much determination as he did. "I realize that. But I've been thinking about how to make it safe."

A muscle in his face twitched. "You've been *thinking* about how to make it safe? You're going to turn me into a homicidal maniac, and you're not absolutely *sure* how to reverse the process?"

"I think 'homicidal maniac' is a bit of an exaggeration, don't you?"

"No."

She chose to ignore his objection. "When I put you under, the first thing I do will be to give you a trigger phrase that will bring you instantly out of the trance. The phrase will be 'I'm Eden.' When I say it, you'll know who I am.''

He didn't look convinced. He had so many doubts about what had happened in Leipzig. But one thing he knew instinctively: when the blinding rage came out, he wasn't going to be able to control it. "And how can you be sure—how can *I* be sure it will work?''

"Before we get into anything heavy, we'll try it several times. I'll tape-record it, and you'll be able to hear that it worked.''

Only part of the tension went out of his face. He was torn apart by what this woman was willing to risk for him. Yet she was offering him a chance to unlock that secret part of his mind that was a stranger to him—and probably a lethal enemy to his future.

He had told Eden at Pine Island that he wasn't the man she had known before. Despite his recent victories, nothing had really convinced him otherwise. Something unspeakable had been done to him in Hans Erlich's clinic. Did he dare find out what? Either way, the consequences were terrible, but he knew which choice he was going to make.

He sighed heavily. "All right. I'll go along with your crazy plan, but only if you take some more precautions. You're going to have to tie me up, in case that trigger phrase of yours doesn't work instantaneously. That way, I won't be able to get at you.''

She wet her lips. The idea of strapping him down went against all her instincts. But she knew he was right. What's more, giving him a measure of control over the situation was a way of minimizing the threat for him.

"Then we'll do it your way," she agreed.

The preliminary tests went as she had predicted. With a little practice, she was able to put him under, almost as easily as he had done it himself. When she played back the recording of the exchange, he could hear for himself that the trigger phrase had brought him out of the trance.

"So are you ready for the real thing?" she asked when they'd turned the recorder off.

His face was pale, the scars standing out like angry welts. "As ready as I'll ever be, I guess."

There was a comfortable chair in the living room with wooden arms. They had agreed that she would secure him there with the heavy cord they'd found in the toolshed.

Mark instructed her on how to tie him so the bonds would hold. Before she put him under, he tested the ropes and was satisfied.

She stepped back and studied his face. He looked like a man who was waiting for someone to pull the switch on the electric chair.

"Mark, it's going to be all right. I promise." She bent over and gave him a tender kiss.

"You're going to have trouble convincing me Erlich did anything like that," he quipped, but she could hear the tension in his voice.

Despite the success of their previous trial runs, it was harder this time to put him under. He was resisting. But she wasn't willing to give up and finally did succeed.

First she oriented him to the date, place and time. Then she used his own words to describe the crash. As she spoke, she could see terrible spasms of pain rack his body. He was back there again, and it took all her strength of will to continue.

"Let me introduce myself," she went on. "I am Dr. Hans Erlich. I will personally see to every detail of your convalescence."

She heard a growl deep in Mark's chest, and his arms pulled against the bonds. All at once she was very glad that she had agreed to restrain him.

"Your wounds are extreme," she explained. "You are in great pain, Colonel Bradley, no?" This was the hardest part she had ever played.

Mark didn't reply, but she saw the answer.

"I can ease that pain. All you have to do is cooperate with me."

"No. Never."

"Bravely spoken, but you'll come around to my thinking sooner or later." The words were like sawdust in her mouth. But she had to say them.

There was worse to come, and she didn't even know what the script was.

"We have been enjoying each other's company for three weeks now, Colonel Bradley," she kept on, subtly dispensing with a large block of time. "Why don't you summarize what you have told me."

"I've told you nothing," Mark spat out.

"Really, nothing?"

"Nothing."

"But you have learned from me, Colonel."

"Yes." The admission was torn from his throat in a burst of agony.

"Then, perhaps you will be so good as to repeat the lessons."

Mark's eyes were glazed, his breathing shallow and rapid. For a few moments, he could only groan in pain. He was *there* again with Erlich. He saw the pale face with its light eyes and almost nonexistent brows.

He was strapped on a gurney on his way to the operating room, and Erlich was right beside him, padding softly down the corridor.

The man tied in the chair began to speak. But this time he was not saying the words of Mark Bradley but those of Erlich.

*"Today we are going to work on your face. Such a shame it is so smashed up. It will require many operations. It hurts me not to let you have any anesthetic, but until you give me some information about your mission, I simply can't allow you anything to lessen the discomfort. Suffering is a great teacher, don't you agree?"*

In horror Eden watched Mark writhe in the chair. God, plastic surgery with no anesthetic. Erlich must be a fiend from hell to use such tactics.

She sat frozen in her seat, listening as Mark recounted more vivisection, more agony—and always the questions that he wouldn't answer. But there was something else going on besides the quest for information. It was something that not even Mark could fight.

*"I don't know exactly who you were working for—CIA, air force Intelligence, or someone else—but it doesn't really matter. They don't count anymore. They have abandoned you. They have left you in my care. And even if I can't get you to tell me what your mission was, I believe that we can work together very successfully from now on. You belong to me now. You will act on my orders. When we return you to your own people, they won't know that you have switched your allegiance to me."*

"And what have I asked you to do?" Eden whispered.

"Deliver to you what I left in Berlin. Other instructions will follow."

Mark glared across at Erlich's colorless face. Hating him. Wanting to smash that look of satisfaction into a thousand pieces. His arms strained at the bonds that held him now. Strange to be sitting up. Where was the hospital bed? But details like that didn't matter. He was going to get that bastard sitting across from him so calmly like the angel of death he was.

"Do I know what the delivery is?" Eden/Erlich prodded.

It was a trick question. What was Erlich up to now? "You know I haven't told you," Mark growled.

*"But you will, Colonel."*

No. He couldn't let it happen. His silence was the only victory he had to cling to. His mind spun. Erlich thought he could keep this up because Mark Bradley was weak and helpless. But by some miracle he had gotten his strength back. He could feel it surging in his arms. He had freed himself once before—on Pine Island. He shook his head in confusion. Somehow the sequence of things had gotten tangled up in his mind, but it didn't matter. He had to deal with Erlich here and now before the angel of death destroyed him.

With a tremendous effort, he wrenched at the ropes once more. They held. But the arms of the chair broke apart.

Eden gasped. It all happened so quickly, there was no time for her to speak the trigger phrase. One moment Mark was tied down. The next, he was across the room with a murderous look in his eyes and reaching for her. Pieces of turned wood hung around his wrists. They crashed against her body as his hands closed around her throat.

The air to her lungs was instantly blocked off. She couldn't speak, and the blows she rained on his chest might as well have been puff balls.

Above her Mark was mumbling imprecations—mixed with a jumble of numbers. 002-72-52, 002-72-52. If she hadn't been struggling for her life, they might have sounded familiar.

All she knew was that she had convinced Mark Bradley too well. He was going to kill Erlich. He was going to kill *her*.

The room swam. She felt her eyes bulging, her head filled with pounding blood. Desperately she tried to mouth the words that would save her. But nothing came out.

Mark looked down at the face of the man he had sworn to kill. Something was wrong. Something he couldn't understand. Victory didn't feel the way he had imagined it.

For a moment his hands loosened around the doctor's throat. In an instant, he heard a choked syllable come from the swollen lips.

"Eden . . ." That was all she could manage.

Something snapped in Mark like a piece of movie film tangled in a projector. The Leipzig hospital room vanished. The Irish cottage materialized around him. He looked down. His hands were around Eden's throat. He was choking her to death. For a heart-stopping instant the terror in her eyes drilled into him, and then she lost consciousness.

WHEN SHE CAME TO, her face was wet. Someone was rocking her and sobbing. It was Mark, and she knew the moisture on her cheeks was from his tears.

She stirred slightly. She wanted to tell him she was all right, but when she tried to speak, only a tiny gasp came out. Her throat hurt terribly.

"Eden, forgive me, Eden."

She groped with her fingers and found his hand, squeezing with all the strength she had. It wasn't much.

He moved then, and the remnants of the wooden chair arms rattled. Impatiently, he stripped them away. Then his arms went around her again, holding her close against his heart.

The reaction had begun to set in. She couldn't hold back her own tears. She finally understood now what Erlich had done to him—and what she had put him through herself.

But right now he was still caught up in the guilt of the horrible thing he had almost done to her. She pressed more closely against him, trying to let him know that it was over.

"How can you?" he rasped. "How can you still trust me after I tried to strangle you?"

"I love you." It was a thin whisper. But he heard, and his heart contracted painfully. He shifted her so that his eyes could meet hers.

"How can you?" he repeated.

"Easy." She laughed. It was a hoarse croak. "Talk later."

He carried her to their bed then. Brought her water. Smoothed hand cream on the bruises on her neck. She saw the effort it took for him to keep from breaking down again when he did that.

"My fault," she whispered, fighting overwhelming exhaustion. But when he tried to leave her alone, she gripped his sleeve.

"Do you want me to stay?"

She nodded. It was safe to sleep now.

While she lay quietly against the white sheets, he looked down at her, seeing the peaceful expression on her face. How could she feel safe with him now? Yet she must.

His mind went back over what had happened—and also over the words and images her bravery had unlocked. Since she'd first come to Pine Island, she'd refused to take no for an answer. She'd pushed against all his resistance. She'd forced the memories out of him, and now just about all of his experience in East Germany was there. The recollections were terrible, but he could face them. The trauma had been dulled by time, and he even had a small sense of victory. The hypnotic techniques he'd learned from the Falcon had helped block the incredible pain. He knew that now—and that he hadn't told his captor anything.

However, he also knew what he had been afraid to contemplate: he was in some way still linked to Hans Erlich. The knowledge only strengthened his conviction that he couldn't take Eden with him to Berlin.

For several hours he sat on the edge of the bed watching her sleep as he thought about what he had to do. He left her side only to light a hurricane lamp when the late-afternoon shadows darkened the room.

When she finally opened her eyes, he held his breath. How was she going to react to him now that the shock had worn off?

She read the anxiety in his expression. "I'm fine," she assured him. Her voice was almost back to normal.

"What can I do for you?" he whispered.

"Make love to me."

Her simple request brought a look of incredulity to his face. "God, Eden, a few hours ago I was trying to kill you."

"Not me—Erlich."

He sighed. No matter how she tried to excuse his actions, the outcome had almost been fatal for her.

"Mark, I knew what kind of chance I was taking. I deliberately put you back in that man's clutches."

"Eden..."

"Let me finish. He was threatening your very survival. The will to survive is one of the most basic of man's instincts. That's why you attacked. And it was Erlich you were going after, not me."

He shook his head. "Intellectually, I know you're right. But I can't help feeling frightened—and horrified—by what I almost did to you."

"I was frightened, too, but we came through it together."

"I don't know what would happen if I met Erlich on the street some time. But back in that hospital situation, I had to break the hold he had on me. You're right, I was acting instinctively."

"I can understand why you would attack him. What he did to you was terrible."

Mark looked away, glad that the light from the hurricane lamp didn't highlight his features. Let her think his actions had been provoked by Erlich's past sins. But that was only part of the motivation. The attack had really sprung from his fear of what the man might be able to do to him in the future. Maybe Eden was right, it was a matter of survival.

She reached her arms around his neck and pulled him down to her. "Don't let him come between the two of us. Give me that, at least."

He couldn't offer her any assurances. But for now he could lay old ghosts to rest in her arms. Tenderly he nuzzled his face against hers, remembering her words of love. More than once he had wanted to confess his own feelings. That hadn't seemed fair before. But maybe now it was better to tell her, especially since he was planning to complete this mission without her. That way, she might be able to forgive him for leaving her behind even if she couldn't understand his motives.

"Eden, I love you," he murmured. "I've loved you for a long time, even before I admitted it to myself."

"Oh, Mark, you don't know how I've longed to hear you say that."

He drew back and looked into her azure eyes that brimmed with tears. "I shouldn't be telling you now."

"Why not?"

"Because of the life I have to lead. Because I can't offer you any security. You have roots. Working for the Falcon means it isn't fair to tie myself to anyone." His hands gripped her shoulders. "Even if I could have admitted that I loved you five years ago, I wouldn't have been able to do anything differently. I would still have left you and accepted the Middle Eastern assignment, knowing full well how dangerous it was. Do you understand what I'm saying?''

''Yes. But what I'm trying to tell you is that I'm willing to settle for whatever we can have together. No strings attached.''

He was about to answer when the faint noise of footsteps on gravel outside made him freeze. Years of training had sharpened his senses.

''What is it?'' she whispered.

He put a finger to his lips. ''Someone's out there. I'm going to find out who. You stay put.''

# Chapter Fourteen

Mark doused the lamp, then reached into the drawer of the bedside table for the gun. How many men were outside? How were they armed? And who were they? He'd better leave the gun with Eden, in case he didn't make it.

He pressed the weapon into her hand. Her eyes were wide with fear. Yet his calm, matter-of-fact manner couldn't help but steady her.

"Be careful," she whispered.

He slipped into the kitchen and took a carving knife from one of the drawers. Under the circumstances it was the best he could do. There was no back door, but he could get out through the window. Perhaps they wouldn't be expecting him to circle around the house.

Outside, he listened again for any clues to where the intruders might be. He could hear the crunch of gravel off to the right, then something solid hitting the ground. It could have been a body. In the protective shadows of the stone-walled cottage he moved toward the action. A few feet from the house one man was kneeling over another. Friend or foe? And which one? His only option now was to attack first and ask questions later.

He judged the distance carefully, then sprinted forward. The kneeling man looked up, startled. He had just been slipping the butt of a gun back into the waistband of his pants. When he saw someone bearing down on him, he automatically grabbed for it again. Before he could get off a shot, the weapon was wrestled from his hand.

Mark flung him to the ground, and their eyes met. It was Ryan O'Connor.

"What the hell's going on?" Mark rasped.

"There wasn't time to warn you, lad. Someone's on to you."

Mark jerked his head toward the man on the ground.

"Followed him across the moors from the village," Ryan explained. "He'd been acting like a nosy parker all day."

"What did you do to him?"

"Struck him over the head with my pistol."

"Better tie him up, then, and gag him. There's rope in the living room."

Ryan raised questioning brows, but Mark didn't explain. Together they dragged the unconscious man toward the front door. Ryan shoved it open with his shoulder, straightened and turned. "Holy mother of God!"

Panic gripped Mark. Something had happened to Eden. He dropped the unconscious man's feet and pushed past Ryan.

Eden was standing in the tiny living room, her bare feet braced and both arms extended with the heavy revolver pointed straight at the door.

A wave of relief mixed with admiration washed over him. "Don't shoot. We're the good guys."

She tried to smile. But her arms were trembling as she lowered the weapon and surrendered it to Mark. "What happened?"

"An uninvited caller," Ryan volunteered. He and Mark were already tying the fellow up. Only when they were satisfied that he was immobilized did they search him for identification. There were no labels or laundry marks in his clothing—which looked European rather than American. His passport was Swiss, and there was a Beretta in a shoulder holster under his arm.

"Did he have an accent?" Mark questioned, handing the weapon to Ryan.

"British. He should have known that was only asking for trouble in the oppressed provinces." He laughed harshly. "You've got to get out of here tonight. Where there's one bloody rotter, there's bound to be more."

Mark nodded. Unfortunately, Ryan was right. Someone had found their hideout, and he had no way of knowing who. The sooner he left, the better.

"I've arranged for a small lorry. It will be here in less than an hour. Better get your things together."

Mark opened his mouth to object and then closed it again. His plans for the next two weeks had not included Eden. But when he had made them, he had thought this place was safe. Now he knew he had to get Eden out of here, too.

The man on the floor began to stir. Without a second thought, Ryan helped him back to sleep.

Eden winced. The young Irishman was obviously used to playing rough. He was also quite well connected: the lorry, which sported a bicycle repair shop logo on the side, arrived on schedule. Mark and Eden had only time to stuff a few belongings into a canvas tote. Ryan's comrades would take care of removing any evidence that they'd occupied the cottage.

The van took them southeast to Rosslare Harbour, where they would catch a boat for Le Havre. It was a seven-hour trip across the country. Eden was grateful that the back section had been fitted with mattresses. If she had felt like a fugitive before, that was nothing compared to the tension gripping her stomach now. There was no way to see out, and as the vehicle bounced along the narrow roads, she kept wondering if someone else with a gun was going to stop them. However, they reached County Wexford without incident.

They were unloaded directly into a cavernous warehouse near the busy port. Though it was the middle of the night, this particular way station was a beehive of activity. Rifles were being individually wrapped in heavy plastic and packed in flour barrels—doubtless for shipment to Northern Ireland.

Ryan grinned as Mark and Eden looked around at the operation.

Mark's hand gripped hers. "Necessity makes odd bedfellows," he whispered.

Eden knew he was right. It wasn't for them to judge with whom the Falcon had chosen to deal. They were being hunted by the East Germans, the Russians and even the Americans. They had to accept help where they could get it.

"We have a pipeline that will have you on the continent before tomorrow night," Ryan assured them. "I hope you don't mind traveling in a crate designed to hold a restaurant freezer. It's really not any worse than the lorry."

Mark nodded. "At the moment it sounds like the only way to go." He gave Eden a quick glance. But she didn't protest.

Ryan turned to her. "Godspeed, darlin'. Anytime you want to join the cause, give us a word. We can use a good fighter like you on our side."

Eden acknowledged the compliment with a smile, remembering how Ryan had ignored her at the beginning. "Glad you're on our team," she said. Then, silently, she let him help her inside the rough wooden planked crate stamped with large letters: This End Up in English, French and Dutch.

The crate offered less room than the lorry had. But whoever had designed this conveyance was obviously aware of what was needed. Besides a thin mattress and blanket, there was a small cooler of food and drink, a compact chemical toilet and a powerful battery-operated flashlight. But Mark knew they would have to use the light sparingly. The batteries had to be preserved, and the illumination could give away their hiding place if it showed through the air holes.

As they were nailed inside, Mark felt Eden shivering. He knew he had to be calm for her sake. Yet he was fighting his own claustrophobic reaction. It was going to be a long time before he completely got over the horror of being locked up at night. But there was more to his apprehension, he acknowledged. He didn't just *want* to go to Berlin. He *needed* to go there, and he didn't like the way the feeling had taken hold of him—like a compulsion. Was he acting on his own desire to complete this interrupted mission? Or was some master puppeteer jerking his strings? That fear made him want to claw his way out of the darkness.

The box gave a lurch and they were thrown into each other's arms in the dark.

"Just the crane," Mark whispered.

Eden pressed her face against his shoulder. In the blackness, he stroked her hair.

His uncertainties were magnified by the guilt of dragging her into more danger. Yet at the same time, having her with him was a source of strength. The two emotions seemed to be pulling him like the rope in a tug-of-war.

They waited in tense silence while the crate was lowered into place in the hold. Once the ship began to move, Eden felt Mark's lips against her ear.

"How are you doing?" he asked.

"I wouldn't want to make a habit of traveling this way."

"The no-frills European tour. You can't see anything. But hopefully, they can't see you, either."

She laughed nervously.

"What are you thinking about?"

"The time that my Dad took me to an amusement park when I was seven. We went on one of those rides in the dark where your car jerks around on a little track and you keep stopping in front of scary scenes with fluorescent paint and black light. You know, spiders jump out at you and witches cackle in the dark."

"Yeah, there was one of those at Euclid Beach in Cleveland. I remember it smelled like a machine shop."

"Did the electricity ever go off while you were inside?" He felt her tense at the memory.

"No."

"You've probably guessed we weren't so lucky. Everything came to a grinding halt, and we were trapped inside in pitch-blackness. Dad wouldn't let me get out of the car because of all the machinery. I don't know how long we sat there, but it seemed like forever. I kept imagining all sorts of things creeping up and grabbing us in the dark." Even now, over twenty years later, her skin crawled when she talked about the incident.

"What happened?"

"The guy running the equipment apologized and gave us tickets for free rides later. But I didn't want to go. You wouldn't get me inside one of those things again if my life depended on it."

The words had made her realize again the gravity of their situation. Under normal circumstances she would never have allowed herself to be nailed inside a box like this.

Mark felt her reaction. "I don't like it much, either."

"Let's talk about something more pleasant," Eden suggested.

"I'll vote for that." There was a moment of silence, and then Mark's warm laugh filled the blackened chamber.

"What's so funny?"

"Oh, I was just thinking about at least one compensation this travel compartment offers."

"What?"

"Unless there's another passenger in the next crate, I believe we have quite a bit of privacy here."

"That's a compensation?"

"It is if you have unfinished business. Didn't you ask me to make love to you before we were so rudely interrupted by the scuffle outside the cottage?"

That seemed like a world away now. But inside this packing crate they were in a little world by themselves. Above the vibration of the ship's motor she could feel the steady beat of Mark's heart and his breath against her hair.

"Of course," he murmured, nibbling at her ear, "if given the choice, I wouldn't opt for making love to you in the dark. I'd much rather be able to look at you. But in my mind I can see the way your eyes turn smoky blue-gray when you want me and the way your lips pout when they've been very thoroughly kissed."

"Mark."

In the blackness, his voice was sensual and coaxing, sending her own imagination racing. She felt his hands tracing up her ribs and then moving higher still to cup her breasts.

Despite the terrible knowledge that they were fleeing for their lives, or maybe because of it, she felt her own desire kindling to meet his. She was beginning to understand that danger could be a very potent aphrodisiac. For all she knew, this crate could end up as their coffin. But with the heat of Mark's body pressed to hers, for the moment all that existed were the two of them and what they could give each other.

RYAN HAD WARNED them to expect a wait on the dock at Le Havre. But they weren't prepared for the argument that erupted between two rough-sounding men about an hour after their crate had bumped to a standstill on the unloading platform. The exchange was in vernacular French. But Mark understood enough to know their hiding place was the subject of the altercation.

"The guy who had to get this thing into a warehouse wasn't expecting us so soon. He's not sure he can make the arrangements," he whispered to Eden.

The disagreement was punctuated by loud Gallic curses that even Eden had no trouble interpreting. She and Mark waited tensely, feeling the heat from the strong September sunlight raise the temperature inside their traveling compartment. Mark reached for the gun that was never far from his side now. She had no doubt that he was prepared to shoot their way out if necessary.

A few minutes after one set of feet stamped off, the remaining man outside tapped on the side of the crate.

"Your early arrival necessitates a change in plans, monsieur."

"Yes?"

"Additional funds will be needed. Can you handle it?"

"Yes." They were in a hell of a position to be negotiating. Yet he knew from experience that gold coins spoke a language all their own.

An hour later they were in another warehouse. As the first nails were drawn out, Mark sheltered Eden in back of him. When light penetrated their darkness, it glinted on the revolver in his hand.

"No need for that, monsieur," a more cultured French voice assured.

"As long as I have the money."

"Let us not be crass. But also do not forget that this operation doesn't run on charity."

Mark nodded tightly. He had felt a kinship with Ryan but was reluctant to trust these thugs. However, he was also a realist. Right now he and Eden didn't have any choice.

As it turned out, Eden thought, they got quite a bit of value for their money—two new Canadian passports, airline tickets to Berlin and several Yves St. Laurent outfits for her. These people might be mercenary—and obviously on the wrong side of the law—but they were efficient. She wondered who their usual clientele were. Drug smugglers? Spies? Terrorists? They probably weren't too picky. Yet she was reassured by a feeling of honor among thieves. Once they took your money, they weren't going to knife you in the back. That might be bad for repeat business from a patron as generous as the Falcon.

She would be traveling to Berlin as the wife of a rich Canadian industrialist meeting her husband at the German Industry Exhibition held every year in September. Mark was an architect making a pilgrimage to the Bauhaus Museum to study the roots of modern design. They had to pretend to be total strangers. It made Eden nervous that they wouldn't be seated together. She would be flying first class, and Mark would be half a plane away in the tourist section.

The flight was scheduled to leave from Paris that evening. Once again, preparations were hectic. This time, after Eden had been outfitted in a dark wig and heavy makeup that made her look like the sleek, sophisticated woman in the passport photograph, she hardly recognized herself. She hoped the same would be true of anyone interested in her arrival in Berlin.

Mark still sported his silver hair. But now his scar-covering makeup made him look prematurely gray rather than aged. His clothing was tweedy—almost professorial. There was a well-used pipe in his pocket and a pair of wire-framed glasses on his nose. Even his brown penny loafers were well scuffed.

The idea of clearing customs alone and under an assumed identity was terrifying to Eden. But the instructions she received before they left for Orly were excellent. As far as she could tell, no one gave her a second glance. She crossed her fingers that Mark had fared as well.

Unfortunately, there were a lot of people on the lookout for one Col. Mark Bradley, and they now had agents posted at all European airports with flights into Berlin. Despite all precautions, he was recognized at Orly. One international phone call and agents in Berlin knew he was on his way.

But the Falcon had prepared for such an eventuality. After the plane landed at Tegel and they'd cleared customs, Mark slipped into a busy men's room, where he was able to exchange part of his clothing, pipe and glasses with a man in the next stall who was a dead ringer for the architect. Luckily, the decoy drew the reception committee. By the time the pursuers realized they were following the wrong man, Mark and Eden had changed cars twice and were in a bakery delivery van on the way to Meinekestrasse.

This time there was only a narrow bench along the wall of the van amid the metal trays of hearty brown bread and *Pflaumenkuchens*. In fact, for authenticity, they made two delivery stops at restaurants in the city.

The bakery itself turned out to be their ultimate destination. It was run by Gustav and Berdine Hofmann, a couple in their forties who had worked with Mark on his last assignment in Berlin. Both had the solid look of the German working class. Gustav was a ruddy, brown-haired man of medium height. Berdine had probably been an attractive blond fräulein. Her face, topped by blond braids in a coronet, was still pretty, but her ample figure attested to years of sampling her own baked goods.

Unlike the French connection of the day before, the couple's ties to the Falcon involved a good deal of personal loyalty.

Although Gustav's father had been conscripted into Hitler's army, he had never supported the dictator. And when a young American Intelligence operative disguised as an S.S. officer had been captured behind German lines, he'd helped the American escape.

The Falcon always paid his debts. After the war he made a point of finding the man who had saved his life. Like so much of the city, the elder Hofmann's bakery had been destroyed in the Allied bombings, and his family was destitute. With his private income, Amherst Gordon was able to set the man up in business again.

But Hofmann had had his pride, too. He would only accept the help in exchange for services he could render. In a sector surrounded by a communist regime, that turned out to be a valuable exchange. The son had continued the family tradition, and he'd been so effective that Gordon had relied heavily on him for years. Berdine was an equal partner in her husband's covert business. Her enthusiasm came from a hatred of the East German Communists. She had crossed the border just before the wall went up. Her sister and brother-in-law had not been so lucky. They were shot while trying to swim across a canal to freedom.

Eden was relieved to find that among the couple's talents was a good command of English, since she didn't know how to say much more than *guten Morgen* in German. Over coffee and strudel topped with heavy whipped cream, the foursome discussed their strategy in the kitchen of the living quarters behind the Hofmanns' shop. Under the table, their Doberman, Fritz, rested his chin on his master's foot.

Berdine gave Mark a welcoming smile. "Oberstleutnant Bradley, for months we thought you were dead, until the Falcon told us what happened after your plane crashed last year."

Mark shrugged. "One of the risks in this business."

Eden knew the casual disclaimer didn't fool their hosts. Mark's experience was etched on his face. But she could see more. He was holding himself in tightly, as though he was afraid of losing control. After the devastating session under hypnosis in Ireland, she understood why. And she knew that his doubts were not entirely unfounded. Erlich had done his utmost to implant orders in his patient's mind. He wanted whatever Mark had left in Berlin, and the man sitting across from her had no way of knowing whether he would deliver it or not.

"You will want to know what happened when we inquired about the Ludendorft campaign diary at Schultz and Stein."

Mark leaned forward. "Herr Gordon told me you called and tried to claim the diary, using my name."

"That is correct. The first person I talked to only knew it had been scheduled for the 15 September auction. When I informed him it was private property and insisted on talking to the gentleman you left it with, Herr Glück, I was transferred to a manager who gave me the—what do you call it—run about?"

"Runaround," Mark supplied.

"Yes. They told me Herr Glück was on vacation in the Tyrol."

"Do you think they were telling the truth?" Eden questioned.

"We had the place of business watched. He didn't go in or out for several days. So our next tack was to send in a prospective buyer for the diaries. When he asked if he could see them, the clerk explained that they were being carefully inspected for authenticity because of the extreme interest in these particular papers. He said they wouldn't want to have another scandal like the 'Hitler Diaries.'"

Eden sighed. Unfortunately, that was the perfect excuse.

"But our man was able to get the gentleman into a conversation. It seems that there has been a lot of foreign interest in the Ludendorf material. Even the Russians sent in a 'collector' to have a look. The clerk remembers his name was Aleksei Rozonov."

Mark swore under his breath. "Collector, my ass. The Falcon has a file on him this thick." He gestured with his hands spread a foot apart. "The man's a KGB officer—and as smart and deadly as they come. If the Russians have sent him in, they know the real value of those diaries. I'm willing to bet they'll stop at nothing to keep me from getting them."

"But how would they know?" Eden asked.

"That's what I have to find out," Mark replied. "I need to get in touch with Glück." He turned to Gustav. "I suppose it's not a good idea to make a call from here."

"A public telephone cell—I believe you call it a booth— would be best. Let me take you to one."

Thirty minutes later, at a safe distance from the bakery, Mark placed the call. Gustav would drive around the block until Mark came out of the phone booth.

For a moment he debated how to handle this confrontation. Giving his name, he knew, would announce his presence. But from his conversation with Gustav, he suspected that the wrong people already knew he was here.

"This is Oberstleutnant Bradley," he informed the receptionist. "May I please speak to Herr Glück?"

"I am so sorry, Oberstleutnant Bradley. Herr Glück has had an accident."

"What happened?"

"Let me transfer you."

The phone clicked and another voice came on the line. "May I verify that I am speaking to Oberstleutnant Bradley."

"Yes. This is Colonel Bradley."

"So glad you have arrived in Berlin. Would you be able to come in this afternoon?"

"That won't be possible. Can you tell me what happened to Herr Glück?"

"So unfortunate. A bad fall on his holiday in the Tyrol. His neck was broken. I believe he was dead on arrival at hospital."

"Too bad." Mark reached up and automatically hung up the phone. Glück was honest. He'd probably kept the diary out of the Russians' clutches all this time. But they'd gotten him in the end.

He stood for a moment, eyes locked on the receiver he'd just replaced. There was a tight feeling in his chest, and his heartbeat had begun to accelerate. There was one more number he had to call. He had no idea who was at the other end, but the digits had popped into his head as he stood there staring at the phone.

Unhesitatingly, he put in additional coins and dialed 002-72-52. The phone rang and was answered, and then he could hear the call being automatically switched, apparently to another location.

He heard the whir of a tape, and then a chillingly familiar voice. "Colonel Bradley, so glad that you have arrived in Berlin. I am sorry I am not able to answer the phone personally at the moment. But you will hang on and wait for me."

Mark stood gripping the receiver, his knuckles white, his face even whiter. The last person in the world he wanted to talk to was Hans Erlich. But he simply couldn't hang up.

There was another click. "Ah, Colonel. Good of you to call. Where are you?"

"At a phone booth."

"And where are you staying?"

"I won't tell you."

Erlich sighed elaborately. "You are still protecting your organization, I see. But in the end it won't do you any good. Let us try another tack. Where is your business in the city?"

Mark tried not to answer. But the effort made the old familiar pressure build up in his head.

"Come, now, Colonel, you know it won't do you any good to resist. I repeat, where is your business in the city?"

Mark's hand shook. He tried to move the receiver toward the phone. But trying to fight the compulsion was like trying to buck the G-pressure in a rapidly accelerating fighter plane.

"Colonel Bradley?" The voice was sharp and commanding.

"At Schultz and Stein."

"The dealers in historical papers?"

"Yes."

"Well, then, I will look forward to seeing you there, Colonel."

# Chapter Fifteen

Aleksei Iliyanovich Rozonov put down the dossier on Col. Mark Bradley and looked thoughtfully across at the Dürer reproduction hanging on the wall of his four-star Berlin hotel room. The picture was of a ramrod-straight Prussian officer. The symbolism made him shake his head. The East Germans were a proud people who insisted on having a hand in shaping their own destiny. Perhaps if they had learned to defer to Moscow where appropriate, he wouldn't be caught in the middle of a mess that was becoming murkier by the minute.

The Russian settled his lean frame more comfortably into the easy chair beside the desk. He was just short of six feet in height, with straight, midnight black hair, heavy brows and an unmistakable gleam of intelligence in his deep blue eyes. Most people found his rather stern countenance and firm jawline intimidating, and that was an impression he chose to foster. He had kept his own counsel for years, and perhaps that had contributed to his rapid rise in the KGB. Although few called him a friend, most officers who knew him gave him their grudging respect. He had a record of getting results where others had failed. Now he had been summoned to Berlin to try to make the best of a bad situation. Not many would have relished the task. But he took a certain grim amusement in having been recommended for the job.

The dossier on Bradley was as complete as Soviet information sources could make it. Yet there were intriguing gaps. Although there had been considerable effort to conceal the facts, the man had almost a regular pattern of disappearing from his assigned duty stations and then turning up, sometimes months later, as though he'd simply stepped out to lunch.

He picked up a pencil and twirled it between his long fingers. Soviet Intelligence hadn't even been aware of the man's activities until he was assigned to the Orion project. At that time Bradley had been tagged for heavy surveillance. Though he'd been quite proficient on his job as consulting engineer and properly circumspect in his Intelligence-gathering activities, it had become clear that he was interested in more than he needed to know. In other words, he was working for *somebody* besides the U.S. Air Force.

As Aleksei looked at the file now, he had a good idea who it was. But he had decided to keep that knowledge to himself for the moment.

All of that background information should have been of no importance now. The KGB had blown up Bradley's plane. But a few months ago the colonel had come back from the dead, compliments of a certain megalomaniac named Hans Erlich. And Moscow had started scrambling for explanations.

The pencil between Aleksei's fingers snapped. Despite Erlich's obvious talents, the East Germans were playing out of their league again. When would they learn that running half-baked operations behind the KGB's back could only lead to retribution?

When Bradley turned up alive, after all, Moscow had no option but to mount a cleanup operation that would have been worthy of a major oil spill in the Persian Gulf. There was the matter of stealing Bradley's air force medical records so the Americans wouldn't be sure they had the right man, planting an operative at Pine Island, and now this showdown in Berlin.

He himself had just been called on to the case. Maybe that was the only lucky thing about this whole mess. He was in an excellent position to take care of a very tricky problem—with a minimum of damage.

IT TOOK ALL OF Mark's efforts to go calmly through the motions of briefing Gustav and Berdine about the developing situation at Shultz and Stein. But he knew as Eden watched his tense features that she wasn't attributing his distress to Herr Glück's untimely death.

Mark would have preferred to remain sitting around the kitchen table drinking Gustav's dark German beer and munching from the platter of ham sandwiches and pickles Berdine had set out. But Eden pointed out that they had traveled most of the night before and needed a rest. The moment she got him alone in their tiny room over the bakery, however, it was apparent that she had anything but rest on her mind.

"All right, what happened when you made that phone call?"

He turned his back and began to unbutton his shirt. "You were sitting at the table. Weren't you listening?"

"Yes, I was listening. But I was also watching your face. You might be able to hide something from them, but I know you too well. Whatever happened this afternoon in that phone booth has shaken you down to your toes."

"Get off my back!" he exploded. "When I agreed to bring you along on this trip, I must have been crazy."

Eden winced. His harsh words stung as though he had slapped her in the face. If she hadn't understood what was motivating him, she would have turned away. Instead, she held her ground, aware that Mark was using anger as a defense. Well, let him; she'd fuel him until she cut through to what was really bothering him. "It's being back in Berlin, isn't it?" she tried.

His jaw was rigid. "No."

"All right then, you must be afraid that you don't have what it takes to complete this assignment."

He whirled and grasped her shoulders, his fingers digging into the delicate flesh. "Don't you ever say that to me again," he threatened, his voice like a pitchfork grating across cement. At the same time, he gave her several rough shakes.

"It might be more effective if you grabbed me around the throat. Then I wouldn't be able to talk."

His eyes darted to her neck where the faint marks of his fingers still lingered. "Lord," he whispered. This time it was half apology, half a cry for help.

"Mark, it's all right. I understand."

"I doubt it."

"Then tell me." There was still no reply. Tentatively Eden reached out and touched his cheek. "Mark, I've been to hell with you and back. Surely you know you can trust me now."

Despite her words, he still had to fight the impulse to turn away. In that phone booth his worst fears had been confirmed. He felt like a prize marlin on the end of a line. The hook was buried deep in his head. And though he could put up a fight, the outcome was almost certain. Hans Erlich was going to reel him in. How could you talk about something like that? he wondered. Yet at the same time, he had come to realize that if anyone could wrench that hook out of his psyche, it was Eden Sommers.

She waited, watching the signs of an inner struggle.

"All right," he finally conceded. "See what you can do with this. After I made that call to Schultz and Stein, there was another number that suddenly flashed into my mind."

"002-72-52?"

For a moment his mind spun crazily. Was this some nightmare where he was going to wake up and find that Eden had been working for Erlich all along?

She saw the panic and anger on his face. "Mark, don't think *that* of me." The plea was the same one he had used when she had come to his room at the Aviary and then been afraid he was repulsed by what Marshall had done to her.

He recognized his own words, and some of the tension went out of his rigid body.

"At Pine Island," she continued, "when I took you back to the plane crash, you recited that number just before you told me you couldn't remember anything else. And then in

Ireland when I hypnotized you into thinking I was Erlich, you said it again. But I wasn't in any shape then to realize its importance."

Comprehension wrinkled his brow. "It was when I was strangling you, wasn't it?"

"Yes. But I won't let you keep blaming yourself for that. What matters is beating this thing—together."

"You mean 'if' we can beat it."

"We will." She looked around the tiny room. The high double bed, chest and armoire had left no space for a chair. "We might as well make ourselves comfortable," she observed, propping up pillows against the headboard and sitting down on the bed in an effort to dispel some of the tension.

Mark followed her lead. "I thought getting in bed with your patient during a therapy session was against the guidelines of the American Psychological Association," he remarked.

"There aren't any guidelines to deal with something like this."

He nodded, sobering again.

"Okay, quit stalling. What's the significance of that number?"

"It's a local phone number. But I'm sure it switches to a microwave link that goes across the border to East Germany."

"You called it?"

"Yes. Erlich answered."

"But how...?"

"He had an answering machine set up just for me. But within two minutes he was on the line himself. God, I tried to hang up, but my fingers were locked around the receiver as though I had rigor mortis."

His fingers had gone rigid at the memory, and Eden reached out to stroke them. "What happened?"

He briefly summarized the conversation. "I couldn't resist him. He still has me in his power."

"That isn't entirely true."

"How can you say that?"

"Think about it. You didn't give away anything about Orion. You didn't give me away, or jeopardize the Falcon's contacts in Berlin."

"But I told him about Schultz and Stein!" His self-accusation stabbed the air. "All Erlich has to do is make a few phone calls and he'll figure out what's going on over there."

"Then we'll be ready for him."

"How?" The question was edged with despair.

Eden realized suddenly that this was match point. If she couldn't convince Mark to believe in himself now, the game was lost. "We'll fight Erlich with his own weapons. Mark, you resisted him in almost every way. But he had you for so long and in so much pain, that you couldn't hold out on every front. However, your basic integrity has remained intact. You wouldn't be upset about any of this if that weren't the case."

A glimmer of hope kindled in his dark eyes. "What are you getting at?"

"Another posthypnotic suggestion—this time from me, not him. Remember, you didn't give away anything about the Orion project. We'll use that resistance to negate any power Erlich still has over you."

He felt like a drowning man who suddenly sees a life preserver bobbing in the water. "Do you really think it will work?"

"Yes." Her voice rang with confidence. *God, I pray it does.*

"Then when are we going to try it?"

"We can do it right now. Let's go into the induction routine."

This time it was easier than ever to put Mark under. He was so desperate to clutch for the life preserver she'd thrown to him that within less than a minute he was breathing slowly and evenly.

"The Orion project totally depends on you," she began, knowing that this suggestion could go either way. It had the power to protect him; it also had the power to destroy him. She knew his mind would turn it into another test. If he couldn't measure up, the guilt might break him.

"Do you understand?" she continued.

"Yes."

"If you have any more contact with Erlich, you will file your secrets in the Orion project. Orion will fill your mind—Orion, Orion, Orion."

"Orion, Orion, Orion," he repeated.

MAJ. ROSS DOWNING set down his glass of schnapps and looked around the restaurant terrace at Blockhaus Nikolskoe. For the afternoon he was dressed as a tourist, in a brown corduroy sport jacket and khaki pants. He sat with his back to a rustic wall and his face to Lake Havel. This well-known restaurant in the suburbs of Berlin had been built in the style of a Russian log cabin. In fact, it had been a wedding present from Friedrich Wilhelm III to his daughter Charlotte when she married the future Czar Nicholas I more than 150 years ago.

It was a strange place in which to be waiting to meet the German who had called him last night at the bachelor officers' quarters. But his curiosity had been aroused. He had been beating the bushes here in Berlin for the past three days. And so far he'd netted a big fat zero. He took another sip of his drink and waited.

At a table not too far away, but discreetly in the shadows, Aleksei Rozonov waited, too. Although the setting held a certain interest for him in its romanticized portrayal of old Russia before the revolution, the restaurant wasn't what had motivated him to take the short drive from the city this particular afternoon. He'd known about Major Downing's arrival in Berlin since the man had stepped off a military plane at Templehof. He'd observed the American's efforts to locate Bradley with a certain amount of apprehension. Downing was an unknown quantity in this little drama.

If Aleksei were to believe Wayne Marshall's reports, the major was a hard-nosed security type who never left a job unfinished. Was that why he'd found it necessary to come here personally? Downing couldn't have the whole picture. But whatever his motives, the man still had the power to interfere. There was no way to put him out of commission at this point, so the best Aleksei could do was look and listen and find out as much as he could.

He watched as a stocky German man made his way toward Downing's table. He wore a loden jacket and an Alpine hat with a small feather in the band, the very picture of a well-dressed tour guide.

"Herr Downing?" Gustav Hofmann asked, inclining his head slightly.

The American officer nodded.

"Thank you for agreeing to meet me here. I'm sure I can give you a specialized city tour that will meet all your requirements."

"We'll see," Downing observed dryly.

The German pulled out a chair. "May I?" Without waiting for an answer, he sat down and gave his cover name. "Herr Schwartzkopf at your service. Let me show you a proposed itinerary."

Downing accepted a brightly colored brochure. Inside were several neatly folded sheets of paper. He had time for only a quick glance, as the waiter was approaching with menus.

"The wursts here are quite good," Gustav remarked. "I think I'll select one for lunch."

"Fine," Downing agreed. The sooner they got the ordering over with, the sooner he could begin evaluating this fellow's information.

Just before the waiter left, Gustav asked for directions to the men's room. Then he excused himself.

Downing opened the neatly typed pages and began to read. It was an effort to keep his expression neutral. He hadn't known what he was expecting. But this story sounded like a Grimms' fairy tale.

Yet, if it was true, it explained so much about what had happened, both at Pine Island and before. When he finished reading, he had a thousand questions, and he waited impatiently for the man who had delivered this startling information to return.

But as the interval lengthened, Downing suspected that the courier wasn't coming back. Finally, when two orders of wurst and sauerkraut arrived, he sighed and began to eat his portion, wondering if they'd meet again at the auction gallery where Schultz and Stein were holding court.

Aleksei thought about taking the second plate of wurst off Downing's hands. He could just picture the major's face if he pulled out the empty chair at the table and started a conversation about their common interest—Col. Mark Bradley. From the stunned expression on Downing's face, he'd bet those innocent-looking travel folders duplicated some of the information in the dossier back in his hotel. And why not? In this case, Washington and Moscow had certain objectives in common. Both of them were out to get the microdot Bradley had left with Schultz and Stein.

The Russian shook his head. He'd hate to be in Bradley's shoes right now. The colonel had been burned, beaten and all but buried, and he was still on his feet and fighting. His was the kind of indomitable spirit that couldn't be bought. Bradley must have a fierce loyalty to his country, and Aleksei respected him for that. He couldn't help feeling that it would be a damn shame if the colonel ended up as a sacrifice now.

"HOW DID THE Falcon respond, Herr Hofmann?" Eden asked Gustav anxiously that evening. She had managed to corner him alone after dinner and before the briefing they would all be attending at 2100 hours.

"He decided we need reinforcements. Luckily there was an American security officer already in Berlin. His name is Maj. Ross Downing. I brought him up-to-date this afternoon."

Eden closed her eyes. Ross Downing of all people!

"You don't approve?" Gustav questioned, reading her troubled expression.

"Downing's the man who was doing his best to break Colonel Bradley on Pine Island."

"*Gott im Himmel!* I thought it was odd that Herr Gordon gave me strict orders not to inform the colonel. That must be why. Herr Gordon knew he would be upset."

Eden stared at him dumbly. Finally she whispered, "Yes," knowing it was a lie even as she said it. The Falcon had certainly considered Mark's reaction to Downing. But that wasn't his primary concern. No, he was hedging his bets. He didn't know how Mark would respond to Erlich if the German doctor showed up. And he wanted to make sure there was someone else on hand to pull his chestnuts out of the fire if Mark tossed them in.

And they were under strict orders not to tell Mark. God in heaven—she unconsciously echoed Gustav's exclamation—she felt like a traitor, part of a conspiracy against the man she loved.

The Falcon had given his orders. She could choose to disobey them. But she knew she wouldn't. Ever since they'd talked about Mark's second phone call yesterday, she'd been helping him get ready. Knowing about Downing was a distraction he didn't need.

"All right," she told Gustav resolutely, "we'll play it according to Herr Gordon's rules."

He nodded. "I'll tell Berdine we're ready to begin the strategy session."

A few moments later the four of them pulled up chairs around the kitchen table. Again Berdine had set out the makings for hearty sandwiches so that they could enjoy a meal while they talked.

"The auction is scheduled for 1100 hours tomorrow. Because it's such a big event, it's being held at a gallery instead of Schultz and Stein's regular location." As Gustav spoke, he pulled out an illustrated catalog and handed it to Eden.

This was the first she'd known about the change of location. She took the catalog and began to thumb through the pages. Apparently a great deal of money was being lavished on this sale in expectation of high returns. Besides the diaries, there were various historical letters—a number dating back to the Bismarck era—some art prints and a good deal of Nazi memorabilia—including early architectural sketches by Albert Speer.

"I didn't realize so many things were included in this auction," Eden murmured.

Gustav had put a marker on the page where the diaries were featured. Eden studied the photograph. They were three burgundy leather-bound volumes that looked rather ordinary.

"I thought somehow they'd be etched in gold," she observed.

"It's not the exterior that makes them of particular interest to most of the bidders," Mark remarked dryly. "Remember, I picked those diaries up nine months ago for a relatively modest sum."

Berdine set down her wurst sandwich and nodded. "There are more showy items in the catalog, but this collection so far has drawn the most interest. The other exhibits going on the block will be available for inspection starting at 0800 hours. But the diaries are sequestered in a special room. They'll only be on view from 0930 to 1030 hours. Gustav inquired and found out that they'll be in a glass case—with a special guard."

Frustration was deeply etched across Mark's forehead. "Well, at least the East Germans and the Russians won't be able to look for the microdot before I do. Of course, I still don't know when I'm going to get a crack at it, either."

"Actually, the situation isn't quite so grim. We're going to have a friend on the premises tomorrow," Gustav remarked, obviously enjoying the revelation.

Eden shot him a startled look. What was he talking about? He wouldn't tell Mark about Downing, would he?

The German met her gaze for a moment before turning back to the other man at the table. "Because of the value of the collection, the gallery has hired extra security guards."

Mark shot him a questioning look. "Does one of them work for you?"

Gustav chuckled. "Yes. Wolf Felder does a bit of moonlighting for us. After the bidding on the diary begins, Herr Felder will make sure he's on guard duty. He has agreed to let you have a few minutes of privacy with the diaries. But you're going to have to be quick, and I had to promise that nothing would happen to the material. Otherwise, his job could be in jeopardy."

Eden felt the electric tension in the room. These people were sitting around the table as though they were discussing plans for a bird-watching expedition the next morning. Yet in fact they were hatching a very dangerous, high-risk scheme, and the stakes were equally high. If everything went off as planned, this little group had the opportunity to tip the balance of world power. Berdine was enthusiastically slathering spicy mustard on her second sandwich. Apparently the discussion had made her hungry.

But if the moment was heady for the two Germans, it was even more so for Mark. Eden could see the gleam of excitement in his dark eyes. What he'd gone through to protect the information hidden in that diary would have killed most men. But Mark Bradley wasn't most men, and now he had the opportunity to make it all count.

She reached under the table and squeezed his knee. He looked at her, his face giving nothing away. But when he pressed his fingers over hers, she could almost feel the adrenaline pumping through the artery at his wrist.

"Schultz and Stein think they have a hot collector's item. If they had the slightest idea of what's really in those diaries, they'd have them under lock and key in Spandau Prison, rather than on the premises. Lucky for us they don't." Mark's voice was vibrant with an undercurrent of triumph.

They went on to rehearse their parts for the next day's activities. While Mark was getting the dot, Eden was to be out front with the well-heeled collectors literally buying him time by bidding on the diaries.

As the intricate plot unfolded, she couldn't keep the look of doubt out of her eyes. Again she was going to be asked to play a role for which she hadn't auditioned, and Mark's life might depend on how well she could pull it off.

"Don't worry about how high you have to go. I can guarantee the Russians will keep topping you," Mark assured her, misreading her concern. "All you have to do is keep the bidding going for at least ten minutes. If I can retrieve the dot while everybody's attention is focused on the auction, the Russians will never know it's missing until months later, after they've examined every bit of that manuscript under a microscope."

Eden suddenly realized just how critical the time factor was in all this.

"Once I get the dot, you can drop out," Mark added. "Just buy me those ten minutes. It won't take any longer than that."

But what if it does, she wanted to shout. She felt as though she were being swept along by a tidal wave. The espionage trio at the table had built a lifeboat. If it withstood the storm, they were heroes. If it didn't, God help them all.

Berdine interrupted her thoughts. "Gustav will be waiting in a car for the colonel, since he has to get out of the gallery instantly with the material. But don't worry. By the time you get to the door, I will be there to pick you up."

Mark glanced at his watch. It was almost midnight. "We'd better turn in," he said. "We have a busy day tomorrow."

That was the understatement of the year, Eden thought as she followed him upstairs.

When he had closed the bedroom door, he turned to her. "Okay, I was picking up some strange vibrations from you down there. What's wrong?"

Eden swallowed and sat down on the edge of the bed, avoiding his penetrating gaze. At this moment Mark reminded her of the quarterback on a team going into the Super Bowl the next morning. He might have his secret doubts, but for her he was putting on a great show of confidence.

Yet there were so many unknowns—including the way Mark Bradley was going to react tomorrow if Erlich showed up.

She would have liked to use this time to reinforce the posthypnotic suggestions they'd worked on yesterday. But she couldn't. If she suggested he needed any help now, she could make him lose the fine edge of his self-confidence. That was the last thing she wanted. But there were other issues she could address.

"Mark, have you stationed me in the auction gallery because I can really help out there? Or is it just a ploy to keep me out of your way?"

He sat down on the edge of the mattress beside her and took her hand. "Eden, I've got to be honest. The last place I want you tomorrow is that gallery. But I know you won't have it any other way."

"That's right."

"Well, somebody must keep that bidding going. So you really are an important part of this. But if you hear any shooting, run the other way with the rest of the crowd."

How could she tell him she'd run away? Yet, as she studied his anxious face, she knew that was what he needed to hear.

"All right, I promise to stay out of the line of fire. But nothing's going to happen, is it?"

"I'm positive it's going to go off like clockwork."

They were both lying to each other now.

His fingers were caressing her shoulders, feeling the tense muscles. The massage felt wonderful, and she tried to let it work the worry from her mind. Although in one sense it relieved her tension, in another sense it did little to relax her. Mark's touch was awakening familiar sensations of wanting and needing.

His lips caressed her hair. His tongue explored the delicate whorl of her ear, and she shivered in response.

He felt the reaction. In one swift motion he turned her to him, and his lips found hers in a hungry kiss that told her he felt as she did. And now there was a new element that gave this night an ever-sharper focus.

She understood what it was: the knowledge that if anything went wrong tomorrow, this might be their last time together. She realized with sudden painful insight that it had been this way for Mark that night five years ago before he'd left her. She hadn't known what was generating the intensity. Now she understood perfectly, because she felt it too.

She was running before the destructive force of the tidal wave, desperately trying to outdistance it. The shelter she sought was in Mark's arms. As her body molded itself to his and her fingernails dug into his back, she knew that their coming together tonight would have the force of the tidal wave itself.

## Chapter Sixteen

The auction gallery was located on Kurfürstendamm, not far from the Europa Center. The avenue, one of Berlin's main shopping areas, reminded Eden a bit of Forty-second Street in New York with its mix of shops, restaurants and hotels. But the German penchant for orderliness created a somewhat different effect than she would have encountered in an American city.

The gallery itself was definitely in one of the more prosperous buildings. It had a stone front and a circular drive. Carefully manicured evergreens in huge cement pots flanked the Roman arch at the entrance.

Gustav was driving the bakery van and would let Mark off a few blocks away from the gallery at a restaurant where he regularly delivered pastries. Then he would change vehicles.

This morning Eden had helped Mark smooth out his scarred face with the makeup he'd worn for their flight to Ireland. She hoped fervently that the makeup and his silver hair would be enough to protect him from recognition by the Russians and the East Germans.

As the Hofmanns' green Volkswagen pulled up at the gallery's main entrance, Berdine reached over and gave Eden's hand a quick squeeze. "Good luck," she whispered.

"Thanks."

The small automobile looked out of place in the line of Mercedeses letting off passengers. But once Eden stepped from the car, she fit in very well with the rest of the sophisticated auction/gallery crowd. Her gray-blue suit provided by the French connection had simple lines—but with "designer" stamped all over it. White kid gloves, matching gray pumps and bag and a conservative picture hat completed the ensemble. She only hoped no one would look past the props. Inside, she was quaking. It took an effort to walk through the doors into the gallery as though she had nothing more on her mind than adding a German lithograph to her collection.

As Mark had suggested, she stood slightly back at first, observing the rest of the assemblage. An atmosphere of excitement seemed to charge the air. Around her, conversation swirled in a dozen different languages. From what she could gather, a number of items coming up for sale were of great interest.

There were a few other women in the crowd, most of them dressed to the teeth. All except Eden seemed to be accompanied by men. In fact, the majority of the patrons were male. But then, that was to be expected with all the war memorabilia being offered.

Her gaze scanned the room as though she were looking for someone she had come to meet. A few men tried to make eye contact, but she dismissed them with a cool lack of interest. Yet she couldn't help wondering the reason for the attention she was receiving. She knew it wasn't unnatural, since she was a good-looking, unaccompanied woman. But each man—or woman—in the room was also a potential enemy. She might even have something to fear from the armed guards who stood at the doors and at intervals around the walls. It suddenly occurred to her that if Gustav could get a man inside, the East Germans and the Russians might be able to do the same thing.

She'd never thought that she'd actually hope to see Ross Downing again. But strange as it was, as her glance moved around the room, she was hoping for just that. At least, if the Falcon was right, the man was on their side. Her spirits dropped when she didn't see anyone who looked like the Pine Island security chief. Perhaps he was there but in disguise.

She was also looking for someone else, someone she prayed she wouldn't see. So far she'd encountered no one who fit Mark's description of Herr Doktor Hans Erlich. Maybe he hadn't been able to slip across the heavily guarded border. Or perhaps he had decided that the game he was playing was too dangerous, after all, and he wasn't going to show up. It was hard to believe he'd give up now. But his absence, at least for the time being, helped bolster her confidence.

Her first real task was to register, using the false passport she'd originally acquired from the Falcon. Unlike the one she'd used in France, it matched her present appearance. While the young clerk studied her picture, she felt her heart pounding as though it might break through the wall of her chest. But when he returned the passport, he simply smiled and handed her a card with her assigned number.

Next she drifted into the room where most of the items to be auctioned were on display. After twenty minutes of pretended interest in Nazi papers, Bismarck letters and nineteenth-century steel engravings of battleships, she went to find a seat in the small auditorium. It was already filling up, but she was able to get a place where she could see the door and much of the crowd. And she was still close enough to the front to attract the auctioneer's eye when the diary came on the block.

Glancing at her watch, she wondered if Mark had arrived. Her stomach was churning, and the effort to appear cool was taking all her concentration. There were still twenty minutes to go before the auction started. If everything was proceeding according to schedule, Mark was probably having a look at the infamous diaries now.

MARK HAD TIMED his entry to avoid the bulk of the crowd. He didn't bother to register but asked where he might see the Ludendorf material. A guard directed him through a door that led to the back of the building. Most of the other doors were bolted to keep the traffic out. But discreet signs directed him toward a room at the end of the corridor.

Before reaching it he passed an open set of double doors leading to a large room that must be the gallery's staging area. Jumbled about the cement floor was an amazing assortment of objects—everything from antique carousel horses to the towering Germanic wardrobes known as *Schranks* and gilt-framed mirrors. Over everything, suspended from long metal poles, were several elaborate crystal chandeliers. At the door to the loading dock across the room a uniformed guard stood with his hands behind his back. When he saw Mark, he called out a warning that the area was restricted.

"Just looking for the inspection room."

"Follow the signs."

Mark nodded and went on. The viewing room was behind the next door. When Mark stepped inside, another man was bent over a glass case that must be protecting the campaign diaries.

Mark froze, his heart leaping to his throat. In his imagination he pictured Hans Erlich straightening and turning toward him. His first instinct was to reach for the snub-nosed revolver in the holster under his left arm. But in the next moment, as the man turned, Mark realized that he was taller and darker than Erlich. Though he wore a gray, conservative suit, there was something about his bearing that suggested military training.

The two of them exchanged glances, each taking the measure of the other. The tall man seemed particularly interested in Mark's face and hair.

"Do I have the honor of meeting Col. Mark Bradley?" he finally questioned. The English was grammatically perfect. But the words were tinged with an unmistakable Russian accent.

So much for his disguise, Mark thought grimly. It had taken Maj. Aleksei Rozonov less than a minute to see through it. But why had the Russian deliberately chosen to give himself away when he could have walked out and left his identity in doubt? What kind of game was he playing?

There was no point in denying who he was now. "Yes," he admitted, his voice unfaltering.

"Your reputation precedes you, Colonel."

"So does yours, Major Rozonov."

The Russian permitted himself a tight smile. "In our profession, we take compliments where we can get them." He stood regarding Mark for another moment. "You'll find the case with the diary is electrified," he said.

Was that a warning or a threat? "Thanks for the tip."

"Just saving you some time, so you can find a seat with the rest of us in the auction gallery."

"I'll bet," Mark muttered under his breath.

The Russian left, and Mark made his own inspection of the security precautions, while pretending his real interest was in the Ludendorf material. Rozonov was right. Anybody who tried to break into that case without a key would get a bad shock—as well as set off an alarm.

He glanced at the uniformed guard with his prominently holstered revolver. The man didn't fit the description that Gustav had given him of Wolf Felder, who should be taking over the next shift. If Felder didn't show, that would mean trouble. He'd have to overpower the guard, use the special tools in his pocket to short-circuit the sophisticated electronic system and get the microdot—and all within ten minutes.

Mark sighed. There was nothing to do now but bide his time. For a moment he considered slipping into the loading area and waiting behind one of the *Schranks*. But when he walked past the double doors, the same guard was looking in his direction. Besides, if he were hiding, he wouldn't know when the bidding on the diary started. Better to wait inconspicuously at the back of the main hall.

Up front, the auction had already started. After seeing how the bidding was done with a discreet nod or hand signal, Eden made a couple of offers on some lithographs to let the auctioneer know she was participating. However, a group of Nazi papers was on the block now, and she simply couldn't bring herself to raise her hand for something so distasteful—even if she planned to drop out quickly.

Many in the crowd, however, did not have her reservations. The bidding was intense, and she saw how quickly the price of an item could rise if two or three collectors had their hearts set on it.

Out of the corner of her eye she noticed Mark slip into the room, and her heart gave a little lurch. Thank God he was all right so far. It took an effort not to let her relief show, but she didn't dare even acknowledge that they knew each other.

Others, too, had noted Col. Mark Bradley's arrival. One was a nervous-looking East German agent in a boxy off-the-rack brown suit who wished he fit into this crowd better. Another was Maj. Ross Downing, who was not far from the exit, although he had been careful to sit out of Eden's line of vision. He had spotted her shortly after her arrival and had been watching her carefully ever since, noting the tapered haircut, sophisticated makeup and expensive suit. She was one cool customer, he thought. She had strolled into this gallery just the way she'd come to Pine Island, as though she had every right in the world to be there. Only now she was dressed like an heiress rather than in the casual skirts and tops she'd worn in Georgia. Her arrival had confirmed at least part of the information he'd received yesterday from the German "tour guide." And now Bradley—looking a good ten years older than he had last month—slipping into the room was another piece of confirmation. Still, the presence of the two of them here didn't explain what was really going on. There were more holes in his information than in a piece of Swiss cheese. The agent at the restaurant yesterday could have been setting him up, and he was going to make damn sure that wasn't the case before he took even a tiny nibble of the bait.

Several historical letters came up and were quickly sold for about fifteen hundred marks each.

When the auctioneer announced the next item, a buzz of conversation filled the auditorium. Eden caught the word *Ludendorf* and felt her stomach knot even more tightly. This was it. She closed her eyes for a moment, took a deep breath, and let it out slowly. She supposed the auctioneer was explaining the historical background of the campaign diaries, and why they would not be brought to the front as was customary during the bidding.

Eden glanced at her watch. It was eleven thirty. She wanted to look toward the door to make sure Mark had left, but she couldn't call any attention to him, or to herself. Instead she listened as the auctioneer began to speak again, mentioning the figure twenty-thousand marks. She had heard him announce his expectations for each auctioned item. Usually he had turned out to be quite close to the final price. This time, she judged, he might be a bit low.

Someone to her far right started the bidding off at a thousand marks. A solid-looking man with a Russian accent offered two thousand. With a little nod of her head, she made it three. Her heart was hammering. She risked a look at her watch. There were eight minutes to go. The East German suddenly came into the competition and jumped the price to five thousand.

There was an undercurrent of excitement in the room now as the crowd sensed the competition.

Almost all eyes had been riveted on the auctioneer when Mark slipped quietly out of the room and into the hall. As the door closed, he stopped dead in his tracks. A guard who hadn't been there before was stationed at the entrance to the back of the building.

Mark walked in his direction and asked the most natural question that might be expected from someone leaving the hall at this particular time. *"Wo ist die Toilette?"*

The man pointed.

Mark stepped closer, pretending to look uncertain.

When the guard turned to point more directly, Mark gave him a quick chop at the back of the neck and watched him sink to the floor. Evidently he still had his touch. The man would have a hell of a headache when he came to in a half hour. But his neck wasn't broken

However, a minute of precious time had just been lost. Mark glanced over his shoulder, then pulled the guy after him through the entry to the back of the building. When he'd been here earlier, he'd noticed one door that wasn't locked. As he'd suspected, it led to a janitorial closet, where he stowed the unconscious guard.

He hurried down the hall, glancing into the loading dock as he passed. It was now unoccupied. Maybe the guard was outside. But there wasn't time to worry about that now.

When he pulled open the door to the room where the diary was being held, another uniformed guard looked up expectantly.

"Herr Felder?"

"*Ja*, Oberstleutnant Bradley."

"Do you have the key?"

"Not on me. It's taped underneath the bottom of the top desk drawer on the right."

Even as Gustav's man spoke, Mark was across the room and retrieving the key. "Stand by the door and let me know if somebody comes," Mark directed as he turned his complete attention to the case. It took only a moment to turn off the electricity. But getting the dot was a more delicate matter. That had to be removed with a special piece of tape and put in a dust-proof container. The one he'd brought looked like an aspirin tin. In fact, he had two identical cases, one with a speck of flea dirt he'd removed from Gustav's dog. It was taped inside, just as though it was the super-reduced Orion specs. Using it as a decoy had given him a grim laugh.

The tiny piece of film was exactly where he'd put it, dotting the *i* in the word *eins* at the bottom of page 78 of Volume Three.

He had just slipped the case back into the upper-inside pocket of his suit coat when he heard what sounded like a rheumy cough. It was followed almost instantly by a *thunk*. He whirled, suspecting what he was going to see. Wolf Felder was slipping quietly to the floor, a red stain spreading across the back of his uniform. Above him stood a tough-looking man with the physique of a prizefighter. He was holding a Luger fitted with a silencer. The specially equipped, high-caliber weapon was capable of slicing through steel with the quiet efficiency of a laser.

Under ordinary circumstances the gun and its owner would have riveted Mark's attention. But in this case his gaze was drawn like a magnet to the figure standing a little to one side of the slayer.

"You look surprised, Colonel Bradley," observed the doctor whose sadistic visage had haunted his nightmares for months. Once again Mark was confronting the reality of the deep-set eyes, the heavy brows, the hair that curled across the high forehead, the prominent mole on the right cheek. Suddenly he realized in horror that he knew the face better than his own.

"Erlich." The word rattled in his throat like a curse.

His nemesis smiled, sending a chill down Mark's spine. "What have you taken from the diary?"

The old familiar feeling of helplessness hovered around the edges of his mind like an octopus closing in on its prey. The atmosphere in the room had suddenly become stifling. He felt like a deep-sea diver whose air hose has been severed—just as the tentacles closed in around him.

"Please relieve Colonel Bradley of any weapons he may be carrying, Günther," Erlich instructed his companion.

The muscular man stepped forward and reached inside Mark's coat, pulling the small revolver from its hidden holster. Quickly he checked for others. The feeling of being trapped increased as Mark watched Günther slip the gun into his own waistband.

"And now tell me, what have you taken from the diary?" Erlich repeated.

Mark bit down on his lip, struggling to remain silent. But against his will, the words came out syllable by grating syllable. "A mi-cro-dot."

"Very good. Then give it to me."

Mark's fingers clenched. There was something he had to remember. It floated somewhere at the edge of his consciousness. Desperately, he tried to hook his mind around it and pull it into focus. It was like trying to hold on to a greased life preserver. He'd think he had it in his grip, only to find it had scooted five feet beyond his reach. He thrashed toward it again. Then, all at once, it came shooting back in his direction. *Orion, think Orion.* Eden's voice screamed in his brain. *You won't give away the Orion project.*

His eyes locked with Erlich's. He pictured himself lashing out at the man who was determined to compel his actions. Instead, his hand moved to the inside pocket of his coat.

*Orion, Orion, Orion, Orion,* he chanted silently, trying to block everything else from his consciousness. Erlich didn't know there were two cases. He could give him the one with the flea dirt inside. In his mind, he tried to force himself to retrieve the right one. But as his fingers closed around the cold metal, he honestly couldn't be sure which pocket he had reached into.

"Let me have a look," Erlich demanded. For emphasis, Günther flicked the wrist that was holding the Luger. Could he take him out? Mark wondered, estimating his chances against a trained killer. Without his gun, they were almost zero. Maybe they'd improve later—if there was a later.

Mark handed Erlich the case. As his hand brushed the blunt, well-manicured fingers, he shuddered. It was impossible not to remember the pain he'd suffered at those hands.

Erlich felt the reaction and smiled. "Ah, so you haven't forgotten the lessons I taught you."

Suddenly the room seemed to press in against Mark more heavily. He wanted desperately to escape. But more than the gun held him here. If he was going to get himself out of this, he had to concentrate.

*Orion, Orion, Orion,* his mind began to chant again. It was like a silent mantra. *Orion, Orion, Orion.*

"All right, let's go, Colonel," Erlich instructed as he handed the case to Günther for safekeeping.

There was another menacing gesture with the gun. Yet even as he followed Erlich down the hall, Mark's own sense of being in control was strengthening.

"This way," the doctor directed, stepping into the staging area. He began to wind his way among the odd assortment of goods stowed about the room. In one of the gilt mirrors, Mark caught a glimpse of the three of them. They made a grim procession, with Günther and his revolver bringing up the rear.

As he followed Erlich, Mark's eyes darted from cabinet to statue to rolltop desk, wondering if there was anything he could use as a weapon. Several yards ahead he saw a pair of black-booted feet just sticking out from behind a large *Schrank*. Now he knew why the guard hadn't been at his post at the door.

His mind raced. Erlich's companion had two guns—not three. Probably the guard's was still in his holster—if Günther hadn't tossed it away.

If it was there, could he get it? Mark wondered. It might be his only chance. He was just passing one of the carousel horses, which was propped precariously against a marble Grecian column.

*Now,* his mind screamed and his body obeyed. He turned slightly, his leg catching an upturned hoof. It was enough to throw the heavy wooden horse off-balance and into Günther's path. At the same time, Mark dived in the direction of the boots. He wasn't quite fast enough. He heard another coughing noise and then felt a sharp, stinging pain in his calf.

"No, you fool!" Erlich's voice shrieked. Mark didn't know whether the words were for him or Günther, and he didn't give a damn. Then the East German doctor's voice took on a different—yet horribly familiar—quality. "Colonel Bradley, stand up and come to me now!" The command was imperative; his puppet had been programmed to obey.

Gritting his teeth, Mark focused on the pain in his leg, willing that to slice through the power Erlich was trying to wield. In one sharp, agonizing maneuver he rolled over the body of the guard.

"Colonel Bradley! You will do as I say!" Erlich screamed.

In a matter of seconds, Mark's hand had closed over the cold metal of the man's revolver. He felt a stab of elation that he had resisted Erlich's command.

As Günther came around the corner, Mark squeezed the trigger twice. From the string of profanity he heard, he knew at least one slug had done some damage. But despite his own injury, the East German got off another round before jumping back.

Mark heard spitting noises above his head as wood shattered around him. At the same time he felt a searing pain in his shoulder, then something warm trickling down his arm. Sweat broke out on his forehead. The only consolation was that the second hit was on the left side. It wouldn't affect his ability to aim a gun.

Dimly he heard other feet and then a sharp command in Russian. God, was he going to have to fight off Rozonov too?

OUT IN THE GALLERY the auctioneer's voice had taken on the fervency of a man who knows he is presiding over a drama of high excitement. "Thirty thousand marks, I have a bid of thirty thousand marks. Do I hear thirty-five?" He looked expectantly from Eden to the Russians who had been systematically topping her bids.

The offer of thirty thousand had come from the East German in the back. Eden stole another glance at her watch. A minute to go to make ten, but she was going to give Mark more time, just in case. After all, she thought with almost hysterical logic, he was supposed to get the money from the sale since the diaries belonged to him.

She raised her gloved hand.

"I have thirty-five," the auctioneer announced. "Do I hear . . ."

His words were drowned in a series of small explosions from the back of the building. Most of the audience reacted with stunned silence.

Eden saw Downing leap up and dash toward the exit at the rear of the hall just as another loud report rent the air.

*"Artilleriefeuer!"* a man shouted.

"Terrorists," another man screamed. It took only a moment for panic to break out. All at once the well-dressed patrons were scrambling over each other in their haste to get out of the building. Eden was on her feet, too. But her intentions were quite different.

However, as the human wave swept forward, she was helplessly dragged along with them and carried through the exit. Once in the hall, she somehow managed to press herself against the wall. She couldn't let herself be propelled out of here along with the rest of the frightened patrons. Mark had told her to run the other way if there was trouble. She'd known then as she knew now that she wasn't going to do it. She had to get to him.

Another volley of shots rang out. Instinctively she turned in that direction and edged along the wall. Someone grabbed her shoulder and shouted, *"Stoppen!"* She wrenched away and continued down the hall. When she was free of the crowd, she started running toward the gunfire, afraid of what she might find.

Ross Downing had beat the mob out of the room and was several minutes ahead of Eden. Like Mark, he had cased the building earlier that morning. He couldn't picture a gun battle going on in the little room where the Ludendorf material had been sequestered. So where was it?

The only other possibility was the staging area by the loading dock. He had no idea what he was going to find there, but he reached the door with his own revolver already drawn.

A flicker of motion in a gilt-framed mirror caught his eye. He whirled in that direction and in the reflection saw Mark Bradley pulling himself up against a row of filing cabinets. His slow movements indicated that he was wounded. There was a ping from somewhere to the left, and a bullet whizzed past his own ear. Automatically Downing ducked for cover behind a suit of armor.

Another slug exploded into the desk to his left. It was followed by the screech of a ricochet off the armor. The careening bullet hit a mirror, sending up a burst of glass shards. One hit Downing just below the right eye and he gasped. Then two shots rang out from the right, drawing the fire that had been directed at him. It was the tall, mili-

tary-looking man he'd pegged earlier as a KGB agent. He'd
assumed the guy was here to finish off Bradley. But he
wasn't shooting at the colonel, he was aiming at two other
men near the exit—one dark and tough looking, the other
blond and more aristocratic—who were shooting at both
him and Bradley. The Russian was drawing fire away from
Bradley and himself.

What in the name of God was going on? Ever since Pine
Island he'd been trying to put the pieces of this crazy puzzle together. Was Bradley a pawn of the Russians, the East
Germans, or just a poor son of a bitch trying to fight his
way out of a death trap? He'd thought he'd been able to fit
some of the picture together. But now he felt as though
someone had just kicked the table and sent the pieces of the
puzzle flying across the floor of this impromptu shooting
gallery.

Downing peered out from behind the armor's metal
shoulder. Where did *he* fit into the picture? He was on strict
orders to bring Bradley back alive. And for the moment,
that was going to have to take precedence.

Another volley of shots rang out. A crystal chandelier
crashed to the floor, sending more glass flying. And then
Bradley fell backward, vanishing behind the cabinet.

The men who were heading toward the door sprinted
from behind the cover of a marble statue. Downing fired in
their direction. So did the Russian. Marble chips flew as
one man went down. The other made it through the door,
but Downing noted with satisfaction that he was doubled
over. A trail of blood marked his progress across the floor.

The Russian, his hand bleeding, was out from behind his
cover and running forward as the bulky man slumped to the
floor. "This one's finished," he growled. Downing saw him
remove something from the man's hand and pocket it. The
Russian looked back at him. "You help your man, I'll go
after the one who got away."

"Wait," Downing began, oblivious to the blood trickling down his own cheek. But the Russian didn't stop. He
was already out the door.

Downing took a step in the Russian's direction. Then he heard Eden Sommers call, "Mark! My God, Mark."

She must have been watching the battle from the doorway. She was across the room and kneeling behind the cabinet before he could put a restraining hand on her arm.

"Get an ambulance," she ordered. "He's going to bleed to death if you don't get an ambulance."

Now that the rain of gunfire had stopped, the room was suddenly full of German police. Then in the distance there was the wail of a siren.

Downing could see Eden cradling Bradley's head in her lap. She was leaning over him murmuring something too low for anyone else to catch.

"Eden . . ." the voice was barely audible, but there was a look of triumph in his eyes. "I gave Erlich the wrong one."

She leaned closer to catch his words. The wrong what?

"In my breast pocket...the microdot in a metal case. See that the Falcon gets it."

"Mark, you're going to make it," she promised, even as she took the metal case. Then her fingers entwined with his, trying to give him her strength.

His eyes fluttered closed. With what appeared to be a great effort, he opened them again and looked up at her. "I love you," he whispered, just before he lost consciousness.

## Chapter Seventeen

It was amazing that even halfway around the world an American military hospital waiting room still looked the same, Ross Downing thought as he opened the door and glanced toward Eden Sommers, who was sitting with her eyes closed on a hard plastic couch. From the rigid way she held her body, however, he knew she couldn't be asleep.

For a moment he studied her. She was still dressed in the same designer suit she'd been wearing eighteen hours ago when he'd first seen her at the auction gallery. Only now it was rumpled and stained with Bradley's blood across the bottom of the skirt.

The woman had guts, he thought again. She had been right all along, and now he was going to have to say something to her about it.

He rubbed the bandage on his face where the flying glass had cut him. It hurt, and the pain was a reminder of unfinished business. Nevertheless, he hated apologies, especially when he had to make them.

Just hours ago, over the secure military communications link between Berlin and the Pentagon, he'd had a most informative conversation with the Under Secretary of Defense. He had a pretty good idea that until a few hours ago the Secretary hadn't known what was going on, either. The insight didn't make him feel any less of a fool for his own part in this colossal fiasco.

"Dr. Sommers?" he began tentatively.

Her eyes flew open, and for an unguarded moment she seemed to flinch away from him. Then she visibly pulled herself together.

"How is Colonel Bradley?" he asked, taking the seat beside her.

"Lucky to be alive. He lost a lot of blood, and it seemed as though he was in surgery half the night. But he's resting fairly comfortably now, and they've told me he's doing much better."

"Have you seen him?"

"For ten minutes. But he was pretty much out of it from the anesthetic." She glanced at her watch. "They're going to let me go back in when he wakes up."

"I'm glad."

She searched his face. "Then you've changed your mind about Mark?"

"Yes." That might be as close as he came to an apology. "I have a message for you," he continued. "The information Colonel Bradley gave you has been delivered."

A weight had been lifted off her shoulders. "Mark almost died getting that evidence. I hope it was worth it."

"It looks like it. There was an arrest in Washington this morning. Someone you've probably never heard of named Humphrey Strickland. But he was right up there in the inner circle at the Pentagon."

"They can arrest someone that quickly?"

"In a case like this. The evidence Mark had on that microdot proves Strickland was a Russian agent, and an extremely effective one because he was so trusted. Apparently that was why Bradley was assigned to the Orion weapons project in the first place—to expose the spy."

Eden nodded, as though the information were some sort of revelation. It was better not to give away how much she knew.

Downing paused and then seemed to make a decision. "Strickland was in my chain of command, too. He's the one who was pressing for me to get results down at Pine Island."

Their eyes locked for a moment. Both of them understood very well what those results would have meant for
Col. Mark Bradley.

"And was he the one who ordered you to use the RL2957
on Mark?" Eden asked quietly.

"Yes." The former chief of station would never be able
to look back on that particular episode without feeling uncomfortable. He wanted to argue that he'd just been doing
his job. But he knew that in future he would be less likely
to blindly obey commands that might be immoral. Maybe
if he'd listened to Hubbard, the two of them could have
done something. But he'd been too arrogant to take the
doctor seriously, and now Hubbard was dead. That, too,
was a regret he'd have to live with. The thought triggered
another.

"I didn't know it at the time, but Strickland also pulled
some strings to get Wayne Marshall on the Pine Island
medical staff," he admitted.

The mention of that name made the blood drain from
Eden's face. Suddenly Downing wondered just what had
happened on that beach before she and Bradley had escaped. He'd only heard Marshall's version of the incident.
Now he remembered the pair of handcuffs at the foot of
one pine tree and the ropes around the trunk of another.
God knows what the male nurse had done to her.

The woman sitting across from him was clenching her
hands tightly in her lap. Wayne Marshall was one person
she hoped she'd never see again. Now she wondered if she
might end up facing him in a courtroom. "I presume he's
under arrest now, too," she ventured.

Downing shook his head. "No, he vanished from the
hospital at Robins Air Force Base. The Pentagon is pretty
sure he's on his way to Moscow—and good riddance."

She nodded. It was almost a relief to hear he'd skipped
the country. But at the same time, she couldn't help wishing that he was going to be locked up and the key thrown
away.

The major shifted slightly in his seat. He'd been shaken
to the core when he'd found the installation at Pine Island

had been infiltrated, and by more than one agent. In retrospect, he was damn grateful that one of them was on the right side—although he still didn't have the vaguest idea where Dr. Eden Sommers's orders had originated. The idea that there was some supersecret Intelligence agency almost nobody in the U.S. government knew about was preposterous on the face of it. Yet he had the evidence of its existence sitting next to him. "I'd like to know who *you* were really working for," he remarked. "But I've been too indoctrinated in security precautions to ask."

Eden managed a slight smile. "I wouldn't want to damage your record. Besides, I've had my own indoctrination."

"I understand."

While they were speaking, the door had opened and a stout, blond German woman came in carrying a canvas tote.

"Eden." The name was spoken with respect, and gentleness.

She looked up at Berdine Hofmann.

"I know you don't want to leave the hospital. So I've brought you a change of clothing."

Eden's emotions were so close to the surface that the thoughtful gesture brought tears to her eyes.

"Thank you," she murmured.

The two women embraced.

"Will you excuse me?" Eden asked Downing.

"Of course." Who was the German woman? he wondered, as the two of them left together. Another idle question that would never be answered.

Getting out of the rumpled suit had a reviving effect on Eden. She saw Mark several times. But he was still too weak to have much of a conversation.

The waiting set her nerves on edge, but she wanted to be there when he needed her. The staff seemed to understand and did everything they could for her. They even let her spend the night in an empty room on the same floor as Mark's. But it was almost impossible to sleep. She tossed and turned for hours on the hard, narrow bed thinking about Mark and praying that he was going to be all right. She finally fell asleep just before dawn. But the clatter of morning activity in the hall woke her when the sun came up.

She felt as though she'd been run over by a truck. Sighing, she decided she might as well get up. Just after she'd gotten dressed again, a cheerful-looking nurse came in with some good news. "Dr. Sommers, Colonel Bradley is awake and asking for you."

Her eyes lit up at the news, and suddenly she felt much better. As she followed the nurse down the hall, she noted that the MP who had been at Mark's door yesterday was on duty again. Even though he'd seen her before, he asked to see her temporary hospital identification card.

As she entered the room, she looked quickly toward the metal bed in the corner. The last time she'd seen Mark's scarred face, it had been almost devoid of color. Now he looked almost imperceptibly better. She noted the change and rejoiced.

However, his eyes were closed and his chest was still swathed in bandages. She knew from the raised outline of the covers that there was a cast on his left leg. The needle from an IV bottle was firmly taped to his left arm. She could see a clear liquid flowing down the tube.

Quickly she crossed to the chair by the bed. As she sat down, Mark opened his eyes and looked at her. Something in their depths seemed to come alive as he focused on her.

"Eden."

"How are you this morning?" she whispered, leaning over and stroking her hand down his cheek.

"Better . . . now."

Her fingers groped for his. "They told me yesterday that the Falcon got the information, and they've arrested the mole in the Pentagon."

He pressed her fingers. "Good."

For a few moments they sat without speaking. Words weren't necessary for the two of them to communicate now. Bringing his hand up, she pressed it gently against her heart, wanting to affirm the physical contact with this man she loved so much. She had almost lost him so many times.

Two days ago at the auction gallery he might have been killed. Now she was greedy for his touch. Even in this unlikely setting, her senses stirred in reaction, and she knew from the look in Mark's eyes that he felt it.

"I didn't think I was very dangerous right now," he said, his voice rough with emotion.

"For me, you're always very potent. But then, I do love you so much."

"I wish I deserved it."

"Mark, how can you say that?"

"Why don't you ask how I could have left you five years ago?" She heard the self-accusation in his voice.

"I think I understand why. But that's all in the past. Just promise me one thing now."

He waited, his eyes questioning.

"That you won't just disappear again without telling me. I love you. I want us to try to work things out together."

"That's what I want, too."

She brought his fingers to her lips. "Thank you."

The silence lengthened again, but now there was an understanding that seemed to flow between them.

"How does beating Erlich make you feel?" she finally asked.

Despite the pain and the injuries, he grinned weakly. "I did, didn't I?"

"Yes."

"I couldn't have done it without you." He knew that wasn't just an idle observation.

"You trusted me enough to let me help."

His eyes closed again. She could see that even this short visit was tiring him. She should let him sleep. "You need to rest."

His gaze focused on the circles under her eyes. "You do, too."

"Later. But maybe I could use some breakfast. I'll come right back when I'm finished."

"Take your time. I'm not going anywhere."

She smiled. It was a good sign that he could joke about his situation. "All right."

Eden had been to the cafeteria once before. It was downstairs and in the next wing. As she walked down the hall one of the nurses stopped her.

"Are you after some breakfast?"

"Yes."

"There's a cart that stops at the station near the elevator. You can get coffee and a *Brötchen* there."

"Thanks for the tip." A roll was about all her stomach could tolerate at the moment.

As she stood in the short line waiting her turn, she looked around at the familiar military hospital setting. They were giving Mark one hundred percent here, and she was grateful that he was on his way to recovery. But she was grateful for a lot of things. He was finally safe. And now that the Orion project was secure again, they were going to have the opportunity to obliterate the last of Erlich's legacy. More than that, there would be time for the two of them to work on their personal relationship.

Eden was buttering the light-textured breakfast roll when the elevator doors slid open and an orderly came out pushing an empty gurney. He was bald and swarthy. And like many of the other personnel he was dressed in a green cotton uniform. Something about his face stirred her memory. His jaw was set in a hard line, as though he was concentrating intensely on something.

Her gaze flicked to his hands. They, too, looked familiar. Had he been in one of the V.A. hospitals where she'd worked? she wondered idly as she stirred sugar into her coffee. She followed his progress down the hall, noting the muscular hunched shoulders.

She watched him head toward Mark's room. He stopped for a brief exchange with the guard at the door, and she could see him showing his identification pass. He left the gurney outside and disappeared from view.

And then all at once she *knew*.

"My God!" she screamed, and dropped the cup of coffee. The scalding liquid seared her leg, but she didn't even notice.

Everyone in the little group around the breakfast cart pivoted in her direction, startled looks on their faces.

"Take it easy," one of the doctors soothed.

"What's wrong?" someone else asked urgently, rushing to her side. A comforting hand was laid on her shoulder.

They seemed to think she'd flipped out from the strain.

"No! Let me go! That man's here to kill Mark."

Fear gripped her chest like an iron vise, and she was running down the hall toward his room even as she shook the comforting hand off her shoulder. A few moments ago she had been thanking God that the nightmare was finally over. Now she had been startled awake to find that the horror was still going on, here, now.

At the door the guard took in her wide-eyed appearance and stepped protectively in front of the barrier.

"Let me in. He's going to kill Mark," she repeated.

The guard hesitated, searching her face. Eden reached for the doorknob, ducking and shoving the wooden barrier with her shoulder at the same time. The momentum carried her halfway across the room and she stumbled against the bed.

Mark's eyes flew open. "What?" And then he, too, saw who was standing over him. An expletive formed on his lips.

Wayne Marshall had almost finished injecting the contents of a small hypodermic needle into the tube leading from Mark's IV bottle. He turned in surprise at the commotion.

From her half crouch on the floor, Eden reached up and wrenched the IV needle from the back of Mark's hand. He groaned as the clear liquid dripped slowly onto the floor. Marshall grabbed for the tube, his gaze darting from Mark to Eden.

"Bitch," he growled. "I should have finished you off at Pine Island when I had the chance."

Mark's eyes were alert. If he could, he would have taken Marshall on. But in his weakened condition it was a struggle to move. Yet Eden saw him edging away from the deadly needle.

As she watched, her anger flared white-hot. It blotted any fear for her own safety, and she sprang at Marshall, her fingernails clawing at his head and face.

But her attack was nothing against his strength. Even with the gunshot wound she knew he had sustained two weeks ago, he was able to throw her off. She landed in a heap against the wall, gasping for breath. Mark was half-out of the bed on the side away from Marshall. Thank God there was a solid object between the two of them now. He hit the floor and muffled his own scream of agony.

The whole scene from the time she'd entered the room couldn't have taken more than thirty seconds, yet it seemed like a lifetime. Was this nightmare ever going to end?

The guard had regained his balance and drawn his gun. Quickly he sized up the situation. "All right, fellow, don't move," he commanded.

He stepped into the room and two other security men followed.

A look of defeat washed over Marshall's face. In one swift motion he raised the IV tube and plunged the needle into his own arm. As Eden watched openmouthed, he slumped to the floor. There was a gurgling noise in his throat, and his body convulsed. Then he went completely still. Eden didn't have to be told that he was dead.

God, that was what Marshall had planned for Mark! She crawled blindly toward the man she loved so much, tears streaming down her cheeks. Then she was pressing her face against his bandaged chest, and his good arm came up to press her close.

"Eden, it is over now. I promise you it's all over now," he said.

EDEN NOSED the rented Buick down the twisting lane. Through the broad windshield she could see the oaks and maples of the Virginia countryside ablaze with scarlet and gold, and she could feel an autumn crispness in the air.

When they reached the beveled, wooden No Vacancy sign by the gate, she looked over at her passenger and grinned.

Mark smiled back. They both knew that the information didn't apply to them. There was definitely a room ready and waiting for them at the Aviary.

At the top of the drive Eden stopped the car and went around to help Mark out. The cast was off his leg, and with his hair back to its natural raven darkness, he'd shed the extra ten years he'd taken on as a disguise. All in all, the man in the passenger seat looked handsome and fit in his blue air force uniform. But he was still under doctor's orders to use a crutch. The edict hadn't pleased him, but he'd found over the last several weeks that the woman beside him had a great respect for doctor's orders. The only times she'd bent the rules had been when she'd propped a chair under the knob of the hospital room door and given him her own brand of physical therapy. Of course, with his leg in a cast, she'd been on top of matters there, too. But he hadn't exactly minded.

She caught the expression on his face and suspected they might be remembering the same thing.

"I trust you're going to leave some details out of your full report to Gordon," she teased.

He raised an eyebrow. "Lie to my superior?"

"No, just protect my modesty."

He looked at her for a moment, thinking of everything she had gone through for him, and an overwhelming feeling of tenderness welled up inside him. "I'll protect you," he whispered. "And to prove it, I'll warn you that Gordon's got a hidden TV camera and mike trained on the entrance to this place. So we'd better quit talking and go in."

Eden studied the topiary birds guarding the door, the triangular pediment and the carving around the bull's-eye window, seeing nothing out of the ordinary. The surveillance equipment was well hidden. But after all she'd learned about the Falcon, she shouldn't be surprised about the precaution.

Her thoughts were interrupted as the door swung open, and Constance McGuire came down the steps.

"Eden, Mark, welcome back," she said, giving them each a quick hug.

The younger woman returned the greeting with fondness. Through the ordeal of the past several months, Constance had been a touchstone—someone who had planned for everything from her well-dressed spy's wardrobe to the equipment Eden and Mark had needed for their escape from Pine Island.

"I'm glad to be back," Mark said as they followed her down the hall.

Eden gave him a quizzical look. Her feelings about the Aviary and everything it symbolized were still ambivalent. The Falcon had brought her here to save Mark. Yet when she'd first joined his very dangerous game, she'd been little more than a pawn. It was only later that she'd become one of the decision makers. But that role had carried its own responsibilities. The security of the free world had been hanging in the balance during their private ordeal.

Spymaster Amherst Gordon was standing where she'd first seen him in the solarium. Cicero was on his wooden perch. To her surprise the brightly colored parrot flapped its wings and squawked a greeting to her as she entered the roomful of tropical foliage. Outside it might be fall. But it would always be summer in here.

"You've just received a high honor," Amherst Gordon observed. "Cicero doesn't give his approval lightly."

Eden inclined her head slightly as she acknowledged the compliment.

"I'd like to add my congratulations for a job well-done." He turned to Mark. "And on your promotion to full colonel."

Eden and Mark exchanged glances.

"Congratulations," she whispered.

"Thanks."

They pulled up chairs at the wrought-iron table and Constance came in with a tea tray. Eden was struck with a feeling of déjà vu. It had all started like this, she remembered.

"By the way, the President has been fully briefed on what happened in Berlin. He adds his thanks to mine," the Falcon said.

After stirring sugar and cream into his tea, he continued. "I'm sure the two of you still have questions. Let me give you some tidbits that I didn't dare discuss outside these four walls. I have an informant in Madrid, code-name Raven. He verified that your decoy microdot got back to Moscow. They're furious about losing their man in the Pentagon."

"That almost makes me feel sorry for Rozonov," Mark admitted.

The Falcon raised a questioning eyebrow. "Why?"

"It isn't in my report, but there's a good probability that he saved my life."

"Undoubtedly he was sent to Berlin not just to get the microdot but also to make an example out of Erlich. That part of his mission must have been successful. I'll wager the East Germans will think twice the next time they butt into a Soviet Intelligence operation," Gordon said.

Eden nodded as a few more pieces of the picture fell into place.

Mark finally introduced the topic she hadn't wanted to bring up. "And what about Wayne Marshall?"

"What about him?" the Falcon asked.

"How did he get into that military hospital in Berlin?"

"When I went back through his records, I found he'd done a tour there. So he knew the hospital and its routine. He must have kept his identification card. As for the Kojak disguise, that was probably the easiest way for him to change his appearance with limited time and resources."

"We assume he was acting on his own twisted initiative," Constance added, looking at Mark. "Killing you must have become an obsession with him after you escaped from Pine Island."

Under the table, Eden's fingers gripped the edge of her chair. She knew firsthand how dangerous someone with a twisted mind like Wayne Marshall's could be. Thank God he wasn't going to be a threat to her or Mark ever again.

They went on to discuss Humphrey Strickland's arrest, along with the arrests of several other agents in his spy network.

"You'll be happy to know Ross Downing is in charge of the interrogation," the Falcon informed them.

"Poetic justice," Eden murmured.

"And what's your assessment of the damage Strickland did to Orion?" Mark asked, looking across the table at Gordon.

"By catching him now, we have minimized the damage. If he had gone undetected much longer, the contracts would have been awarded, and it would have been astronomically expensive to change any of the designs. All the Russians have now is overviews that won't do them a damn bit of good once the project is operational. Downing's job will be to find out what other projects he may have jeopardized, along with the identities of other Soviet agents we haven't yet picked up."

For the next two hours they discussed other aspects of the operation. Eden couldn't believe how quickly the time slipped by. It was late in the afternoon when Constance finally asked if they wanted to relax for a few hours before dinner. Several times during the discussion she'd silently slipped out of the room. Each time she'd returned with a preoccupied look on her face.

Connie's suggestion could have been made for Mark's benefit. After all, he was still recovering. Yet from the woman's expression Eden guessed that the director of the Peregrine Connection and his assistant probably had urgent business they needed to discuss.

"I've given you the Jefferson room, and your luggage is already unpacked," Connie informed them crisply. There was no pretense of their being assigned separate quarters this time.

Once they were alone, Eden glanced at Mark. He was a remarkable man, and her love for him knew no bounds. Yet she'd heard the old enthusiasm in his voice when he'd recalled the Orion mission.

When they'd talked about Mark's immediate future, Gordon had ruled out fieldwork for him. He was scheduled for three months R and R, during which they would continue his therapy program. When he returned to active duty, he would be assigned as an air force liaison in the Situation Room at the Pentagon. She wondered if that would satisfy his need to be where the action was. He would no longer be in physical danger. But he'd certainly be handling crises on a global scale.

And if that wasn't enough, perhaps she could help supply the element of adventure he needed in his life. She'd already started putting out feelers for a job in the D.C. area.

"Well, where do we go from here?" she asked.

He looked across at the wide bed with its quilted damask spread. "How about over there for starters?" As he spoke he tossed the crutch against a high-backed armchair and pulled her body tightly to his. As always, she melted against him, and her head tipped eagerly upward for his kiss.

When his warm lips finally lifted from hers, he splayed his fingers out across her cheeks. "I love you," he whispered.

She tucked that knowledge into a corner of her heart. "I love you, too."

But she didn't need to cling to Mark for strength. Over the past few months she'd found a reserve of fortitude she'd never known she possessed. She'd fought for the man she loved, and won. That knowledge made her sure she could do the same with whatever lay ahead in the future.

*More to come from the Peregrine Connection*

*Amherst Gordon and Constance McGuire moved into the Aviary's shielded operations office.*

*The Falcon took in the grim expression on his assistant's face. "All right, let's have it," he demanded, his gruff voice reflecting his fears for one of his agents.*

*Connie handed him a newly deciphered message.*

*After reading the text, Gordon whistled through his teeth. "So the Raven is on to some new developments in the Russian chemical warfare strategy."*

*"Yes."*

"He's got to get the details before I can go to the Pentagon."

"If he probes any further, he could blow his cover." She didn't go on to state the obvious. If the KGB figured out who he was, he was facing torture and death.

Gordon settled into his padded desk chair, his mind making assessments and evaluating risks. The balance of power in the world was in danger of shifting. One man called the Raven might be able to bring it back to stability. "Tell him to keep digging. But give me an update on that contingency plan for getting out of Madrid, just in case."

"I've got it right here."

Gordon took the sheets of paper, wondering if the plan had a chance in hell of working. His inner doubts must have been reflected on his face.

"You're doing what you have to do," Connie said gently.

"I know. I still can't help hating myself. He's had a rougher life than most people could ever imagine. He deserves some happiness. But I can't guarantee him anything. All I can do is ask him to risk his life."

"He's gotten out of some pretty tough spots in the past."

"I'm just praying he can do it again."

\*     \*     \*     \*     \*

*Don't miss the next Peregrine Connection—
#301 FLIGHT OF THE RAVEN, coming next
month—only from Rebecca York and
Harlequin Intrigue.*

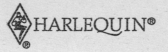

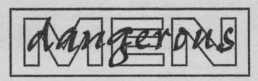

## HARLEQUIN®

# INTRIGUE®

# COMING NEXT MONTH

**#301 FLIGHT OF THE RAVEN by Rebecca York**
*Peregrine Connection #2*
Julie McLean was a rank amateur on the trail of the Raven, the most noto-
rious spy in the Western world. Was he Aleksei Rozonov, the smooth
Russian whose kisses made her as hot as Madrid in summer...
and made her forget she was a woman on a mission?

**#302 I'LL BE HOME FOR CHRISTMAS by Dawn Stewardson**
When Ali Weyden's dead husband called, it was to say he had their son
and was holding him for ransom. Ali had no place to turn—except to
crime writer Logan Reed. She knew he could handle the situation, but she
hadn't expected him to offer her tender loving care....

**#303 THE KID WHO STOLE CHRISTMAS by Linda Stevens**
To Shannon O'Shaughnessy, little Joey, heir to the Lyon Department
Store fortune, was like the son she never had. But then a week before
Christmas, he was abducted—and the only suspect was the new store
Santa, a sexy but secretive man she hired—and loved...

**#304 BEARING GIFTS by Aimée Thurlo**
There was nothing like attempted murder to chill all Christmas cheer.
Relations between softy Mari Sanchez and cynic J. D. Hawken were
already icy—until their sudden joint custody of a gutsy, endangered little
girl landed the duo in perilously hot water....

# AVAILABLE THIS MONTH:

**#297 EDGE OF ETERNITY**
Jasmine Cresswell

**#298 TALONS OF THE FALCON**
Rebecca York

**#299 PRIVATE EYES**
Madeline St. Claire

**#300 GUILTY AS SIN**
Cathy Gillen Thacker

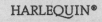

## HARLEQUIN®

 **I N T R I G U E ®**

*A Decade of Danger & Desire*

**Harlequin Intrigue invites you to celebrate a decade of danger and desire....**

It's a year of celebration for Harlequin Intrigue, as we commemorate ten years of bringing you the best in romantic suspense. Stories in which you can expect the unexpected... Stories with heart-stopping suspense and heart-stirring romance... Stories that walk the fine line between danger and desire...

Throughout the coming months, you can expect some special surprises by some of your favorite Intrigue authors. Look for the specially marked "Decade of Danger and Desire" books for valuable proofs-of-purchase to redeem for a free gift!

**HARLEQUIN INTRIGUE
Not the same old story!**

DDD

# "HOORAY FOR HOLLYWOOD" SWEEPSTAKES

## HERE'S HOW THE SWEEPSTAKES WORKS

### OFFICIAL RULES — NO PURCHASE NECESSARY

To enter, complete an Official Entry Form or hand print on a 3" x 5" card the words "HOORAY FOR HOLLYWOOD", your name and address and mail your entry in the pre-addressed envelope (if provided) or to: "Hooray for Hollywood" Sweepstakes, P.O. Box 9076, Buffalo, NY 14269-9076 or "Hooray for Hollywood" Sweepstakes, P.O. Box 637, Fort Erie, Ontario L2A 5X3. Entries must be sent via First Class Mail and be received no later than 12/31/94. No liability is assumed for lost, late or misdirected mail.

Winners will be selected in random drawings to be conducted no later than January 31, 1995 from all eligible entries received.

Grand Prize: A 7-day/6-night trip for 2 to Los Angeles, CA including round trip air transportation from commercial airport nearest winner's residence, accommodations at the Regent Beverly Wilshire Hotel, free rental car, and $1,000 spending money. (Approximate prize value which will vary dependent upon winner's residence: $5,400.00 U.S.); 500 Second Prizes: A pair of "Hollywood Star" sunglasses (prize value: $9.95 U.S. each). Winner selection is under the supervision of D.L. Blair, Inc., an independent judging organization, whose decisions are final. Grand Prize travelers must sign and return a release of liability prior to traveling. Trip must be taken by 2/1/96 and is subject to airline schedules and accommodations availability.

Sweepstakes offer is open to residents of the U.S. (except Puerto Rico) and Canada who are 18 years of age or older, except employees and immediate family members of Harlequin Enterprises, Ltd., its affiliates, subsidiaries, and all agencies, entities or persons connected with the use, marketing or conduct of this sweepstakes. All federal, state, provincial, municipal and local laws apply. Offer void wherever prohibited by law. Taxes and/or duties are the sole responsibility of the winners. Any litigation within the province of Quebec respecting the conduct and awarding of prizes may be submitted to the Regie des loteries et courses du Quebec. All prizes will be awarded; winners will be notified by mail. No substitution of prizes are permitted. Odds of winning are dependent upon the number of eligible entries received.

Potential grand prize winner must sign and return an Affidavit of Eligibility within 30 days of notification. In the event of non-compliance within this time period, prize may be awarded to an alternate winner. Prize notification returned as undeliverable may result in the awarding of prize to an alternate winner. By acceptance of their prize, winners consent to use of their names, photographs, or likenesses for purpose of advertising, trade and promotion on behalf of Harlequin Enterprises, Ltd., without further compensation unless prohibited by law. A Canadian winner must correctly answer an arithmetical skill-testing question in order to be awarded the prize.

For a list of winners (available after 2/28/95), send a separate stamped, self-addressed envelope to: Hooray for Hollywood Sweepstakes 3252 Winners, P.O. Box 4200, Blair, NE 68009.

CBSRLS

## OFFICIAL ENTRY COUPON

## "Hooray for Hollywood"
### SWEEPSTAKES!

Yes, I'd love to win the Grand Prize — a vacation in Hollywood — or one of 500 pairs of "sunglasses of the stars"! Please enter me in the sweepstakes!

This entry must be received by December 31, 1994.
Winners will be notified by January 31, 1995.

Name _____

Address _____ Apt. _____

City _____

State/Prov. _____ Zip/Postal Code _____

Daytime phone number _____
(area code)

Account # _____

Return entries with invoice in envelope provided. Each book in this shipment has two entry coupons — and the more coupons you enter, the better your chances of winning!

DIRCBS

---

## OFFICIAL ENTRY COUPON

## "Hooray for Hollywood"
### SWEEPSTAKES!

Yes, I'd love to win the Grand Prize — a vacation in Hollywood — or one of 500 pairs of "sunglasses of the stars"! Please enter me in the sweepstakes!

This entry must be received by December 31, 1994.
Winners will be notified by January 31, 1995.

Name _____

Address _____ Apt. _____

City _____

State/Prov. _____ Zip/Postal Code _____

Daytime phone number _____
(area code)

Account # _____

Return entries with invoice in envelope provided. Each book in this shipment has two entry coupons — and the more coupons you enter, the better your chances of winning!

DIRCBS